# PAST IN THE PRESENT

## SHERRYL D. HANCOCK

# VULPINE
## PRESS

Published by Vulpine Press in the United Kingdom in 2019

ISBN 978-1-83919-281-4

Cover by Claire Wood

www.vulpine-press.com

Also in the *MidKnight Blue* series:

Building Empires

Empires Fall

Where Loyalties Lie

Treachery Rising

Betrayals Stand

For all Intents and Purposes

Blood in the Water

Means to an End

# CHAPTER 1

"Okay, do you two have anything?" Midnight said as she glanced up, her gold-green eyes flicking to her husband of twelve years, Rick, and then her partner of sixteen years, Joe Sinclair.

Both men looked up, thinking in unison how tired Midnight seemed. Midnight Chevalier-Debenshire singlehandedly ran the San Diego Police Department as the Chief of Police. She'd avoided hiring an Assistant Chief in the four years she'd held the post. Rick was fairly sure it had everything to do with the distasteful memories she had of a previous AC who, when she was still a lieutenant, had sexually harassed her, telling her he would promote her to captain if she slept with him. Rick had particularly enjoyed taking the man into custody when they'd bugged his office during an interview with Midnight.

Now, years later, she was trying desperately to keep up with her ever-growing popularity in the media and law enforcement community, as well as her ever-growing department. Many of Midnight's closest friends had been suggesting she hire an Assistant Chief for a year or more, but she'd been stalling. Rick suspected she'd been hoping Joe, her best friend as well as her former partner, would change his mind about taking the job. Joe had resoundingly turned her down time and again, citing his lack of desire for such a political position.

Recently, Midnight had finally given in to the pressure from her husband and friends and had put out a Law Enforcement Bulletin

1

advertising an opening. She'd been flooded with applications and resumes almost immediately. It had taken days to wade through them. Rick and Joe had been assisting her. This particular evening, the three of them were sitting in her office reading over the applications.

Noting her husband resting comfortably, stretched out on the couch, and Joe sitting casually in one of her chairs, his long legs out in front of him and crossed at the ankles, Midnight was unable to keep the grin off her face. Here sat the two most important men in her life, and as usual, they were helping her with an excruciatingly boring task.

"You know what this makes me think of?" she said.

"What?" Rick asked, his English accent still strong after many years in the States.

Midnight looked at Joe and grinned. "The time I was looking for a second to help me run FORS." She was referring to the gang task force she'd created years before, which she had run quite successfully with Joe's help.

Joe grinned widely, his light blue eyes twinkling in amusement. "I don't go in for any of that chasing around the desk crap," he said, his accent as clear as Rick's, his smile growing wide as he quoted the words Midnight had said to him the day he'd applied to be her second-in-command at FORS.

"Good," Midnight replied, smiling as well. "'Cause I don't do any chasing around the desk crap." She began to laugh as Rick's grin started, and Joe nodded.

"Damned right!" he said, laughing. She had remembered his reply to her just as well.

"I don't see your application here, Deputy." Midnight raised her eyebrow at Joe. The title was one he'd held long ago when he applied with her.

"Nor will you, Chief," Joe replied smoothly, giving her a mocking stern look as he pointedly called her by her current title.

"Ugh!" she said in disgust, throwing herself back in her chair. "Joe, you know I can't do this without you!"

"Bullshit," Joe replied, unruffled. "You've done quite well for the last four years."

Midnight narrowed her eyes at him, then looked at her husband, who was grinning at the exchange.

"Don't give me that look, Night," Rick said, sitting up. "You know damned good and well you need help. Joe just meant you've *been* doing it for this long without *him*." Rick gave his best friend a sour look, for making Midnight think she could avoid hiring an Assistant Chief at all. "You don't have to live with her burnt out all the time, man. If you did, you'd know where I'm coming from."

Joe nodded. "I know what you mean, I just don't want the job. You think I want to look like *that* all the time?" he said, gesturing to Midnight, then promptly ducked the pen that came flying at him from her direction.

"Still got good reaction times for an old man, Sinclair," Midnight said, laughing even as she narrowed her eyes at him.

"You know I think you're beautiful, Midnight," Joe began soothingly. "You just look like shit right now."

"Nice," Midnight said, giving both men a vile look. "Well, let's get this done so I can schedule interviews and get it all over with."

They did just that, selecting four candidates.

3

Rick was surprised the following week when she informed him of her plan for the candidates—interviews were that day.

He was sitting at their kitchen table having his morning coffee when Midnight walked in, stunning him with the simplicity of the outfit she wore. As was the style of the time, Midnight's skirt was long, to her ankles, but had slits up both sides to just above her knees. The skirt was white, and set off her ever-tanned legs nicely. She wore an emerald green silk Oxford blouse and the emerald-and-gold necklace and earrings Rick had given her for an engagement present twelve years before. Her copper-blond hair was held back from her face at the crown with a white hair clip. Her makeup, as usual, was light, but effectively highlighting her finely boned face, sun-kissed skin, and gold-green eyes. She was the picture of health, vitality, and youth, even at thirty-seven years of age. Rick found her endlessly attractive, and never could figure out how she still managed to surprise him even after almost twelve years of being together.

"Wow," he said, his eyes and the look on his face saying all that his single word hadn't.

Midnight laughed and shook her head, never sure what it was her husband saw that made him react the way he just had. She poured herself some coffee and sat down at the kitchen table, looking him over as she often did. Rick, too, was still incredibly attractive to her, with his light brown curly hair still worn a few inches past his shoulders. His deep blue eyes, set in a handsome, finely boned face, could glitter with laughter or darken with passion, and still held her hypnotized so often. His swimmer's body, all lean strength and hidden power, was still long and lean, standing an even six feet. He could excite her with a look, or infuriate her just as quickly. Theirs was still

4

a fiery relationship, but there wasn't a person alive who could come between them.

"Interviews this morning?" Rick inquired, raising an eyebrow at her.

"Uh-huh," Midnight replied. "Have to pick up the first one at nine."

"Pick up?" Rick looked perplexed.

"Yeah," Midnight said, shrugging casually, even as her hand tightened on her coffee cup. She knew she was about to argue with him on this. "I'm picking each of them up at the airport."

"Why?" Rick asked, his eyes narrowing slightly.

"Because I want to see how they react to—"

"You?" Rick interrupted, tense. "You don't intend to tell them who you are, do you?"

Midnight was quiet for a moment, then raised her eyes to him. "Eventually."

"I don't like it," Rick said, shaking his head.

"I'm not asking you to like it," Midnight replied mildly.

"Midnight…"

"Richard…"

"Okay, tell me why," Rick said, changing tactics.

Midnight narrowed her green eyes at him, sensing the change instantly. "It's simple. I have to work with this guy a lot."

"Okay… and?" Rick prompted, knowing there was more to the answer.

"And," Midnight sighed, sitting back, "I need to know I can trust him implicitly. Like I would have trusted Joe or you, or any of our friends."

"What are you afraid of?" Rick asked, his voice softening.

Midnight was quiet, her eyes dropping to the tablecloth in front of her.

"You're afraid he'll be like Dearborn, aren't you?" Rick asked gently, referring to the Assistant Chief who had treated Midnight like a body to be used and tossed aside. Rick felt his insides tighten as Midnight nodded after a long pause. "So you're going to test them," he continued—it was a statement, not a question, but his tone of voice betrayed his distaste.

Midnight raised her eyes, and he could see the fire already starting behind them. "Should I just take my chances, Rick?" she asked. "Should I wait to see if the guy will fight me on everything, or not back me when I need it, because he doesn't *really* think women belong in law enforcement?" Her eyes sparkled with anger. "Should I wait and see if he'll try something with me because he assumes any woman that hires a guy to work closely her with must *need* a man?" She'd hit a nerve with that question; she knew because Rick's eyes widened in surprise and anger.

"If any guy you hire *ever* tries something with you, he'll have me and five of the nastiest people he's ever met to deal with." Rick's eyes were blazing at the very thought of any man trying to force his attention on the woman he loved so dearly.

"I know that," Midnight said softly. She knew the people he'd referred to were their extended family—Joe, Dave, Tiny, Kana, and Spider. He was right—they were a fairly scary group to have after you. They had all been incredibly fierce gang members before joining

Midnight and her crusade to rid her city of gangs. Even if they were all fine, upstanding peace officers now, they still had a tendency toward strong-arming anyone that harmed or threatened to harm the people they loved and respected. Midnight was at the top of that list for all of them. "I know the gang would back me on this, but I don't want them to have to, okay?" she said, giving him a beseeching look. "I don't want to have to go through that. I want my first choice to be my best choice."

Rick didn't say anything. He simply leaned back in his chair and blew his breath out in a defeated sigh. Midnight smiled slightly, knowing that Rick's sense of fair play was warring with his need to protect his wife.

"Look, I'm not going to *make* them say anything out of line. I'm just going to give them a chance to show their true colors before they know who I am, okay?"

"So, what are you going to do, let them think you're some secretary or something?"

"Exactly—I'm not going to lie. If any of them actually know anything about my department, then they should know who I am, right?"

Rick pursed his lips, nodding "True." He hadn't actually thought about that. Midnight was a highly publicized public official. Anyone applying for an Assistant Chief's job really should know something about the department and its head. It wasn't like Midnight was some obscure figurehead no one ever saw. She was on the news all the time, making huge strides in improving the quality of life in San Diego as well as the work environment for her officers. She was well known. "So, who's first?"

"Moss," Midnight said, her tone slightly amused. Rick hadn't agreed with her and Joe on this candidate. He was older—fifty-five—and he'd been in law enforcement for thirty-seven of those years. Midnight and Joe saw it as experience; Rick saw it as old and stodgy. Midnight was inclined to agree with Rick, but knew it wasn't fair to exclude the man because he was older than her. The other hindrance was that he was actually at retirement age, but Midnight intended to find out if it was his intention to retire soon.

Predictably, Rick rolled his eyes and nodded.

Driving along in her car later that morning, Midnight was thinking about the other three candidates. They ranged in age from a young thirty-five—"the pup," Rick called him—to forty-five as the next oldest down from Moss. The thirty-five-year-old Taylor seemed overly eager to both Rick and Joe, but Midnight thought he was pretty smart for having achieved Assistant Chief status with the Phoenix Police Department at such a young age. Rick and Joe had said he'd probably slept his way into the job. Midnight had given them a dirty look, until she'd remember that the Chief of Police for Phoenix was not only male but reported to be gay as well. She'd found it necessary to swat both men then.

The next highest in age was forty-two, older than Midnight by five years. His name was Barbary, and he was currently a captain for Sacramento Police Department. He ran the vice unit, and from what Midnight could determine, he did so quite well. His service record was littered with accomplishments, although his education level was no more than high school graduation. Joe had liked the man's application, citing the fact that he had a great deal of street experience combined with the running of a fairly complicated division in law enforcement. Joe knew about that all too well, since he ran the vice unit for Midnight. She had taken his advice and scheduled the man for an interview.

The fourth candidate, Masterson, forty-five years old, was the most impressive on paper. He was an Assistant Chief for New York Police Department. He ran an entire borough. He was an ex-Navy Seal and had two bachelor's degrees, one in business administration and the other in philosophy. Both were from Harvard University. He had been a cop since his honorary discharge from the Seals and was nineteen years in. His service record reflected experience in a number of fields, including narcotics, vice, patrol, homicide, and internal affairs. Midnight was anxious to meet the man in person. Joe and Rick had figured him for a snob right off the bat, considering where his degrees were from. Midnight had given them both a sour look, reminding them that their inheritances and trust funds didn't mean *they* were snobs, so why should a degree from an Ivy League college mean Masterson was? Rick and Joe had nothing to say to that one.

Pulling into the airport terminal area, Midnight parked her white convertible Sebring at the curb. She glanced at the officer on duty and could see that he recognized her. He grinned and inclined his head to her as she walked by. Even as she did, Midnight heard some woman complain, "Why can *she* park here and not me?"

As she entered through the terminal's double doors, Midnight heard the officer say, "Because she's the Chief of Police, ma'am, and if I give her a ticket, she'll fire me." Midnight laughed, hoping in the back of her mind that the officer didn't really believe that. She wouldn't blame him for giving her a ticket, but she had no intention of dragging Assistant Chief candidates through the airport parking lots. Midnight got to the gate to meet the first of them early, counting herself lucky that at least half the candidates had included pictures of themselves with their applications. Moss hadn't, so she was nervous about trying to recognize him from the description one of his coworkers had given. It might help that Moss was most likely going to be in uniform. Her next problem was her last interview, Masterson; she'd been unable to garner either a description or a picture of him. She figured she'd wing it. Just in case, she had made a sign with his name on it, kind of like the limousine companies did. She knew she'd feel like an idiot holding it up, but if that's what it took, she didn't mind too much.

As it turned out, she recognized Moss right off the bat. He was the epitome of old-time cop. He was silver-haired and narrow-eyed. He looked her over, and from what Midnight could tell, wrote her off as fluff. His comments in the car didn't do much to dissuade this assumption. He criticized her driving skills, her music, her age. When Midnight informed him she was thirty-seven years old, he accused her of lying outrageously. Midnight was more than a little fed up with his attitude when her car phone rang. Without thinking, she picked it up and barked "Chevalier" into the receiver. It was Joe calling about a warrant. She answered his questions, glancing over at Moss and noting that he was watching her with narrowed eyes. When she hung up he was silent for a full minute.

"What did you say your name was?" he asked, his tone still condescending.

"Actually," Midnight said evenly, "I didn't say."

"You answered the phone 'Chevalier'—is that your name?" he asked, as if he were an interrogating officer.

"That's part of it, yes," Midnight replied, her eyes glittering with malice.

"Are you related to Chief Chevalier?" he asked, his tone dripping with contempt for what he obviously believed was nepotism.

*Oh God, he has no idea!* Midnight thought.

"No, I'm not related to her," Midnight said, pausing a moment to let that sink in, then went for the kill. "I *am* Chief Chevalier."

It was apparent Moss was aghast, but Midnight soon discovered it wasn't due to his own behavior.

"You, you—" he sputtered indignantly. "You tricked me! What kind of circus are you running here?"

"It's no circus, sir, I assure you," Midnight replied coolly. She already knew she could not work with this man. "I am very careful about who backs me up."

"Backs you up?" Moss echoed cryptically, his tone almost a sneer. "You are no longer a street cop, Chief Chevalier. You no longer require backup officers."

"No, I require someone who knows when and where to make critical remarks, and also knows better than to judge people by their age, sex, or who he thinks their family is."

"You're saying I've judged you?" Moss replied, looking affronted again.

"Oh, you've judged me. You had me all figured out, right up until you knew who I was."

"I don't like games, Ms. Chevalier."

"It's Chief Chevalier, or Mrs. Debenshire—pick one," Midnight replied, her voice cold enough to freeze fire. It was her standard answer to anyone that called her Ms. Chevalier. She knew using the term "Ms." was a way to put her in her place, and she wouldn't stand for being put anywhere for long.

"I see. Well, Chief Chevalier, I don't appreciate this kind of behavior from a Chief of Police," Moss said, determined to make his point.

Midnight looked thoughtful for a few minutes, then said, "Well, I don't like being talked to like a child either. So I guess that makes us even."

Moss gave her a sour look and refused to speak again during the drive to the office. Midnight gave herself a mental shake, reminding herself that this was not part of the interview, only a way of seeing what these people were really like. She knew she was going to have a really hard time being objective toward this man now, but that was why she had an interview panel to work with her.

She had selected three other people to be on the panel. One of them was Spider Nguyen, a longtime friend and a lieutenant in her narcotics division. He was an original member of Midnight's gang task force, and formerly a gang leader himself. He was quiet and reserved, but his mind was always working and the term "still waters run deep" fit Spider quite well. In the years she'd known him, he'd surprised her frequently with his depth of understanding of the human psyche. For someone that had never had any formal schooling in psychology, to Midnight's way of thinking, Spider was still a master of the science. She also knew Spider didn't always agree with her way of thinking; however, when he argued with her, he did so with no emotion. It was always a nice change to have one man that actually discussed things with her rather than ranting and raving, as she was used to with Rick and Joe.

Midnight had also selected an officer from patrol, Tim Simmons. He was a ten-year veteran of patrol, and had fairly good insight into what people really meant when they said something. He was used to deciphering verbal skirmishes on the street; his intuition was excellent. Midnight was fairly sure she could get a highly unbiased opinion from him. She also felt it important to have someone from each rank in on the interviews. Midnight knew that different levels in her organization had different takes on the kind of person they thought would make a good Assistant Chief. Midnight wanted the benefit of those differing opinions.

Midnight's third choice was the person she called her "transplant." Jessica Ako, who was now married to a member of Midnight's original task force, Tiny, was a very good addition to the department. Jessica had come to San Diego to "visit" Joe Sinclair during a very rough time in all of their lives when things were in a major upheaval. Rick and Midnight had been separated; Joe and his wife, Randy, had been as well. There had been a dirty cop playing both sides against the middle, and he was winning when he and his drug dealer friends had snatched Joe out of his bed one night. It had been Jessica's insight that had given them the break they needed in figuring out who was behind the abduction. She had put them on the trail of a cop, and had eventually led them right to Dick Dickerson, a dirty cop working with the drug cartel. Midnight had been forever grateful to Jessica for her help in that case, and had gladly given her a job with San Diego Police Department when she applied. Jessica had quickly worked her way up to sergeant and was now part of the internal affairs unit.

Walking into the interview room, leading a still-disgruntled Moss, Midnight glanced at her panel. She saw Spider's eyes narrow immediately, and knew he sensed the antagonism from Moss. She introduced each member of the panel, stating their names and ranks and the units they worked for. When she got to Simmons, she could see that Moss was surprised that a patrolman was on the panel. *Good*, Midnight thought. *Let him be surprised.*

The interview began, and Moss answered every question, but did so with little or no embellishment. His answers were to the point; he did not give any details of his experiences, merely listing his assignments. When asked what he felt was most important in a work environment, he looked directly at Midnight and said, "I don't feel that law enforcement should be reduced to a series of games."

Midnight looked back at him, her face impassive, staring right back into his eyes with no trace of the shame or guilt he obviously expected to see in hers.

Spider took that cue and pursued the issue. "What kind of games would you be talking about, sir?"

Moss glanced at Spider, noting the almost guileless look on the man's face, and cleared his throat. "I was talking about power plays, young man. When people feel they have an advantage and use it to put others at a handicap. It is a poor way to do business."

"So you're saying," Midnight began, leaning back in her chair, "people should always proclaim themselves, so mistakes won't be made in judgement?" Now she leaned forward, putting her elbows on the table, folding her hands together, her gold-green eyes piercing his. "Wouldn't you say it is the responsibility of the individual to moderate themselves, with all levels of people?" She smiled then, a wintery smile that didn't reach her eyes. "I mean, today's gang leader could be tomorrow's Chief of Police, right? One never does know."

Moss stared back at her, obviously taken aback by her attitude and the fact that she was quite soundly chastising him for his behavior without actually sounding to the others like she was doing any more than posing a philosophical question. It was at that moment he realized he had made a fatal error in misjudging this woman. He had taken her for another token female in a field dominated by men. Granted, this one had done quite well for herself, but again, he had attributed that to the political climate of the time. Hell, there had just been a female United States Attorney General, right? And look what a debacle that had been! It didn't mean anything. This woman, however, he had misjudged, and in realizing that, and knowing it was too late to change his tune now, Moss merely inclined his head in acquiescence. She was right, after all, to a point. Besides, she was the Chief of Police; no matter why he thought she was there, she had the final say over everything in the department. Moss knew he wasn't getting that job, but he had gained a new respect for the chief of the San Diego Police Department.

Later, Midnight sat in her office, thinking over the interview. She knew that in the end Moss had conceded defeat, and while she felt he had sorely needed the setting down she'd given him, she hoped he understood that his attitude wasn't the only reason he wasn't getting the job. She intended to call him at a later date to explain. Reflecting on it now, she knew that Moss, given time, could come around to her way of thinking, but Midnight didn't think she could be patient enough to take the time to dispense with all of his mindsets and prejudices. She realized he had thought her a simple piece of fluff, part of the department as "window dressing," to make the city council look good. She appreciated that in the end he had obviously changed that thinking, but it was still only a first step. She knew it would take a lot of time to make him believe that she really did know how to run her department, and that she needed someone to back her all the way on issues, or offer valuable opposing opinions, without prejudice or malice. She didn't think Moss would be ready for a partnership like that for a long time, and she didn't have time to wait. She needed help now.

Her next interview was with Barbary. He was a salty dog, which Midnight had no problem with. He didn't recognize Midnight when she picked him up at the airport, but he made no off-color comments either, nor did he speak down to her. When she pulled into her parking space at the department, marked with a sign that said "Reserved for Chief Chevalier-Debenshire," he glanced over at her and said, "Don't you think the chief will get mad you're parking in her space?"

Midnight laughed in spite of herself, and said, "No, I won't get mad at me." It took Barbary a moment or two, but then he started to nod as if he finally got it.

"So you're the chief, huh?" He sounded nonplussed, which to Midnight was a good thing.

"Yes, sir, I am," she replied, getting out of the car. He followed suit.

"Heard you looked young for your age," he said, his tone not depreciating at all.

"Well, thanks, I think," Midnight said, laughing a little. He seemed nice enough, but a bit on the colorless side. *Of course*, she thought, *all the men I know are so colorful most of the time it's blinding! Normal might not be a bad thing.*

They went into the interview room, and again, Midnight made the introductions. Barbary gave no indication of having a problem with the ranks in the panel. The interview began, and Midnight was quickly disappointed in his lack of enthusiasm for law enforcement. When asked what he felt was most important about the job, he said, "It's a paycheck." Midnight cringed inwardly. Now she knew why he was still only a captain after so many years with the department. He had no real drive. She wasn't sure what had motivated him to apply for the Assistant Chief's job, but she knew it wasn't a desire to improve things.

In truth, Barbary had applied because his wife, Edna, had told him she thought San Diego would be a nice place to eventually retire in, and wouldn't it be nice if he could draw a bigger pension. Barbary would do anything for Edna, even if it meant being stuck as some Assistant Chief in a big department. He knew the suits never really did any of the work; they always had someone to do it for them. Ever since he'd made captain at Sacramento PD it had been a free ride. He had lieutenants that did all the work. All he had to do was sign the paperwork they put on his desk and kick back the rest of the day. How much harder could Assistant Chief be? It would be a bigger check, and probably even less to do.

After the second interview, Midnight went back to her office feeling rather despondent. She was halfway through her candidates and so far there was no hope whatsoever. As if he could sense her need for support, Rick appeared in her doorway.

"Lunch?" he asked lightly.

Midnight looked up at him, and he could see her despair instantly. He walked over and pulled her out of her chair. He hugged her close, nuzzling her temple with his lips.

"That bad?" he asked softly.

17

Midnight nodded against his chest.

"Come on," Rick said, taking her hand and walking toward the door. He led her out into the outer office, where her secretary sat. Cassandra looked up and smiled. Rick grinned back at her, silently thanking her for calling and telling him that Midnight "needed" him. He said, "The chief is out to lunch for about two hours."

"Yes, sir." Cassandra smiled. She absolutely adored Midnight Chevalier, and she thought Rick Debenshire was the best man on the planet for a husband. She envied the love that they shared, and hoped to find that for herself one day soon. In the meantime, she enjoyed helping out when she could, like the call she'd made to Rick's office a few minutes ago. She'd seen immediately when Midnight walked into her office that she was very unhappy. Cassandra knew how important hiring an Assistant Chief was for Midnight's own well-being, but she also knew how difficult it was going to be to find anyone able to handle Midnight's independence, quick wit, intellect, and work ethic. Cassandra hoped the next two interviews would go better, and that Rick could get Midnight back in a better frame of mind.

In his Mustang, Rick didn't say much, just drove. He knew Midnight was busy thinking things through and trying to get a game plan for the next two interviews. He could see how desperately unhappy she was, and he knew eventually she'd tell him all about it. Rick knew his wife well enough to understand he didn't need to push her to get her to tell him what was wrong; he just needed to give her time to assimilate it first.

They were seated on the outside deck of an ocean-side restaurant when Midnight finally started talking. Rick listened to the entire story without comment. He'd ordered her wine, and watched her drink two glasses while she talked. He also ordered their food without asking her, knowing her preferences as well as his own, and that she needed to get some actual food into her stomach before the wine hit her.

"So, now I'm down to two, Rick. Two!" she said miserably, taking note that his eyes were trailing over to the wine glass in her hand, which she had just drained for the second time. "I'm okay," she said, but even as she did, she felt a bit light-headed. *Oh good, Chevalier. Get blasted before your next interview—that'll go over big!* she thought morosely.

"Uh-huh," Rick said, his grin showing that he was unconvinced, and she knew he could tell she wasn't okay. "So, Moss sucked, and Barbary sucked worse?" Rick summed up in his usual fashion.

Midnight laughed at the simplistic statement. "Well, Barbary didn't suck, he just... he was kinda lifeless, ya know?"

"Doesn't sound like he's in it for the job," Rick stated, aware that that was what was bothering Midnight.

"Nope, and I just can't work with that. Now, Moss I might have been able to work with, but he would need a lot of substantiation to show him I know what I'm doing before we could ever work as a team." She scrubbed at her face in frustration. "I don't have time for that!"

"No, you don't," Rick said, looking thoughtful for a long minute as they food arrived. After the waiter had walked away, he said, "But if worse comes to worst, he might be a good choice. He's already shown you that he can change his attitude. That's pretty good for someone that set in his ways."

"True," Midnight said, taking a bite of the fish he'd ordered for her. "Oh, this is good." She smiled at him. It was amazing that he knew her so well that he knew exactly what she'd like, even though they'd never been to this restaurant before. "So, do you think I should change my tactics with the next two?" she asked, worrying that she was putting the candidates off.

Rick thought about it for a minute, then shook his head. "No, because I think that knowing they don't know who you are, or do, gives you a feel for how interested they are in the department versus just the position itself. It doesn't sound to me like you're doing anything that makes them act any differently than they normally would."

Midnight laughed and shook her head. "Well, I'll tell you, for a minute there I was ready to shoot Moss. I haven't been talked down to like that since I was a rookie."

"Well, he probably thought you were the young, beautiful secretary to some high-up official, getting light goof-off duty," Rick said, grinning.

Midnight smiled. "Oh, sure, butter me up now." She loved that he always complimented her, even if she never seemed to know how to handle it. She reached for the carafe of wine and saw his eyebrow rise. "I'm okay now," she said, and he grinned. "What?" she asked with mock indignation.

"I thought you were okay before," he said, his grin widening.

"Oh, shut up, Debenshire!" She laughed. "Guess I shouldn't, huh?" She looked so appealingly contrite he wanted to pour her the glass himself.

"If you think you can handle it, but eat more of your food first." He knew she was relying on his judgment here, and didn't want her to overdo it when she needed all her wits about her for the next two interviews.

"Yes, dear," she said, grinning.

They talked about other things then, enjoying the chance to spend some relaxing time out of the office in the middle of the day. After their lunch, they took a walk on the beach, holding hands like teenagers. They were a good-looking couple, and people's heads turned as they passed by. When they reached a jetty, Rick leaned against the rocks, pulling her back against him and wrapping his arms around her waist. They stood watching the waves and the seagulls diving into them.

"Feel better?" Rick asked after a long while.

"Much," Midnight replied, leaning her head back against the hollow of his shoulder. She glanced up at his profile, and he tilted his head down to look at her. "Thanks for this."

He leaned down and kissed her temple gently. "Anytime, babe," he said softly against her hair, his lips lingering.

"What do I do if the next two interviews are as bad as the first?" she asked, voicing the concern she'd had all along.

Rick shrugged. "Then we go back through the applications till we find the right one."

"That will take so much work," Midnight said, dejected again.

"Okay, we'll blackmail Joe into taking the job," Rick said, with a smile in his voice.

Midnight laughed. "You have blackmail material?"

"Oh yeah. I've known him a long time, remember?"

"You are evil, Mr. Debenshire," Midnight chided, smiling up at him.

"And you are beautiful, Mrs. Debenshire," Rick replied, moved by the look in her eyes. There were still so many times when he looked at his wife and could not fathom his good fortune at not only finding her, but having her actually fall in love with him as deeply as he'd fallen for her.

Her arms were over his, which were wrapped around her waist, and he took her hand and turned her around. He cupped her face, looking deep into her eyes. Midnight felt her stomach flutter at the look in his eyes, even as his lips descended slowly on hers. Midnight reached up and wrapped her arms around his neck, pulling him closer to her as they kissed. His arms went around her waist again, one hand sliding up her back, his fingers splaying wide to hold her against him. When the kiss ended, his lips trailed across her cheek.

"I love you," he whispered in her ear.

Midnight shivered at the timbre of his voice. She looked up into his eyes. "And I love you," she said, her voice trembling slightly.

It always astounded her, the effect he still had over her. Even after twelve years of marriage, he could reduce her to a trembling set of nerves and desires so easily. If she didn't love and trust him so much, she knew she would be terrified of his influence over her. In years past, she would never have allowed a man to get so close to her that he changed the entire way she thought and acted, but Rick could do just that.

On this particular afternoon, he had taken the negative, desolate feelings she'd been allowing to build up over the interviews, and had replaced them with good, warm feelings of confidence and support. Rick knew her like no one else did, not even her best friend, Joe. Rick could always sense her moods and figure out a way to diffuse them, if that was what he wanted to do. It was a good feeling.

The next interview was with Taylor. Midnight had seen a picture of this young man. He was good-looking in a blond-butch-hair-cut-cop kind of way. She waited near the gate and saw him as he got off the plane. He walked straight over to her and said, "You're Chief Chevalier," giving her an almost appraising look.

Midnight nodded. "Yes, I am. You're Assistant Chief Taylor?"

"That's me," he said, smiling widely. "Call me Matt."

Midnight nodded, but stopped short of giving him the same privilege. She wondered if he'd notice; he didn't seem to. As they walked toward the front of the terminal, Midnight realized she was already categorizing this man and pulled herself up short. Friendliness was not supposed to be a bad quality; nor was confidence.

Once in the car, Matt began the conversation, and Midnight felt her stomach lurch immediately.

"You look even better in person than you do in your publicity pictures."

Midnight gave him a sidelong glance, tempted to say, *Are you sure you want to start out the conversation that way?* Instead she said, "I do, do I?"

"Oh yeah, you do," Matt replied, grinning. Then he looked around at the scenery. "Beautiful place."

"We like it," Midnight said, her tone almost normal.

"Yeah, this is a lot better than Arizona, with the ocean and all— great place to have fun," Matt said, and Midnight could almost feel the shift in his thinking. He gave her a long, considering look then, his gaze shifting to her tanned legs, exposed from the top of her knee down. With his eyes still on her legs, he said, "You and me, we could have a lot of fun, I'll bet."

Midnight didn't turn her head, her eyes narrowed slightly. "Could we?" she asked, making her tone light.

"Oh yeah, it would be great." Matt stretched his legs out in front of him and leaned back comfortably, exuding male confidence.

Midnight glanced over at him. Her expression, which was slightly amused, could have been mistaken for playful. "I don't know if my husband would like that too much."

Matt didn't bat an eyelash. "Oh yeah, your husband. He works for the department too, doesn't he?"

"Yes, he's a lieutenant in charge of FORS," Midnight replied mildly.

Matt looked thoughtful for about two seconds, then shrugged. "I'd outrank him—what could he do?"

"Outrank him?" Midnight repeated, not sure she'd heard him correctly.

"Yeah," Matt said, his tone almost chiding now. "He wouldn't give us any trouble. Rank does have it privileges."

Midnight was literally stunned into a momentary silence by his complete lack of respect for either her or for the unknown husband he was already pulling rank on without even having gotten the job yet. She decided a change of subject was necessary and soon, before she took him back to the airport and dumped him on his head.

"So, how did you move up so quickly in Arizona, if you don't mind me asking."

"No, I don't mind you asking," Matt said, his voice almost a caress, and Midnight had to keep herself from shuddering. It only got worse as he informed her of his tactics. "Let's just say I know who to throw dirt on, and how to do it."

Midnight nodded, feigning admiration for his methods. "So the other guy wasn't as good a candidate?"

"Hell no. He was an old coot. I deserved that job, and I got it. You do what you gotta do, you know?"

"Yeah, I know. So how do you like being Assistant Chief there?"

"It's great," Matt said, smiling widely. "I get to play all I want, and no one ever bothers me."

"Well, this is a working AC here, you know," Midnight put in, unable to resist.

"Oh, we'll work…" Matt trailed off as his eyes trailed down her body and back up again. Midnight had the wild urge to slap him, but she knew there was a better way to handle this. Fortunately, they arrived at the department then, and she led him to the interview room. After introducing him to the panel, she excused herself for a moment and left the room to make a call. She came back five minutes later and the interview began.

Matt did well, exuding charm and charisma to the maximum. His answers were good, although Midnight sensed he was exaggerating on a number of things. She found herself tapping her foot, waiting for the interview to be over. When it was concluded, Midnight escorted him out of the conference room. Rick and Tiny, a very tall and muscular Samoan also from Midnight's original gang task force, walked up.

Midnight turned to Matt and said, "I have a meeting to go to, but these gentlemen will make sure you get back to the airport."

Matt looked surprised, but nodded. He gave her a brilliant smile and extended his hand. "It was a great pleasure meeting you, Chief Chevalier," he said, his tone thick with undercurrent.

Midnight placed her hand in his, and he covered it with his other hand, almost possessively. She sensed more than saw Rick tense, but managed to smile up at Matt. "It was nice meeting you too. Have a safe trip back."

"We'll make sure he gets back," Tiny said, glancing at Rick. Rick nodded, his eyes not leaving Taylor's hand over Midnight's.

Midnight turned to Tiny and smiled brightly, her eyes trailing over to meet Rick's. "Thank you, gentlemen." She turned and left. Tiny led the way back out to the parking lot, and Rick fell in behind Matt.

At Rick's Mustang, Tiny climbed into the back seat. Matt got in on the passenger's side and grinned over at Rick as they pulled out of the lot.

"Man, the chauffeur service in this department is great. I mean, the chief herself picked me up."

"Yeah?" Rick said, his accent evident.

"Yeah..." Matt said, a wistful smile on his face. "That is some hot-looking woman, I'll tell you."

Rick glanced in the rear-view mirror at Tiny, then over at Matt. "Yeah, she is," he said. In a conversational tone, he added, "She's married, ya know."

Matt shrugged. "Yeah, I know she is. But he's only a lieutenant."

"So?" Tiny said from the back seat, looking confused.

"So," Matt said, almost laughing, "if I'm the Assistant Chief, I outrank him. What's he gonna do?"

Rick looked thoughtful, his lips turning down, then shrugged and looked Matt right in the eye. "He could kill you."

Matt was silent for a moment, his face showing surprise at Rick's comment. Then he burst out laughing. "Come on, man. We're all cops—that ain't gonna happen."

"No?" Rick said, looking as if he wasn't sure.

"Nah, man. Duh, this is reality here." Matt rolled his eyes and glanced back at Tiny, who was smiling and nodding.

There was a long silence that stretched uncomfortably. Matt shifted around in his seat, looking back at Tiny. "So what do you do for the department?"

"I'm a sergeant with homicide," Tiny said, glancing at Rick.

Matt turned to Rick. "And you?"

Rick paused a full beat, then said, "I'm a lieutenant in charge of FORS."

Matt nodded, and then suddenly something clicked. Rick was sure he could hear it, in fact. Matt started to grin, a self-conscious yet "I can fix this" grin. "Nah, you're just messing with me, right?"

Tiny leaned forward, his massive arms on the back of the seat between Rick and Matt. He looked at Rick, and then at Matt. "No, we're not," he said simply.

Matt began to look distinctly uncomfortable at that point. Rick's face had turned to dangerously unreadable. His deep blue eyes, however, were shooting sparks that were impossible to miss. "That was my wife you were making a pass at," he said, his tone like ice.

"Hey, man, I was just messing around. I didn't mean any harm," Matt said, his voice forcibly casual.

"No?" Rick sounded unconvinced.

"No, man, really." Matt glanced at Tiny, who stared back at him with coal-black eyes and a slightly malicious grin on his face.

"You picked the wrong woman to fuck with, man," Tiny said, his tone low.

"Yeah, you did," Rick echoed.

"Look," Matt said, putting his hands out in a placating gesture. "I'm sorry, I should have had more respect for the married thing, okay."

Rick gave a short laugh, shaking his head. "Nah," he began, holding up his left hand and wiggling his wedding band. "This don't mean shit." He closed his hand into a fist and brandished it menacingly. "It's *this* you have to worry about." His eyes narrowed as he pulled up to the terminal. "If you *ever* even *think* about touching my wife again, there won't be any badge big enough for you to hide behind. You got that?" His tone was that of the gang member he'd been years before, and the look in his eyes did everything to back the statement up.

"Yeah, man, I got it," Matt said, glancing at Tiny and then back at Rick as he reached blindly for the door handle. He climbed out, visibly shaken.

Tiny gave him a frosty smile. "I hope you enjoyed your stay."

Matt all but ran for the terminal.

Tiny got out and climbed into the passenger seat, then looked over at Rick. "Think he got the point?"

Rick glanced back at the big Samoan. "Yeah, I think he got it."

They stared at each other for a long moment and then both burst out laughing as Rick put the car into gear.

"They aren't all like that guy, are they?" Tiny asked a few minutes into the drive.

"No, but they aren't much better," Rick said, shaking his head. "She's gonna go bloody insane if this next guy don't pan out."

"Who's the next one?"

"Some guy from New York," Rick said, not sounding very impressed, then added, "Harvard graduate." With that he rolled his eyes.

Tiny chuckled, not real impressed with the Harvard label either. "What happens if he doesn't work out either?"

"Well," Rick said, examining his hands on the steering wheel, "I'm considering blackmailing Joe into taking it."

Tiny laughed again. "Yeah? How come he won't do it anyway?"

Rick shook his head. "He doesn't want that kinda responsibility. I can't blame him—Midnight goes through a lot of hell to do the things she does. She couldn't pay me enough to take a job like that."

Tiny guffawed at the mere thought of Rick as Midnight's Assistant Chief. "Shit, if you became her AC, neither of you would ever get any work done."

Rick chuckled knowingly. "Ain't that the truth."

"Hell, half the time you two can't get through staff meetings together."

"Hey," Rick said with mock indignation, "we're fine as long as we don't sit too close, or look at each other too often." He was laughing all the while. It was true; he and Midnight shared an incredible physical attraction for each other that had not dimmed in the slightest over their twelve-year relationship. If anything, it had grown stronger with each year.

"Yeah…" Tiny said, his voice trailing off as he thought about it, and then reflected on his own marriage. He and his wife weren't quite that bad, but there were definite sparks between them, and he loved Jessica beyond anything he'd ever imagined he could feel for another person.

Back at the department, Rick walked into Midnight's office. She was sitting at her desk, her elbows in front of her, rolling her pen between her hands, obviously deep in thought. After a few moments she glanced up.

"Did you enjoy yourself?" she asked, her tone only half joking.

"Immensely," Rick said, kicking the door closed and moving to sit in the chair across from her desk.

Midnight nodded, then tossed the pen down and gave him a direct look. "Taylor just called from the airport and rescinded his application."

Rick didn't even flinch. His face was perfectly composed when he said, "Good."

"Richard…" Midnight began, her concern for some kind of lawsuit coming to bear.

Rick shook his head. "Night, no guy is going to talk to my wife like he did and get away with it."

"Yes, but—"

"No buts," Rick put in simply. He sat forward, his posture showing his need to defend his actions.

Midnight stared back at him for a long moment, then blew her breath out in a sigh. "Just tell me you didn't hit him."

"I didn't lay a finger on him," Rick replied, sitting back and relaxing now that he knew what she was concerned about.

"And Tiny?" Midnight asked, knowing Rick's penchant for telling half-truths when he could get away with it.

"Tiny didn't touch him either."

Midnight's eyes widened in surprise, and Rick saw the beginnings of a grin tugging at her lips. "What did you tell him?"

Rick shrugged. "Just that if he ever even thinks about touching you again, there won't be any place for him to hide."

"That's all, huh?" Midnight said, grinning now.

"It was simple but effective," Rick said, grinning back at her.

Midnight shook her head. "Apparently."

"Did he say why he was taking his application back?"

Midnight paused for a moment, composing her face into a serious expression. "He didn't feel he could contribute anything to this department."

Rick's grin was sardonic as he shook his head. "Wouldn't have been able to contribute much with two broken arms either."

"Probably not," Midnight replied, rolling her eyes. "I should know better, shouldn't I?"

"You should," he agreed.

"Well, I know I would have wanted that chance if the roles had been reversed."

"And I appreciate that chance."

"As well you should," Midnight countered.

"That so?" Rick asked, grinning as he stood to walk around the desk.

Midnight stood to meet him, looking up at him. "That's so."

He reached out, touching her cheek. "So you're saying I should show my appreciation."

Midnight stared directly into his eyes as she said, "For hours on end."

"Oh…" Rick said, trailing off as he leaned down to kiss her.

They kissed for a while, feeling like teenagers making out in the adult's office. Eventually, Rick went to sit on her desk, with her standing between his legs, his arms around her waist. Midnight's hands were on his shoulders as she gazed up at him.

"So, this last guy is your last big chance, huh?" Rick said, trying to keep his tone light.

"Actually, no," Midnight said calmly.

"Really?" Rick asked, surprised.

"Yeah, really." Midnight reached over and picked up the list she'd been making before he'd come in. "I started going back over the applications and adjusting my thinking a little bit, and I have some other possibilities here."

Rick looked at the list, only remembering half of the names. He glanced at his wife and nodded in admiration for her ability to overcome any and all obstacles.

"Should have known you'd pull out of this one," he said, his smile warm.

Midnight shrugged off the compliment lightly. "I do what I have to do, babe."

"I know," Rick said, nodding. "And you do it quite well."

"Yeah, yeah," she replied airily, smiling to take any sting out of her dismissal of his compliment.

"So when's the next one due?" Rick asked, glancing at his watch and noting it was already four o'clock.

"Not till six."

"Why so late?"

"All the commuter flights were full from New York."

"Oh," Rick replied simply.

"Oh," she echoed, smiling.

"Then you'll be late tonight?"

Midnight nodded. "Pretty much."

"Okay," Rick said, standing and looking down at her. "Guess I better get back to work."

"Never know when the chief might be around."

"Nope," Rick said, grinning. He leaned down to kiss her again, but pulled himself up short. "Think she could be around now?" he asked, shifting his stare to either side of them comically.

"Well, if she is, let her watch and get jealous." Midnight reached up to kiss him.

Two hours later she was still thinking about that exchange as she stood waiting at the gate for Masterson. She was wearing her black leather FORS jacket, because the weather had cooled significantly since the sun had gone down. She realized the jacket had her first name on it, which could easily tip Masterson off to who she was. However, she was tired, and the last thing she felt like doing was freezing her ass off just to test one more person. The line of people had trickled down to almost nothing, and she was worrying that she had for sure missed the guy when she saw him. She did a double take, because the man she'd seen was familiar to her, and she had immediately assumed it was Masterson. She realized then that he was walking straight toward her. But the name that came to mind for this face wasn't Masterson, but Masters. Her mind was working even as she reached out to meet his outstretched hand.

"Chief Chevalier, it's good to meet you," Masterson said, his voice exactly as she remembered, his smile warm.

"Chief Masterson, it's nice to meet you too," she said automatically, even as her mind turned over the possibility that he didn't remember her. It had been years ago, after all.

Midnight had met Kyle "Masters" when he was a new sergeant with the New York Police Department. She had been running FORS as a sergeant then. It was two full years before she'd ever laid eyes on Rick. She and Kyle had been at the same conference in Sacramento. They had been in the same work group and had hit it off famously. Kyle was the definition of tall, dark, and handsome. He stood at six feet, three inches, and he had coal-black hair and beautiful bright green eyes. He was muscular without being bulky, and he had an incredible smile. Of Irish-Italian decent, he loved to party and play, but he had a passion for many things. He had been funny and charming, and was also full of the kind of confidence Midnight loved in men—confident without being cocky.

Kyle had asked her to dinner that night. She'd accepted, and they'd ended up back at his hotel room. It was the beginning of a year-long "weekend-romance" kind of thing. Neither of them were looking for any kind of heavy relationship, just someone to have fun with on occasion. She had told Kyle all about Joe, and how important a friend he was to her. Kyle had told her about all the women that he dated back in New York. There was no pressure in their relationship, and in those days that had been exactly what Midnight had been looking for. Kyle was a voracious but incredible lover, and when he was in town they literally spent most of their time in bed. The members of FORS knew when Masters was around because their leader was "unavailable unless someone is dying," and she'd show up a couple of days later looking both exhausted and sated. Joe's favorite saying had been that "the Masters train had been through town."

Looking up at him now, Midnight realized that he looked exactly the same, except for a couple of gray hairs at his temples, and even those were barely noticeable. As he gestured politely for her to precede him, she was trying to decide if it bothered her that he didn't remember her. On the one hand, if he didn't, he hadn't come here expecting to get the job on memories of a more care-free time, and that was good. But on the other hand, if he didn't remember her, that was a blow to her ego. She quickly tamped down that thought. *If he has all the experience he listed on that resume, I'd be stupid to let my ego keep me from being objective,* she told herself emphatically. By the time they'd reached her car, she had resolved to put the past where it belonged and treat him like any other candidate.

As they got into the car, Kyle glanced back at the terminal. "This place sure has changed a lot."

Midnight nodded. "Oh, yes it has! Driving my guys out here insane with patrol duty."

Kyle grinned. "I can imagine."

Midnight pulled out of the terminal area and headed back down Harbor Boulevard. She saw the accident up ahead immediately. "Oh, great." Her eyes went over the scene as the traffic edged around the accident. "Please let there be someone on scene, please…" she muttered.

"I don't see anyone," Kyle said, leaning to the side to see around the car in front of them.

"Well, that just figures, doesn't it?" Midnight said, rolling her eyes and grinning. She looked over at Kyle. "Wanna get your hands dirty?" she asked, her tone telling him she in no way expected it of him.

He grinned back. "Is this part of the interview?"

"Yeah," Midnight said flippantly as she started toward the emergency lane. "I arranged this accident in our way just to see how you handle day-to-day citizens—you figured me out."

Kyle laughed. "Sure, why not?"

Midnight put her red light up on the dashboard and got into the emergency lane. Cars moved out of her way to let her pass. She pulled up to the scene.

An old, beat-up panel van was sitting across two lanes, its front bumper facing the center divide. A newer-model Cadillac was caught with its front bumper in the right rear fender of the van, and steam was rising from its hood. Two men were standing in front of the vehicles, obviously arguing.

Midnight glanced over at Kyle and, rolling her eyes again, got out. She walked toward the men as Kyle came around from the passenger's side.

"Okay, gentlemen," Midnight said authoritatively as she held up her hands as a sign for them to stop yelling. "I need to know, are these vehicles drivable?"

Both men looked at her, obviously surprised by such a well-dressed woman trying to take charge of the scene. They both nodded slowly after a moment.

"Okay, good. I need you both to remove them from the roadway so we can get traffic moving again and—"

"Wait a minute!" the stockier of the two men said. "I ain't moving nothing till the cops get here."

"Well, the cops are here, sir," Midnight said, her voice still placating, as she pulled open the side of her jacket to show the badge clipped to the waist of her skirt. "So please move this vehicle."

"You ain't no fucking cop!" the same man said, his eyes raking over her.

"I assure you, she is," Kyle put in from right behind her.

"Yeah, well, till a real cop shows up and sees how this dumb fucker cut me off, I'm not—"

"Cut you off?" the other man yelled, throwing his arms up in a gesture of frustration. "You were trying to make an illegal turn back there and I was going straight! You can't blame me if you're not smart enough to turn from the right lane!"

"I was turning from the right lane, you dumb raghead! You were just—"

"Enough!" Midnight yelled, glancing back at Kyle. "Masters, please?" she said, gesturing toward one of the men, who was obviously of Middle Eastern descent. Kyle gave her a strange look, but then nodded and moved toward him. Midnight walked toward the first man.

She took him by the arm. "Yours is the van, right?" she asked, even as she led him over to the driver's side.

"Yeah," the man said, pulling his arm free of her grasp.

"Fine." Midnight took a step back and gestured toward the door. "Get in it and move it, now."

"This is bullshit, that raghead's gonna—"

"Sir," Midnight interrupted firmly. "Move the van, now. We'll worry about the whys and wherefores in a minute."

"This is bullshit," the man muttered as he got in. He moved the vehicle to the area Midnight directed him to, and the Cadillac sputtered in behind. Kyle walked over to Midnight. He was writing on a small pad of paper he'd produced from somewhere.

"What's that?" Midnight asked.

"Drawing the accident scene for the investigators," Kyle said matter-of-factly.

Midnight grinned. "Oh yeah," she said, her tone saying, *I knew that.*

Kyle grinned at her. Just then a patrol car pulled up and two officers got out.

"Hey, Chief," the first officer said.

"Hey, Rollins, how's it going?" Midnight replied.

"Same old thing. What are you doing here?" Rollins asked, eyeing Kyle curiously.

"Your job," Midnight replied glibly.

The other office grinned. "Uh oh, busted back to motor pool again."

"Shut up, Madera!" Rollins said, laughing. Then he looked at Midnight. "We'll take it from here, Chief. Thanks."

"Anytime," Midnight said, rolling her eyes.

Kyle ripped the sheet off his pad and handed it to Rollins. "Thought this might help."

Rollins looked at the paper, then at Kyle. "It will, thanks," he said, his voice tinged with a little respect for the stranger, who was obviously a cop too.

Kyle just nodded in response, then followed Midnight back to her car.

As Midnight pulled away from the curb, Kyle looked over at her for a long moment, not sure whether he should say anything. She'd thrown him when she called him Masters. He had convinced himself she didn't remember him. It had bothered him in a way, but it had also been a good thing, considering the cocksure kid he had been then. Midnight had been one of the most incredible women he had ever been with. She'd pulled him into her the first day he'd met her, and he'd craved her after that. She was the kind of woman a man could just enjoy without worrying about hurting her feelings when he didn't call constantly or visit all the time. She had been completely free-spirited, like him. At first he hadn't believed that she was really capable of having the kind of relationship they'd had—easygoing, no pressure. Until that point he hadn't met a woman that could truly do that, but Midnight Chevalier had changed his mind quickly. After their first lustful weekend together, he'd returned to New York and gone back to work, earning his sergeant stripes. He was young and determined in those days to become the best homicide detective ever.

He'd forgotten about the fiery blond in San Diego for a full month, but then the opportunity to travel to San Diego again had come up unexpectedly, and he had decided to go. When he'd gotten to town, he'd taken a chance and called Midnight. She'd answered her phone sounding distracted. He'd told her who he was, and she had laughed, asking where he was. He told her he was in town. Midnight had asked if he was busy for dinner. He told her no, and she invited him to her house.

"Dinner" had turned out to be Chinese take-out, and they'd barely eaten that before they were back in bed together. There had been no comments about not calling her; there had been no attitude, or questions about when he was coming back. They had simply enjoyed each other's company thoroughly during the times when he wasn't at his meetings or she wasn't at work. He'd met her friends, including Joe Sinclair, and had been easily accepted by them as well. He had left three days later, determined to return again soon. In the end he'd made more than a dozen trips to San Diego in a year, and had seen Midnight every time. Sometimes they stayed at her place, sometimes she came to his hotel. He saw her friends a few times at parties or at the office when he came by to see Midnight for lunch. Every time was as comfortable as the first. The following year, things took off with his career. He was given a chance to really prove himself, and he grabbed it. It had meant no vacations or trips across the country for a while. A year after that he met and fell in love with Barbara Vicente. He'd never seen Midnight again, except on the news, until this night. And he had been sure she didn't recognize him. Now he wasn't so confident.

"What?" Midnight asked, glancing over at him and noting his studying look.

"Earlier, you called me Masters," he said casually. "Does that mean you actually remember me, or was that a slip?"

Midnight grinned. "Both."

"Both?" he questioned, his dark brows drawing together.

"Yeah," Midnight qualified, still grinning. "I do remember you, and I did slip in calling you Masters."

"So why didn't you tell me before that you recognized me?" Kyle asked, still not sure how this was going to affect his bid for the Assistant Chief's job.

"You walked up to me and said, 'It's nice to meet you.' Masters, what did you expect me to say?" There was laughter in Midnight's voice.

"True," Kyle said, rubbing the bridge of his nose nervously. "So do I lose points or gain them for my duplicity?"

Midnight laughed then, remembering what a quick wit he had. She gave him a mock serious look. "I'm sorry, I can't tell you that at this time."

"Ah, okay." Kyle nodded, looking appropriately serious as well, but with a grin tugging at his lips. "So how've you been?"

"I've been good," she said, smiling now. "You?"

"Life has its moments," he replied, with enough severity to let

Midnight know he wasn't kidding.

"So why the move to San Diego?" Midnight wasn't sure how to put it so that it didn't sound like an interview question.

"Let's just say I need a change of scenery for me and my boys."

"You have kids…" Midnight said, trailing off as she realized how that might sound.

"Yes," Kyle said, smiling. "Two boys. Nick is thirteen and Brenden is five."

"Almost the same as mine. I have an eleven-year-old daughter, who's almost twelve, and a seven-year-old boy too."

"And a very intense husband that loves you very much," Kyle added.

Midnight gave him a sidelong glance. "And you know this how?"

Kyle leaned back in the seat, eyeing her speculatively. "Same way a billion other people in this country know it. I saw him burying you three years ago with the world looking on."

Midnight grimaced at the mention of such a horrible time, then nodded. "Oh, that."

"Yeah, that," Kyle echoed. "I was glad to hear it was a mistake."

"Yeah, me too," Midnight replied, a glimmer of her usual humor coming back. She pulled into the parking lot then, and into her space. Shutting off the car, she turned to him. "So what about you? You said a change of scenery for you and your boys. Are you divorced, never married, or shouldn't I ask?"

Kyle took a slow, deep breath, then looked over at her. His green eyes were extremely somber as he said, "I lost my wife about three years ago."

"Oh my God," Midnight said, reaching out to touch his hand, her eyes searching his. "I'm sorry."

Kyle nodded, looking like he was desperately trying to compose himself by taking long, deep breaths. "It's okay, Midnight. You couldn't have known."

"I know, but…" she began, but trailed off as he shook his head. She knew she needed to leave it alone then. It just struck her as so tragic that he had lost a woman he had obviously loved. She knew how hard it had been for Rick, thinking that she had been dead years before when a car bomb destroyed her classic Corvette.

After a few minutes, they got out of the car. She led him up to the floor the conference room was on, then turned to him. "Look, do you need some time to get your head together?" she asked softly.

"Yeah, is that okay?" Kyle asked, his look concerned.

"It's okay, go on. The conference room is just down at the end of the hall," she said, pointing. "Come in when you're ready, okay?"

Kyle touched her on the shoulder, his eyes searching hers, then smiled. "Thanks, Midnight."

Midnight smiled back. She knew it was indirectly her fault he'd lost his composure in the first place. She walked down the hall to the conference room and pulled Spider aside.

"What's goin' on?" Spider asked. She was already fifteen minutes late, and then she'd shown up without the candidate.

"There was an accident on Harbor Boulevard. I was first on scene." She glanced behind him at Jess and Simmons. "Look, do you happen to remember Masters?"

"Masters?" Spider echoed, starting to shake his head.

"From way back at the beginning of FORS—tall, dark-haired guy from New York?"

"The train?" Spider said finally as recognition dawned.

"Oh God! Don't use that term!" Midnight gasped, laughing in spite of herself.

"So what about…" Spider began, but then it was obvious something had clicked in his head. "Masterson."

"Yep," Midnight said, nodding.

"Rick know?"

"Spider!" she whispered fiercely. "*I* didn't even know till I picked him up. I didn't know his name was Masterson—I only ever knew Masters."

"So, you want me to… what? Score him low?" Spider asked, obviously ready to do whatever she wanted.

"No!" Midnight said, ever astounded at her members' loyalty. "I just wanted to tell you ahead of time, so that if you got who he was halfway through the interview you wouldn't blurt out something like 'the train'!"

Spider laughed, and then his eyes trained to the door to the conference room; Kyle had just walked in.

Kyle spotted Midnight talking to another man over in the corner of the room, a conversation which broke up when he walked in. He was wondering what it was about when he saw the man's face. Walking over, he extended his hand to Spider. "Nguyen," Kyle said, pronouncing Spider's Laotian surname properly, as the younger man took his proffered hand. "It's been a long time. How are you?"

"I'm good, Masters. Thanks for asking. Good to see you again," Spider said, smiling.

Midnight introduced him to the rest of the panel, and the interview began.

Simmons asked the first standard question. "Tell us about why you feel qualified to be Assistant Chief in the San Diego Police Department."

Kyle paused for a long moment, obviously formulating his answer. Midnight sat back in her chair, remembering when he would say anything that came to mind regardless of its impact.

"First of all, I think that more than one's job prepares a person for a position like this. Being an Assistant Chief is an important job, and requires a lot of abilities that can't be acquired by just working. A position like this requires a lot of social and political skills, as well as a good work ethic. I've worked my whole life to pull myself up from my humble beginnings. In doing so I have pulled myself up through the ranks of law enforcement. I have a great deal of experience in many aspects of police work, and that is important because I don't feel you can lead without having been led at some point in your life. You can't manage the job unless you've done the job."

He paused, looking at each member of the panel, his eyes stopping at Midnight. "I was a Navy Seal for four years. I have a bachelor's degree in business administration. I have nineteen years' law enforcement experience, including two years on patrol, six in homicide, two as a lieutenant. I was four years in narcotics, as lieutenant in charge of the Southside. I was three years in vice, one as a lieutenant, two as a captain. I was two years in the special crimes unit, as captain in charge of the division. Currently I am Assistant Chief over all major crimes—it's been two years."

It was obvious everyone on the panel was scrambling to process the entire list. Midnight was grinning. Jessica got her thoughts together first and asked a question of her own.

"Chief Masterson, you also have a bachelor's in philosophy, correct?"

Kyle's green eyes settled on Jessica. He was thinking to himself that this department had far too many beautiful women in it, but his face showed nothing. "Yes, that's correct."

"May I ask why?" Jessica said, her own green eyes narrowed slightly in curiosity.

Kyle inclined his head in a nod. "My wife was a philosophy major. Originally I went back so I could win more of our debates," he said, grinning engagingly as the two men at the table chuckled in agreement with the idea. "In the end, it proved invaluable in everyday life. Philosophy gives you a new way to look at things."

Spider asked the next question. "What do you consider more important, the letter of the law or the spirit of the law?"

Again, Kyle paused before answering. "Definitely the spirit of the law. Laws are basically guidelines—it's up to law enforcement to understand the purpose behind those laws and enforce them within the most reasonable means."

Spider nodded as he wrote, unconsciously showing that he agreed with Kyle's philosophy.

Midnight asked the next question, one they'd asked and had really bad answers to in the three previous interviews. "What do you consider the most important purpose of law enforcement?"

Kyle looked back at her for a long moment, picking up the way she leaned forward as she spoke and the intensity in her expression, telling him this was an important question. Again, he paused, gathering his thoughts. Finally he directed his answer to each member of the panel. "It's important that law enforcement positively impacts the daily lives of the people it protects."

"What do you think is the best way to accomplish that?" Midnight asked, her eyes glittering with excitement.

"By listening to the people and altering priorities as the criminal climate shifts."

"Meaning?" Midnight shot back.

"Meaning, a department can't concentrate its energies on one area without a consistent look outward to determine changing needs," Kyle replied, obviously enjoying the faster-paced debate style they'd slipped into.

"Can you give me an example of that?" Midnight asked.

"Sure. In New York, for a long time, the biggest problem was the mafia. A great deal of resources were expended in an attempt to suppress the criminal element that came from that particular arena. Now, the mafia, while still present in New York, is much less of a concern. It is now necessary for the focus of the department to shift to a more urgent need."

"And what do you see as the more urgent need at this time?" Midnight asked.

"Many would say drugs and gangs," Kyle said, his tone belying his own thinking on that.

"But you wouldn't?" Midnight replied, her eyes widening

slightly in surprise at his obvious difference in opinion.

Kyle inclined his head again, as if in deference to Midnight's own priorities. "I think that drugs and gangs are an ongoing problem, and basically a proliferation of lack of education and morals evident in today's society. Definitely a problem, but not the only one."

"What other problems do you see as imperative?" Midnight asked, drawn into his thinking in spite of herself.

"I think that hi-tech crime is becoming a widespread problem, with the advent of the Internet in just about every home in America. That brings dangers, everything from consumer fraud to sex crimes."

"And you don't think that problem is being addressed?" she asked, curious as to whether he'd slam his own department to make points in the interview.

"I think law enforcement as a whole has a difficult time dealing with a crime that is less tangible and much more difficult to pursue."

"And prosecute," Midnight added.

Kyle acquiesced with a nod. Midnight nodded in return, realizing suddenly that she'd monopolized the floor for a few minutes. Looking at her panel members, however, she could see that they'd enjoyed the discussion as well.

"Okay, we can get back to the canned questions now," Midnight said, smiling as her eyes alighted on Kyle again. Kyle laughed, as did the panel.

The interview continued for another half hour, often detouring into side questions from something Kyle said. Midnight liked a free-style interview situation, in which the panel were able to ask questions that would better acquaint them with the candidate. When the interview was over, Kyle shook hands with each of them, and Midnight escorted him out into the hallway. "I'll be with you in a few minutes, okay?" she said, smiling.

He laughed. "I'll just hang out and wring out my tie."

Midnight canted her head to the side. "You were nervous in there?"

"Hell yes," he replied, looking at her like she was crazy to ask him a question like that.

Midnight shook her head slowly, amazed and pleased at the same time. "Couldn't tell."

Kyle grinned. "I play poker a lot."

"Uh-huh," Midnight murmured, unconvinced, then turned and went back into the conference room. Kyle leaned back against the nearest wall, looking up at the ceiling and blowing his breath out. He loosened his tie, then pulled it free from his white shirt. Looking down at it, he remembered the day Barbara had given it to him. It had been Father's Day, not long before she died. He had teased her that she was becoming clichéd in her old age. She told him she couldn't have him looking shabby; it was embarrassing. He had grown sober, and she had laid her hand on his cheek, looking up into his eyes lovingly. He frequently remembered that touch, that look.

"Hey," said a deep voice to his left. Kyle turned. Walking toward him was a man standing easily six feet, five inches, with a large, muscular frame. He had long dark hair, a dark tan, and almost black eyes. Kyle stared at him for a long moment, and then recognition dawned, as it apparently did for the other man as well.

"Tiny, how the hell are ya?" Kyle said, smiling easily.

"Masters, right?" Tiny asked, not sure if his memory was serving.

"That's me." Kyle nodded, extending his hand to the younger man. "How've you been?"

"I'm good, real good. Just waiting for my wife." Tiny gestured to the conference room with his head.

"Oh, so your wife would be the gorgeous redhead."

Tiny looked surprised for a moment, then realized that the only other woman in the conference room was Midnight. "Yeah, that's Jess," he said, pride in his voice.

Kyle nodded, smiling.

"So what are you doing here?" Tiny asked, glancing at the tie in Kyle's hands. "You're not interviewing, are you?"

Kyle grinned. "Yep, Assistant Chief."

"Wow, didn't know that. How come?" Tiny smiled. "They fire you in New York?"

Kyle laughed. "Yeah, how'd you guess?"

"So long as you weren't like that guy right before you, you're okay," Tiny said, rolling his eyes.

"Guy before me?"

Tiny nodded, and proceeded to tell Kyle the whole story about Taylor and his trip back to the airport.

"Oh man," Kyle said, shaking his head, amazed. "He was stupid enough to actually make a pass at Midnight?"

Tiny snickered. "Stupid enough for that, and even more stupid to make the same comments to Rick. He's lucky he left here alive."

Kyle gave a low whistle. "I remember how protective you all were of Midnight. Debenshire sounds worse."

"He's not worse, he just has more to protect," Tiny said matter-of-factly.

Kyle nodded. "True."

They talked for a few more minutes, and then the door to the conference room opened. Spider came out and walked over to Kyle, extending his hand.

"Good seeing you again, man. Take it easy," Spider said, smiling. Then he turned and headed down the hall.

Simmons walked out, nodding to Kyle on the way past.

Jessica appeared then. She too extended her hand, thanking Kyle for his time.

"Thank you," Kyle replied, smiling warmly.

Jessica stepped toward Tiny, who put his arm around her, kissing her softly on the cheek. Tiny put his hand out to Kyle. "Good seeing you again," he said, grinning. "Hope my wife didn't rake you over too many hot coals—she's IA, ya know."

Jessica elbowed him in the ribs, which he didn't seem to notice, except to laugh.

Kyle took Tiny's hand, shaking it and laughing too. "She didn't. You take good care."

With that Tiny and Jessica started down the hall together. After a few moments, Kyle went to the open door to the conference room. Midnight was standing reading something. Kyle leaned against the doorjamb, watching her.

She glanced up, smiling. "I'll be there in two minutes, I promise."

"No rush," he replied easily.

Kyle reached up and undid the top two buttons of his shirt, and started looking around the conference room. Midnight glanced up and watched him wander around. She picked up the papers from the table, put them in a folder, and walked toward him. "I need to take these to my office before we go, okay?"

"Sure," Kyle said, following her out of the room.

Up in her office, Midnight sat down behind her desk. Again, Kyle stood in the doorway watching for a long moment. Then he went inside and started examining her shelves of books. Midnight glanced up, grinning at how comfortable he seemed. After a few long minutes, she rested her elbows on her desk and sat waiting for him to turn around. When he did, it was with a question.

"You know, I forgot to ask. When will you be making a decision on the Assistant Chief?"

"Tonight."

Kyle looked stunned. "Tonight?"

"Yes, the decision has already been made," Midnight replied smoothly.

Kyle shook his head in amazement. "You don't drag your feet around here, do you?"

"Nope." There was a long moment of silence, then Midnight grinned. "When can you start?"

Kyle looked back at her, openmouthed in his astonishment. "Wow," was his only reply.

Midnight gave him a mystified look. "You have no idea how well you did in there, do you?"

"Obviously well enough," Kyle said, as the idea that he'd gotten the job sank in and he started to grin.

"You blew us all away, Kyle," Midnight said, using his first name for the first time.

"My pleasure, Midnight."

"Can I ask you something?" she said cautiously.

"Sure." Kyle sat down in one of the chairs across from her desk.

"Why did you want to come here?"

He thought about it for a minute, then said, "Because I knew you were the kind of chief I could work with. Someone who would listen to my ideas, and give me credit for them when they were good ones." He looked straight into her eyes. "And because I always thought you were an incredible cop, and I think you're an even better chief."

Midnight stared back at him, then shook her head. "All that, huh?" she said, grinning self-consciously.

Kyle smiled. "You never could stand compliments, could you?"

Midnight laughed, shaking her head. "No, I guess not." She looked at him seriously. "So how come you didn't say any of that in the interview?"

Kyle gave her a contemplating look. "And look like a total kiss-ass?" he said, sounding like he had fifteen years before. He shook his head. "I want to get the job on my merits, not on how much butt I kiss."

"How do you know I don't like that stuff?"

"Unless you've changed a lot over the years, you don't. And if you did, I wouldn't want to work for you."

Midnight knew he was serious, and she found she really liked his direct approach. He reminded her of Joe. "Still so direct, huh?"

Kyle nodded. "Yeah, but I've also learned to play the game when I have to."

"Good, I need someone that knows how to play. I'm afraid I still suck at it," Midnight said, laughing.

"I don't believe that for a minute," Kyle replied, narrowing his eyes at her. "Can I ask you a question now?"

"Shoot," she replied, leaning back in her chair and putting a heeled foot on the open lower drawer of her desk.

"Since you apparently didn't know I was Masterson, your husband doesn't either. How is he going to react when he finds out who I am, or was to you way back when? Or do you not intend to tell him at all?"

It was a long moment before Midnight answered. "Oh, I'll tell him. Tonight, in fact, because believe me, it will be around this entire department by morning. And if I don't tell him, someone else will."

Kyle nodded, understanding the way the gossip mill worked in all departments.

"How he'll react, well, that's a different story," Midnight said seriously. "It's hard to tell with him sometimes. There have been times when I expected him to go ballistic about something and he's been fine about it. There have been other times I didn't think anything of an occurrence and he's blindsided me with fury. So…" She held up her hands in a gesture of futility.

"I just don't want him to be too uncomfortable around me if I can help it, you know?" Kyle said.

Midnight shrugged, shaking her head. "He's an adult, Kyle. He can deal with this if we can."

"Well, you know you have nothing to worry about with me, obviously, since you went ahead and hired me."

"Yeah, I do know. And in time so will Rick."

Kyle nodded. He thought for a moment. "Would it help if I came to your place and met him? Rather than here, because then we'd be in his territory."

"Men!" Midnight said, rolling her eyes. "They always think in terms of possessions and territory." She shook her head and grinned. "Actually, I do think that might help. How long are you in town for? Your flight back is tomorrow morning, right?"

"Yeah, but I need to get some leads on a place to live and all that, since I just scored the job," he said, incredibly pleased about it.

"Well, I might be able to help you out there."

"You want me to move in with you, and you're divorcing Rick?" Kyle grinned sardonically as Midnight laughed.

"How'd you guess?" she said. "Actually, I was thinking of Joe Sinclair—remember him?" Kyle nodded. "He has a house that's empty right now. It was the one he bought when he first came to San Diego. He rents it out from time to time to people in the department he trusts. I'm sure it's empty right now, if you think you'd be interested."

"How big is it?" Kyle asked, thinking he needed at least three bedrooms.

"I want to say it has five bedrooms. It's practically a mansion, Kyle—this is Joe we're talking about here."

"Oh yeah, Sinclair the independently wealthy man. If it's that big, how much is he going to charge? I'm only an Assistant Chief, ya know." He grinned again, but was honestly concerned about the price. Two boys weren't cheap to raise on one's own. His wife had left behind money, and life insurance, but he hadn't ever been able to bring himself to use any of it. It had all been put into a fund for the boys, for college and the like. He still forced ends to meet with just his salary.

"Well, you'll have to talk to Joe, but I'm sure he'll work with you on it. Want me to call him tonight and ask?"

"That would be great, thanks."

"And how about you come to dinner at our house tomorrow night?" Midnight said, wanting to get the meeting between Rick and Kyle over with as quickly as possible.

"Sounds good."

"Perfect." She stood up. "Ready to go to your hotel, Chief?"

He smiled. "Yes, I think I am."

The drive to his hotel didn't take long; he was staying in La Jolla. She dropped him off and said she'd call Joe when she got home. He thanked her and told her he'd call in the morning to let her know when he'd be by the office. They had decided to skip the paperwork until the following day.

Driving home, Midnight felt good about things to come. She knew Kyle would be the perfect complement to her style. He was smooth in the areas she was still—and figured she would forever be—

rough in. He had street smarts, which made him better at determining current needs and gave him the know-how on how to treat them. She knew he was going to be an asset to her. Now she just needed to convince Rick. Telling him about Kyle was going to be hard; she knew he hated the idea that she'd not only had men before they had been together but that she'd had a lot of men before they got together. He had patently avoided any knowledge of who she'd been with in the department, but on the few occasions when he'd had to deal with someone she'd been with, he'd been edgy and hard to deal with for a while afterwards. Now, here was Kyle. Not only was Rick going to have to deal with him, but Midnight would be working with him constantly. She had no idea how he would react to this news.

# CHAPTER 2

As they drove home in his Ford Explorer, Jess gave her husband a sidelong look. "So, how do you, Spider, and Midnight know Kyle Masterson?" she asked, in what Tiny considered her best IA voice.

Tiny looked over at his wife of almost seven years. There were still so many days when he was secretly thrilled that she was actually his. She was such a beautiful woman, with an easygoing personality and such a way about her that he found it impossible to believe she'd actually fallen for him. Tiny had always considered himself an all-brawn, no-brains type of person. He'd always thought his power lay in his strength. He'd also always considered himself unappealing to women, especially ones as beautiful as Jessica.

For years he'd had a huge crush on Midnight Chevalier, the woman who had basically rescued him from himself and the life he'd been leading. He'd been laid up in the hospital when she showed up at his bedside and introduced herself. At first he'd been stunned by her beautiful eyes and her flowing copper-blond hair. He hadn't been able to speak at first, because he was just too shy. Midnight had sensed that, and she'd gone about making him feel comfortable in her presence. At first he hadn't known exactly who she was. He'd assumed she was with the hospital staff, trying to get out of him who had stabbed him, literally, in the back. It had been another gang member, one of his own gang, but he wasn't going to tell them anything. Midnight asked about it once, but when he wouldn't answer she dropped it. He found out two days into her visits that she was a cop; she'd worn her badge. That was the day she told him she was there because she knew where he was headed. She told him about her brother, and how he had died, bled to death in her arms because of a gang fight. She'd pointed out that the same thing had already almost happened to him. Did he think he could avoid it forever? Actually, yes, he did, but Midnight Chevalier was a compelling force. She sucked him in, and within a week he was out of the gang and joining her task force, named FORS.

He'd been so dumbstruck by Midnight that he would have followed her anywhere at first, but then he came into his own as a member of the unit. Midnight had made him into someone worthwhile. His crush had deepened, but she was with Sinclair then. Years later she met and married Rick, and Tiny had accepted then that women like Midnight were out of his reach. Then along came Jessica. As luck, or cruel fate, would have it, Jessica was also smitten with Joe Sinclair. She had come to San Diego from Sacramento to visit Joe, whom she had met when he taught a range class in Sacramento. She thought Joe Sinclair was incredible.

One night, Tiny had gone to Joe's to give him news about the Chief of Police at the time, and because Joe wasn't home, he'd had a chance to sit and talk with Jessica. She'd been funny, and nice, and he'd gotten brave enough to ask her out, with her help. He'd been smitten with her the very first time he met her, but he'd never dared to hope. Now here she was his wife, his lady, his love. It still astounded him.

"Nathan?" Jessica queried, using his given name, or a shortened version of it. She was never sure where he went in his mind when he looked at her like that. Whenever she asked, he'd just shake his head and smile at her, as if it was too complicated to explain.

"I'm sorry," Tiny said, grinning sheepishly. "What did you ask me?"

"I asked how you, Spider, and Midnight know Kyle Masterson," she repeated patiently, knowing her husband was always thinking a million things at once.

"Oh," Tiny said, shrugging slightly. "He was with Midnight a long time ago."

"With?" Jessica asked, looking surprised.

Tiny grinned shyly, but with a mischievous gleam in his eyes. "Yeah, with, as in carnally with."

"Wow," Jessica said, shaking her head slowly. "When was this? I mean, not while she's been married to Rick, right?"

"No," Tiny said. He looked offended that she'd say that about Midnight.

"Nathan, I didn't think so—that's why I asked that way."

"Well, it was about two years before she ever even met Rick," Tiny explained.

"I thought she was with Joe before Rick," Jessica put in, ever the intuitive investigator.

"She was with Joe sometimes, but they weren't a constant thing," Tiny said, obviously uncomfortable talking about Midnight's love life.

"Okay, I'm sorry," Jessica said, sensing his discomfort and quick to try and relieve it. "Does Rick know Kyle Masterson?"

"Why would he know him?"

"I was just wondering." Jessica shrugged, then looked at her husband pointedly. "It might make things go smoother."

"What things?" Tiny asked, suspicious.

"Things like the fact that he's our new Assistant Chief," Jessica said, grinning ingenuously.

"Holy shit!" Tiny exclaimed before he could stop himself, then looked over at his wife apologetically. "Oops, sorry."

Jess laughed. "Don't worry about it, hon. I have to agree with you."

"Rick's not going to like this," Tiny said ominously.

"Probably not," Jessica replied, grimacing comically.

Midnight's cell phone rang before she reached home.

"Yes?"

"Hey," Joe said on the other end of the line, his voice somehow soothing her frayed nerves.

"What's going on?" Midnight asked, relaxing.

"I hear you had an interesting interview." Joe's grin was almost visible through the cell phone.

"Jesus! How did you find out so fast?" Midnight asked, shaking her head incredulously.

"Spider."

"That rat," Midnight said, even as a stubborn smile started on her face. Couldn't keep news like this quiet for long.

"Rick know yet?"

"Joe," Midnight deadpanned. "How would he know? I just found out when I picked Kyle up at the airport, and I'm not even home yet."

"Oh," Joe said, and Midnight could feel him grinning again. "So you gonna tell him?"

Midnight narrowed her eyes at the phone, as if it were the one thoroughly enjoying questioning her like this. "Sinclair, I'm not stupid!" she said unnecessarily. "If you already know, you can imagine the rest of the gang will know soon, and if you think for one second any of them would hesitate in telling Rick just exactly who Kyle Masterson is, you can just think again."

Joe laughed. "I was thinking of calling him myself."

"You are such a shit."

"Yeah, but you love me anyway."

"Maybe," Midnight admitted, a grin tugging at her lips. "Just keep it to yourself for a bit, Sinclair. I'm going to tell him when I get home. Is that soon enough?"

"It'll do," Joe replied, a smile still in his voice.

"Yeah, yeah..." Midnight said. "What I wouldn't do for a department of people that respected me, just for ten minutes..."

"We respect you. We just love you more, so giving you constant grief is part of the package."

"I see," Midnight said, rolling her eyes. "How 'bout you love me just a little less over this issue, okay? Rick's gonna be bad enough—I don't need you guys making it worse. Think about Kyle in this—he's gonna have to deal with Rick. You and I both know what Rick's like when he's been pushed too far by good-natured ribbing. Okay?"

"I got ya, babe. I'll inform the crew," Joe said, his tone sobering somewhat. She was right; Rick could be pushed too far when it came to Midnight. Kyle Masterson might end up laid out flat the first time he met up with Rick face to face. Not a good way to start a good business relationship.

"Thanks," Midnight said as she pulled into the driveway to her house.

"Anything for you," Joe said sincerely.

"Now you tell me," Midnight replied, smiling. "Hey, speaking of which—do you think you'd be interested in renting Kyle your old house?"

"I don't see why not."

"I know you usually don't charge people to use it, but I have a feeling he'll expect to pay something, so just go along with it, okay?"

"Ah, pride thing, huh?" Joe said, grinning.

"Yeah, well, what can I say—not all cops are bums." Midnight laughed. She knew Joe had given many of their friends breaks when they needed it. Since Joe was worth millions, money wasn't a big concern of his.

"I'll work out something with him, okay?"

"Thanks, Joe. I'll owe ya."

"Yeah, yeah," Joe said airily. "Goodnight, and good luck."

"Yeah, you too… thanks."


The light was on in their bedroom when Midnight walked in, so she knew Rick was still up. She didn't know whether she was relieved or not. She hung her FORS jacket up in the hall closet and set her briefcase down on the table. When she walked into their bedroom, Rick glanced at her. He was lying on their bed, wearing gray shorts and a black-and-gray plaid sleeveless pullover, unbuttoned all the way, with nothing underneath it. His tanned, lightly defined chest and flat stomach caught her attention and quickened her pulse, as always. His deep blue eyes followed hers dropping to his chest, and he knew what she was thinking instantly. Perfect white teeth showed in a finely boned, tanned face as he grinned and shook his head.

"You know, I'd love to just be respected for my mind," he said lazily, his accent deeper than usual because he was tired.

"Uh-huh," Midnight said, kicking off her shoes and grinning over at him.

"See how dumb that sounds?" he replied, sitting up as she walked toward him. He pulled her down on his lap, his lips finding hers instantly as his arms wrapped around her waist. Midnight's arms went around his neck, and she enjoyed the feel of his curly hair as her fingers laced through it. They kissed for a long while, getting more and more passionate with each moment.

"Mama!" a small voice cried from the doorway, causing a quick end to the passionate embrace as Midnight looked up and laughed guiltily. Ricardo launched himself up onto their bed and crawled across to Midnight's side. Midnight was still sitting on Rick's lap, and she turned around to face the youngster, who immediately threw his arms around her.

Rick laughed at Ricardo's enthusiasm. "I have to admit, Ricardo," he said, grinning at the little boy, whose face was only inches from his own, though half buried in Midnight's copper-blond hair, "that I feel exactly the same way when I see her." Ricardo didn't understand the meaning of that, other than that Papa was happy to see

Mama too, but Midnight got it and laughed.

After a long hug, Ricardo leaned back and looked up at Midnight. "You are late," he said, his broken English still heavily accented with his native Spanish.

"Yes, I am," Midnight agreed.

"Did you call?" Ricardo asked, sounding like Midnight or Rick scolding their daughter, Mikeyla.

"I, um…" Midnight stammered, glancing at Rick for help.

"Yes, Ricardo, she called me," Rick put in, rescuing her from having to explain why adults didn't always have to call when they were going to be late.

"Ah, bien." Ricardo said.

It had been a difficult time at first when Ricardo had come to live with them. His mother, Marta, had been killed saving Midnight's life. She'd pushed Midnight out of the way when the bomb meant to kill the chief exploded under the hood of her Corvette. It had been Ricardo's uncle, Juan, who had pulled Midnight's unconscious body out of view and taken her to his apartment to administer what first aid he could. In the end, Juan had contacted the chief of the Mexican police and told him Midnight was alive. They had allowed the world to think Midnight had been killed, to keep the assassin, Ricardo's own father, from making another attempt on her life before he could be caught and brought to justice.

It had been Juan who had told Midnight that he thought his sister would have wanted Midnight to take the son she loved so dearly. Midnight and Rick had discussed it, and since having another child had not been an option for Midnight, due to a medical condition from her first pregnancy, they decided that Ricardo was exactly what their life needed, that it had been fate smiling on them. Midnight had befriended Ricardo and his mother in a cantina a few days before the bomb had been set in her car. She had broken up an altercation that threatened to turn violent between Ricardo's mother and father. She had humiliated Ricardo's father in front of the entire cantina, because he had threatened first to hit his wife, then when Midnight stepped in, threatened to teach *her* a lesson as well. Ricardo and Marta had been very impressed with the American woman with an excellent Spanish accent and incredible fighting skills, and such a warm smile. Ricardo had been smitten from the moment he'd first seen her.

In the end, Rick's father, Robert, an attorney in England, was able to get through the red tape involved in adopting Ricardo with surprising ease. It did help that Midnight was very well acquainted with the Chief of Police in Mexico, as well as the fact that Rick's family had a good deal of money to smooth over any major problems. Ricardo had been with them for nine months now. Midnight was the only member of the family who spoke fluent Spanish, and at first Ricardo hadn't known any English. It had been a learning process for all of them. Midnight had been very proud of both Rick and Mikeyla for putting forth their best efforts to learn Spanish, and also of Ricardo for not only learning English quickly but for adjusting to their family with ease. His uncle Juan came to the States as often as possible for visits, and commented on how happy Ricardo seemed.

There had been times when he had asked about his mother, and Midnight told him that his mother was a very brave and strong woman who had saved another person's life, giving her own unselfishly. Midnight had made a point of getting a few photographs of

Marta from her brother, and placed them in frames to put in Ricardo's room so he would never forget his mother. She frequently told him that she was not trying to replace her, that she only wanted to love him and raise him to be the best man he could be, which she knew his mother would have wanted for him. It was Midnight's intent to repay Marta's selfless act by giving her son every opportunity she possibly could. Midnight honestly believed Marta was looking down from heaven and watching what was done with her son. She even talked to her every so often, thanking her for her great sacrifice, which had allowed Rick and Mikeyla to get her back. Midnight had no idea how often Rick also talked to the woman he had never met, thanking her for that very thing.

Even now, as Ricardo smiled up at Midnight, Rick closed his eyes and said a silent thank you to Ricardo's mother.

"Shouldn't you be in bed, niño?" Midnight asked, glancing at her watch.

"I told him he could stay up till you got home," Rick said as Ricardo glanced at him.

"Aha, a conspiracy!" Midnight said, grinning down at Ricardo. "Well, come along, little man. Let's get you into bed. Mama has lots to talk to her Ricardo about." Rick laughed, because he knew she meant him. Ricardo grinned, remembering when Midnight had told him that her husband's name was Ricardo too. That had been outside the cantina with his mother. A shadow chased across his small features as he thought of his mother, but then Midnight took his hand in hers and he smiled. His mama had done a great, great thing, saving this woman's life. It was God's will that he be with this new family, and God knew everything, so certainly he knew what was best. His mama was with the angels, and guiding his new mama to keep her safe from harm. Ricardo squeezed Midnight's hand as the emotions seemed to well up in him again. He looked up at her with eyes threatening to overflow with tears. Midnight bent down and picked him up as she continued toward his room. He wrapped his arms around her neck and buried his face in her hair. Rick felt compelled to follow them, at a discreet distance so as not to intrude.

Once in Ricardo's room, decorated in trucks and cars, which were his two passions, Midnight sat down on his bed, a race car with tires and everything. She clutched the little boy in her arms, not sure what had caused his sudden need to cling to her as if he were drowning, but realizing that he needed to be comforted. She stroked his back, kissed the dark curls at the back of his little head, and then his forehead when he turned toward her. After a long moment, he reached up to touch her cheek softly. Midnight looked down at him and saw that his eyes were shining and his cheeks were wet from tears.

"Do you want to talk about it?" she asked softly.

He shook his head slowly.

"Okay," Midnight said. "But you know if you ever want to talk, I'll always listen, don't you?"

This time he nodded. "I talk to her sometimes," he said, his voice soft and a little choked with emotion.

"I do too," Midnight replied quietly.

His eyes widened. "You do?"

Midnight nodded, touching his cheek with her fingertips, gently brushing away his tears. "I talk to her about you, and how you're doing."

He nodded, blinking as if trying to adjust to what she was saying. "Does she answer you?" he asked, his small voice hopeful.

Midnight was quiet for a moment, then shook her head. "No, she doesn't answer me, but I know she hears me."

"How?"

"Because I see her smile in yours every day. I see her eyes in your eyes, and when you smile and are happy, I know that she is too."

That statement made Ricardo smile so brightly, Midnight felt her chest constrict with emotion. She smiled to try and keep her composure. Then she hugged him tightly, tears shining in her eyes. Glancing up, she saw Rick standing in the doorway, and she could have sworn there were tears in his eyes too. She put Ricardo to bed then, tucking him in and reading him his favorite story, then kissed him goodnight. Rick came in to kiss him as well.

Back in their room, Midnight went to their bathroom to shower and change. When she came out ten minutes later, Rick was sitting on their bed, his back against the headboard, his legs stretched out in front of him. He was lazily flipping through the channels, obviously waiting for her. He turned the TV off. Midnight, wearing a green silk camisole that reached mid-thigh, walked over and straddled his legs.

"So how did the last interview go?" Rick asked, his gaze touching on her bare shoulders then moving to her eyes.

"It went really well," Midnight said hesitantly—and Rick picked up on it instantly.

"Oh man, I can hear a 'but' in that statement," he said, rolling his eyes. "What was wrong with this one?"

Midnight was silent a moment, looking at the wall above his

shoulder. Then she shrugged and looked him in the eyes. "Nothing. In fact, I hired him."

"Okay…" Rick said, knowing there was more and trying to figure out what that was.

Midnight took a deep breath, then let it out in a sigh. "Look, the fact is, I know him."

"You know him?" Rick repeated, dumbfounded. "Then why didn't you tell—"

"I didn't know I knew him till he got off the plane tonight," Midnight interrupted, wanting to get this over with quickly. "I met him a long time ago, at a conference."

Rick nodded slowly, his eyes narrowing slightly. "Why do I know there's more?" he asked, his tone chilling slightly already.

Again Midnight took a deep breath, holding it. "Because there is." Her voice took on a business-like tone as she continued. "We met at the conference, we hit it off, we went out."

Rick nodded again, a knowing look entering his eyes. She could feel him tensing under her. "And you slept with him," he supplied when she didn't say anymore.

Midnight swallowed almost nervously, then nodded.

"When was this?" Rick asked, his tone clipped.

"About fifteen years ago," she answered, her voice starting to match his.

"And it was a one-time thing?" Rick asked hopefully.

Midnight shook her head.

"How long?" he asked, rapid fire again.

70

"A year."

Rick stared at her dumbfounded. His eyes took on a hurt look, but his face remained stony as he asked, "You dated him for a year?"

"It wasn't an all-the-time kind of thing—he lived in New York." When it was obvious he was waiting for further clarification, she continued, "We were together when he was in town, which was maybe once a month."

Rick said nothing for a long few moments, looking everywhere but at her. Midnight waited, aware that he was assimilating what she had said. She didn't like the position she was in; she hated being on the defensive. But she also knew that in order for Rick to be okay with this, she needed to let him vent his feelings about it if that was what he wanted to do. Finally his eyes came back to hers, and Midnight felt herself flinch at the pain she saw there. She didn't understand it until he spoke again.

"Did you love him?" he asked, his voice quiet and stricken.

Midnight stared back at him for a long moment, stunned that he was actually worried about that. "Rick…" she said softly, searching his eyes as she reached up to touch his cheek. "I have never loved anyone like I love you." Then she shook her head, because that hadn't cleared his mind. "No, I didn't love him."

He swallowed convulsively, trying to get his feelings under control, as Midnight leaned forward, laying her head against his chest. He nodded, more to himself than to her, as he wrapped his arms around her, holding her close. They stayed that way for a long time. Then she pulled back, looking up at him.

"What else do you want to know?" she asked softly.

"Did he bring it up tonight?"

"The past?"

"Yeah."

"No," she said, shaking her head. "In fact, at first we both pretended we'd never met. When I finally slipped and called him by his old nickname, Masters, he was surprised I did remember him after all. We talked about our kids, you, and about his life too."

"You talked about me?" Rick asked, clearly surprised.

"Yeah, we were talking about his kids and then about Keyl and Ricky, and then he said something about my very intense husband who loves me very much."

"Why did he say that? And how does he know me?" Rick asked, suspicion creeping in.

"He saw the funeral, Rick," she said, her voice softening. She knew how hard it was for him to think about that time.

Midnight had seen so many clips from the media since then. She'd seen him at the gravesite, and watched as he had literally flinched at each shot of the twenty-one-gun salute, and as he had sunk to his knees during the playing of "Taps." She'd seen the agony on his face, and how lost he had looked. It made her physically sick, but it gave her a real understanding of how much he really loved her too.

"Oh," Rick said, understanding exactly what Masterson had seen. He'd watched some of it himself since then, and he knew there was no question in anyone's mind about what would happen to him if he ever lost Midnight for real. "So you trust the guy?"

"Yes, I trust him."

Rick nodded slowly. "Then I'll give him a chance."

Midnight smiled. "That's all I'm asking."

"Good," Rick said, leaning down to take possession of her lips. He was still kissing her as he moved her back off his legs, getting to his knees as he laid her down on the bed. Their heads ended up at the foot of the bed as they kissed for a long time, his body half covering hers. When the kisses ended, he slowly rolled to the right, pulling her with him, moving onto his back. Midnight's head rested against the hollow of his shoulder, her body pressed against the length of his side, her leg over his possessively. He stroked her hair as he stared up at the ceiling, her nails tracing patterns lightly on his bare chest, both of them lost in their own thoughts. That's the way Mikeyla found them twenty minutes later.

Mikeyla Debenshire was a precocious eleven-year-old. She was a perfect mixture of both parents, with Midnight's copper-blond hair and Rick's deep blue eyes and finely boned face. She was a beautiful girl, and would eventually be a beautiful woman, and she couldn't wait to grow up. She had Midnight's intellect, but also her father's wild side, and she'd inherited both parents' passion for everything. There were so many things she wanted to do, but as was inherent in youth, she wanted to do all of it right now. Lately all her friends had been telling her how "great" her parents were, how cool it was that they were so "hot" for each other. Her best friend, Sarah, who was thirteen and a half, said that her parents never looked at each other the way Mr. And Mrs. Debenshire frequently did. Mikeyla was caught in the struggle to grow up and see the world through mature eyes, and yet in many ways she was still a child. Looking at her parents, who hadn't yet noticed her presence, she tried to see them the way her friends did.

She saw her mother's hand on her father's bare chest. His shirt was open and she could see his tan gleaming in the bedroom light. He wore a gold chain at his throat, a series of flat links Midnight had given him years before for his birthday. His light brown curly hair lay around his shoulders and spread out on the sheet behind his head. None of her friends' fathers wore their hair long like her dad did. She liked it in a way, thought it was cool, even though most younger guys were cutting their hair these days. She'd heard her mother threaten her father with great bodily harm if he cut his. There had been many times when she'd walked into the kitchen to find them kissing—her mother's hands would always be in his hair. Mikeyla had also heard her father threaten her mother about not cutting her hair as well. It was funny in a way, that her parents cared so much about that kind of stuff. Kinda like teenagers. Mikeyla looked at her mother's copper-blond hair, lying over Rick's upper arm as he stroked it lovingly. She wondered what it would be like to have a boy touch her hair like that, so adoringly.

There had been so many boys interested in her lately, but she didn't know how to act around them. Many of them had been friends of hers for years. She tended to hang out with older kids because kids her age were just dumb. Being around two dynamic personalities like her parents, not to mention the colorful people that made up their circle of friends, Mikeyla had become so acquainted with adult conversations that she expected the same level from her friends. While the eleven-year-olds she knew were only interested in Justin Timberlake and Britney Spears, Mikeyla was interested in the latest cars, books, and movies. While she liked the music from the popular bands, she didn't spend as much time worshiping them as other girls did. She knew it set her apart, but she'd found some older friends who seemed to get her much better. Sure, they liked the boy bands and stuff too, but they weren't so gaga over them that they couldn't talk about other things. Of course, lately all the talk had been about this one chat room that everyone was logging into. That's what she wanted to talk to her parents about.

Rick glanced up, noticing Mikeyla standing in the doorway.

"Hey, Keyl," he said. Midnight propped herself up on her elbow to look back over her shoulder at her daughter.

"Hi, you two," Mikeyla said, walking into the room. She went to sit on the bed as her parents moved to sit up. Even then, they didn't move away from each other. Midnight turned to face Mikeyla, and Rick sat with one arm bracing himself on the bed, the other sliding around Midnight's waist. It was like they knew how the other was going to sit and they just moved that way together.

"What's up?" Midnight asked. Mikeyla didn't usually pop in for no reason. Lately she'd been busy with her friends a lot.

"Can we get the Internet?" Mikeyla asked without preamble.

Midnight looked back at her daughter for a long minute, then glanced at Rick. He kind of shrugged, and looked back at Midnight, basically telling her it was her call.

"What are you going to use it for?" Midnight asked, knowing all about the latest chat craze. "Well," Mikeyla began, aware they'd want her to use it for school and stuff too, "I can use it for school, to look up stuff for book reports and things."

Rick's grin was lopsided as he said, "Yeah, but what are you going to use it for?" His tone told her she wasn't fooling him.

"Dad!" Mikeyla said, exasperated.

"Keyl!" Rick mimicked. "I know you," he said confidently. "And you said 'I can use it for,' not 'I am going to use it for.' So why do you really want it?"

Mikeyla stared back at her father for a long moment, then at her mother, who was giving her a look that said, *He's got you there.* Once again she cursed having parents who were both really good investigators and readers of body language. "Okay, okay, I want to go to this chat room everyone's talking about."

Midnight nodded, and Rick said, "Uh-huh."

"It's really cool, Dad. All my friends are on there all the time."

"*All* the time?" Rick repeated.

"Well, not during school, of course," Mikeyla put in, though she knew that wasn't always true.

"No, of course not," Midnight replied, grinning back at Rick. "How old are the kids in this chat room?"

"My age, some maybe older," Mikeyla said vaguely.

"Maybe how older?" Rick replied, narrowing his deep blue eyes, telling her that he was getting suspicious with her answers.

"Older, Dad," Mikeyla said. "Like fourteen and fifteen."

"Do people from this chat room hook up?" Midnight asked. She knew generally how the whole thing worked, but not well enough for her comfort.

"Sometimes," Mikeyla said, shrugging.

"Are you planning to?" Rick asked.

"No, Dad," Mikeyla said, sounding petulant and slightly rebellious. "I just want to chat with my friends."

"You see your friends every day out here—what's the point in talking to them in some chat room?" Rick asked, mystified.

"It's different!" Mikeyla said, wishing her parents were more like Sarah's. They didn't care what she did on the Internet as long as it didn't cost them money. She'd already talked on the phone to two boys from it. One she said was really cool, though the other one had been a real creep according to Sarah; he'd wanted to have phone sex. Sarah had hung up on him, happy she hadn't given him her number and that her parents had star-69 blocked on their phone line. Sarah was talking about meeting the first boy though. He was from San Bernardino, and he said he had a car and could drive there to pick Sarah up. It sounded really cool and romantic to Mikeyla. Now if she could get into that chat room and find a boy from San Bernardino too, maybe she and Sarah could have a double date!

Rick was nodding, giving her a knowing look, and Mikeyla glanced at her mom, begging her silently to let her do it. Again, Midnight turned to Rick. He shrugged and nodded. Mikeyla knew she'd gotten it. She was so happy she threw her arms around her mother, hugging her tight.

Midnight laughed. "Okay, okay, but I don't want you overdoing it," she said sternly.

"And don't you give our phone number or address out to anyone," Rick added, his tone even more formidable.

"I won't, Dad, I promise," Mikeyla said, thinking if she did decide to talk to any boys on the phone she'd just get their number and call them from Sarah's house. She knew how paranoid her parents were about their home address and number. She'd never totally understood it, but they had always been that way.

Mikeyla sat back, looking at her parents again. They really did make a gorgeous couple. With her mother's creamy skin and gold-green eyes, and reddish-blond hair that flowed down to her waist, and her father's strong but finely boned handsome face, his deep, dark blue eyes and curly brown hair that fell around his face so casually. They were both physically very fit, so they seemed to go so well together, Rick's tall, lean frame against her mother's petite one. "You guys look good together," she said, still happy that they were going to let her get the Internet without too much of a fight.

"Do we?" Rick asked, grinning down at his wife as she looked up at him.

"Yeah," Mikeyla said, laughing. "Kinda like a rock star and his groupie girlfriend."

Midnight looked stunned at the description, but then started to laugh. Rick was already chuckling.

"Great, I've been reduced to your groupie," Midnight said to Rick, elbowing him in the ribs.

Rick tried to block her move but was unsuccessful. "So get me a beer, will ya?"

"I'll get you a beer…" Midnight said, trailing off ominously.

"On second thoughts…" Rick said, looking contrite. He dropped his head to her bare shoulder and kissed it softly.

"Yeah…" Midnight said, smiling as she slid her hand over his, which was wrapped around her waist.

Mikeyla watched the exchange, starting to see what her friends saw, looking at their hands together, the gold of their wedding rings glittering against their tanned skin. It was kinda cool, having parents who still played and enjoyed each other as much as they did.

Later that night, as they lay in bed together, their bodies still intertwined from their lovemaking, Midnight remembered Kyle was coming to the house the next day for dinner.

"Oh, I forgot to tell you," she said, glancing over at Rick. He was still lying half over her, his arm around her shoulder, his leg over hers.

In response, he moved his head down to her shoulder, kissing it, then inward to her neck, leaving a trail of tender kisses. When he got to her ear, he whispered, "What?"

"Umm... was I saying something?" she joked.

"Uh-huh," he said, grinning as he nodded, his head right next hers.

"Oh, yeah," she said, sounding like she'd just remembered. "Kyle's coming for dinner tomorrow night."

Rick pulled back. "Why?"

"So he can meet you on your own turf," she said simply.

Rick looked thoughtful for a minute. "And you're sure he's not looking to rekindle an old flame with you?"

"Yes," Midnight said with conviction.

"How?"

"Because he was married, and obviously very much in love with her."

"Was? Isn't that the key word there?" Rick asked skeptically.

"She died, Rick," Midnight said solemnly.

"Ouch," Rick said, grimacing. "How?"

She shook her head. "I don't know. But he seemed pretty

crushed by it, and it happened three years ago."

"Wow…" Rick trailed off as he considered that information, then nodded. "Okay, I'll give him all the benefit of the doubt. If you trust him, I will."

"I trust him."

Rick said nothing for a moment, looking down into her eyes. "Then I do too."

"Thank you," she said, moving to kiss his lips softly.

"One question," Rick said, canting his head to the side.

"What?"

"If I had said I couldn't handle it, him being here, would you have rescinded your job offer?"

"Yes," she answered without hesitation.

"Could have cost the department a fortune…" he pointed out.

"Nothing is worth losing you," she said, snuggling closer.

Rick grinned lopsidedly. "You know I'd never put you in that position, right?"

Midnight grinned in response. "Yep."

She fell asleep shortly after that, and Rick slept for an hour or so before an excruciatingly vivid nightmare woke him in a cold sweat. He had dreamed about Midnight's car exploding and her being inside. It was a nightmare he'd had constantly for two months after Midnight's return. He'd finally had to start taking sleeping pills to keep them away.

He got up carefully, put on his discarded shorts, and walked into the kitchen. He stood at the sink for a long time, trying to block out the images from the dream. He knew talking about Kyle's wife dying and Midnight mentioning that Kyle had seen her funeral the year before had brought everything back into specific relief. After a few long minutes, Rick walked over to the bar. After pouring himself a succession of three shots, he began to feel his nerves calm down. "Gotta get a handle on it, Debenshire," he told himself. He knew he couldn't let himself get as run down as he had before.

After an hour he went back into their room. He stood staring down at Midnight. She was sleeping on her side, her hair flowing around her. Her left hand lay on the pillow next to her face. Rick looked at her wedding rings—her band, and the emerald ring his grandmother had left for him in her will, telling him to give it to the woman he loved. He had given it to the right woman, that was for sure. The ring had been a source of a couple of particularly painful memories for him.

There was the time he and Midnight had been in the middle of a divorce, when he'd lost his mind long enough to have an affair, causing Midnight to file divorce papers. Once he'd realized his mistake, it had been too late. Unable to face the prospect of not being married to her anymore, he'd fled home to England to lick his wounds. Midnight had sent him the rings, parcel post. He had closed his hand so tight over them that the emerald had cut into him. He still bore a small scar in his palm from that.

The other time had been three years before, when he believed Midnight was dead. While he was still trying to adjust to the nightmare his life had become, a package had arrived from Mexico. Inside were Midnight's wedding rings. The Chief of Police had returned them to Rick, since the body they believed to be Midnight's was charred beyond all recognition and the rings had been found in the

81

wreckage nearby. He had gone down the hall into his and Midnight's room, closed the door quietly, and proceeded to hurl them across the room, accompanying that with a banshee howl of agony that had pierced the heart of every person in the house at the time. All he had wanted was his wife back; he didn't care what he had to do—he'd even have given up his own life.

Climbing carefully into bed so as not to disturb Midnight, he pulled her into his arms, feeling her stir and then settle comfortably against him again. He lay awake holding her and trying to will himself back to sleep. In the end he didn't sleep at all.

The following day turned out to be eventful. Kyle came into the office shortly after Midnight got there at 6:00 a.m. When he walked in, Midnight was reading a report that had been left on her desk. It was from homicide. A man had been found dead in his apartment the night before at 8:00 p.m. The reason it was of particular interest was the killer's method. The early coroner's report showed that the man had been shot first in the legs, the killer working up the body with a final fatal shot to the heart. It was a cop-style killing, and that was something she wanted looked into immediately. She'd already made the call to make sure it was being checked out.

"Early riser too, huh?" Midnight commented when Kyle walked in.

"Figured you still were," he replied, grinning.

He was dressed more casually today, though still more formally than Midnight was used to. He was wearing black slacks, a long-sleeved jade green shirt, a black leather belt, and black leather dress shoes. His hair, as always, was neat and clean—no long hair for Kyle

Masterson, although she noted that it did reach the top of his collar now and curled slightly at the ends. Midnight was dressed much more casually than she had been the day before, in slate-gray cotton pants with a black silk Oxford shirt and her usual black ankle boots. Her hair was loose, and still slightly damp from her shower. She wore light makeup—mascara and a faint blush, and a light touch of lipstick. As usual, she had the healthy glow of a tan, and she seemed to Kyle to be the same woman he'd known fifteen years ago.

Midnight noticed his assessing glance, and grinned. "What?"

"Well, Chief, the least you could have done was age over the years," he said mildly as he sat down across from her.

"Oh, I've aged," she replied, rolling her eyes.

"Where?" he countered, looking wholly unconvinced.

"Inside," she answered, smiling.

"Uh-huh." Kyle shook his head to counter his comment. "So, how did your husband take it?" he asked, changing subjects quickly.

Midnight shrugged. "He was okay with it—not at first, but in the end he was."

"Good," Kyle said. "Should we get that paperwork done, or do you need coffee first?"

"Coffee might be a good idea."

"Let's go," he said, and stood up.

Midnight suggested they go over to the Pit. Kyle remembered the place from years before. "How's Tom Ryan doing?" he asked.

"He's doing alright. He's not at the Pit as much as he used to be. His nephew Kevin is running it now. Tom got married again about eleven years ago, to a dispatcher from the department who's getting ready to retire this year. They seem pretty happy together."

"That's good," Kyle said, his eyes taking on a faraway look.

"Yeah," Midnight said, and made a point to turn the conversation in a different direction. They had their coffee and went back to the office. The morning was spent working on his hiring paperwork. At 9:00 her phone rang; she picked up, answering as she always did.

"Chevalier."

Kyle glanced up, wondering how her husband felt about her using her maiden name all the time. He knew it would bother him, but his wife had never been a Chief of Police. He knew Midnight had a made a name for herself in the law enforcement community, and Chevalier was the name everyone knew her by. It still seemed odd to him, but he knew he was thinking like an "old-fashioned man," as Midnight would say, with emphasis on the *man* part. Kyle could hear only Midnight's side of the conversation, but he could tell from her face that it was her husband. He tried to be polite and tune out, but he found himself listening with fascination, even as he continued to work on his paperwork. He'd never heard Midnight Chevalier talk to any man like she talked to her husband.

"Good morning," she said, smiling into the phone.

"What are you up to this morning?" Rick asked, sitting at his desk in his office two floors down.

"Paperwork, nothing exciting."

"Well, I'm sorry to hear that," he said, grinning.

"Are you?" she asked, her voice softening.

"Uh-huh," Rick replied, making even that sound suggestive.

"Richard..."

"You have company, right?" he said, sounding even more mischievous.

"I swear…"

"Oh, you're gonna swear now?" he said, his accent deepening. "I like when you swear…"

"Okay, Lieutenant, you want to die, right?" Midnight laughed as she turned her chair around to face her window, putting her booted feet up on the sill.

"Maybe, but only if I get to choose how," Rick replied, his voice losing none of its innuendo.

"This is a testosterone thing, isn't it?" Midnight said, grinning all the while. She remembered a time when he had kissed her deeply right here in this office, in front of another man he'd perceived as a threat. He'd done it to show the younger man who Midnight belonged to, and they'd both known that.

"Could be," Rick replied, laughing finally.

"Is."

Again, he laughed, not denying it. "Have a good day, love."

"You too. Be careful."

"I always am," he said, his voice deepening again.

"Ugh! Men!" she said, laughing again.

"I love you," he said, his voice sincere and serious now.

"And I love you." She could feel his smile on the other end of the line, and smiled herself. "Talk to you later, babe."

"That you will. Bye."

"Bye," she said, turning around to hang up the phone. She

glanced up at Kyle, and saw that he was still working away.

They continued on until the personnel paperwork was done, and then Midnight started to give him a run-down of current projects and plans that she wanted to establish once he was fully on board. Her phone rang a few more times; she dealt with matters quickly and efficiently, giving each person enough of her time to understand the problem but no more than was necessary to solve it. Kyle found he liked her style more with every call. At 10:30, there was a knock on her door, and a call at the same time.

"Come," she called, and picked up the phone. "Chevalier," she said into the receiver.

Joe Sinclair walked in. He was wearing black jeans and a navy collared shirt with the San Diego Police Department logo on the right breast pocket. He wore his standard black shoulder holster over it.

He glanced at Kyle, then extended his hand. "Heard you were coming on board. Good to see you again."

Kyle stood and took Joe's hand. "Thanks. It's gonna be good to be here."

"Well, it's definitely going to be interesting," Joe said, grinning and looking over at Midnight, who rolled her eyes at him.

She hung up a couple of minutes later, then looked at Joe cynically, one brow raised. "I assume you didn't just come here to harass my new Assistant Chief."

"Actually, to harass you," Joe said caustically , his smile bright.

Midnight nodded, grinning back at him. "Okay, what is it?"

Joe moved around her desk to stand next to her chair, laying out the folder he had brought. "Need a signature for a tap."

Midnight looked down at the file, reading the justification attached to the request. Kyle watched the exchange with interest. He knew she'd been romantically involved with Sinclair years before she was with him, and he knew that not only were Joe and Midnight best friends, but so were Rick and Joe. It was an interesting situation, one that would drive any normal person crazy. Midnight seemed to handle that with the same ease with which she seemed to handle everything else in her business life.

"So, why are they moving on this now?" Midnight asked Joe.

He leaned his hip against her desk, facing her. "Campari thinks they're getting close to something on this."

"Close?" Midnight said, looking skeptical. "I don't want hours of tape on conversations about what's for dinner."

Joe laughed. "Yeah, I know. But Campari's convinced that they're getting ready to deal on this one."

"How convinced is he?" Midnight asked, knowing Joe would give her the real story. "What do you think?"

Joe went into an explanation of the case, during which Midnight leaned back in her chair, putting her feet up on the desk next to him. Joe never missed a beat.

"Okay, so you're basically agreeing that a tap's a good idea," Midnight concluded.

"I think at this point if we don't do it, we might miss something important."

Midnight thought about it for another minute, then nodded, sitting up and picking up her pen. As she signed her name to the document, she said, "Is Campari going to do the time on the tap, or do you have someone else in mind?"

"I thought we could get Sloakam to do it," Joe said. He grinned. "He's still in training, and we don't pay him as much to sit on his ass as we do Campari."

"Ah, yes, the bottom line," Midnight said, smiling too.

"I hear the chief is a real pain in the ass about the bottom line," Joe said, glancing over at Kyle.

"Yes, I am, Sinclair, so you better watch yours," Midnight said, sounding almost serious, but the smile on her face ruined the effect.

"So, how'd it go with Rick?" Joe asked as he stood.

"He survived," Midnight replied mildly.

"Mmhmm…" Joe looked unconvinced. He'd seen Rick in the hallway earlier that morning; he didn't look real happy.

"Save it, Sinclair," Midnight said, narrowing her eyes at him. The last thing she needed was Joe making Kyle feel even more uncomfortable about the whole situation.

Joe lifted his head slightly, as if he'd just gotten her message telepathically, then gave her a narrowed look of his own, as if trying to read her.

"In fact," Midnight said, trying to stave off any more questions, "what are you and Randy doing for dinner tonight?"

"Nothin' that I know of. Why?"

Midnight looked at Kyle, belatedly wondering if it would make him more or less uncomfortable to have a group for dinner instead of just them. "Well, Kyle's coming over to the house, and I was thinking it might be cool to have a few other people there."

"To run interference?" Joe asked pointedly, his grin back.

Kyle laughed at that. "Couldn't hurt," he said, looking at Midnight and realizing she'd downplayed Rick's reaction to his presence a little bit.

"Sure, why not?" Joe said, "What time?"

"Seven," Midnight said, relieved that Kyle seemed to like the idea too.

"We'll be there," Joe said, then in afterthought, "What about Blue and Susan?"

"Are they a couple currently?" Midnight replied.

"Who knows," Joe said, laughing. "But they still show up together all the time, so…"

"Yeah, sounds good. Marie can watch Kat and JT," Midnight added.

Joe looked over at Kyle. "When do you want to see the house?"

"This afternoon okay?"

Joe nodded. "Just come down to my office when you get done here, and we'll go take a look."

"Thanks, man. I appreciate it."

"Well, I gotta keep the Assistant Chief happy, right?" Joe said, grinning again.

"Couldn't hurt," Kyle said, laughing as he extended his hand to Joe.

Joe shook it, then looked over at Midnight. "Thanks, babe," he said, holding up the folder. Midnight nodded, and Joe left the office.

Ten minutes later, Midnight's phone rang again. She was on the other side of her desk, going over some details of the job with Kyle, so she reached over and hit the speaker phone button.

"Chevalier."

"Chief," came her secretary Cassandra's voice. "Sergeant Templeton asked if she could have a few minutes of your time sometime this morning."

Midnight glanced at her watch. "Sure, tell her to come up now."

"Okay, will do."

"Sergeant Templeton?" Kyle said, just trying to get familiar with what names belonged to who.

"My biggest failure as chief so far," Midnight said, frowning at the thought.

"Failure? How?" Kyle asked, surprised.

"Well, not her so much as her husband."

"Her husband?"

"Jason Templeton. He was killed in the line of duty my first two months as chief. He was in a pursuit, chasing a suspect who'd decided to make a run for it. Rhiannon, his wife and partner in narcotics, was in the car with him. A child ran out into the road, and in taking evasive maneuvers he rolled the car. He was killed instantly. Rhiannon was hurt, but she survived."

"And Rhiannon is Sergeant Templeton?"

"Yes. She's my property sergeant now, because she doesn't want to go back into the field at this point."

"Okay, so how is his death your fault?"

"We never were able to make an arrest on the guy he was trying to take down when he was killed."

"So, I'd say it's your investigator's fault, not yours."

"Yes, but the ultimate responsibility lies with me."

"Well, not necessarily—" Kyle started, but they were interrupted by a quiet knock on the door.

"Come," Midnight said.

Rhiannon opened the door and walked in. Her eyes went from Midnight to the dark-haired man who was just standing up. Midnight got to her feet too.

"Sergeant Rhiannon Templeton, this is Kyle Masterson. He's going to be our Assistant Chief."

Kyle extended his hand to Rhiannon, noting the sad, closed look in her eyes when she raised them to his. "It's nice to meet you," he said warmly, smiling.

He was careful to keep the look of surprise off his face. This woman was incredibly beautiful in a very haunting way. She had long, dark auburn hair and rich emerald green eyes. She was tall, easily standing five feet, eleven inches in her two-inch heels. She was dressed in a navy blue skirt and blouse. She looked very business-like. Kyle was trying to equate what Midnight had just told him with the woman standing in front of him. The sadness in her eyes seemed to emanate from her very soul, and he knew that she had lost someone very dear to her. His heart went out to her immediately, because he knew exactly where she was, because he was still there too.

"It's nice to meet you too. Welcome to the department," Rhiannon said. Her voice was soft, like she was afraid to speak too loudly.

"Thank you," he said, glancing over at Midnight then back at

Rhiannon. "Should I leave you two alone?"

Rhiannon looked to Midnight, who shrugged. "I don't see why you can't stay," she said, turning back at Rhiannon. "Unless you want him to leave…" Midnight trailed off; she didn't know what the meeting was about. She had a hunch it wasn't about property, since they had a meeting scheduled later in the month to discuss that.

Rhiannon seemed to hesitate, then shook her head. They all sat down at the small conference table. Rhiannon took her time gathering her thoughts before she began. "I wanted to talk to you about my sister, Stevie." Midnight looked surprised, but nodded for her to continue. "I don't know if you know this, but she quit the department around the time all that stuff happened three years ago…" She trailed off, not wanting to bring up bad memories for Midnight.

"I wasn't aware of that, no," Midnight replied.

"Her official reason was 'to pursue other avenues,'" Rhiannon said, her tone business-like, although it was evident from the worry on her face that she was far from calm inwardly. "Midnight, I think my sister is mixed up with Tiempo."

Midnight stared back at Rhiannon, actually confounded for a few moments by her statement. Then she started to nod slowly as things fell into place. Stevie O'Neil was the more reckless of the two sisters. Rhiannon had a good head on her shoulders, and was sensible even when her world crashed around her. Stevie was a fighter, and she'd throw caution to the wind in a heartbeat to get what she thought she had coming to her, even if that meant endangering her own life.

"She's trying to back-door him," Midnight said, summing up Rhiannon's fears.

"Yes," Rhiannon said, but then caution took over. "Well, I think so. She hasn't said anything to that effect. But she's stopped visiting Mother, and I haven't seen her for months again. When I ask her what she's doing, she says 'freelance security.' And then today…" She trailed off, as if suddenly questioning her own conclusions.

"Today what?" Midnight asked, the hairs on the back of her neck starting to raise.

"Today I saw that article about the man found dead in his apartment," Rhiannon said, her voice hushed, as if saying it quietly would reduce the impact.

Midnight sat back, closing her eyes slowly as trepidation poured through her. Another dirty cop. But this one was trying to get justice for herself. She opened her eyes then, leaning forward in her need to know the whole story. "What makes you think Stevie was involved?"

Rhiannon looked at Midnight for a long moment, then shrugged. "The method used—Stevie's a crack shot. She'd know what her limitations were. And the man's a known dealer, and I happen to know he's dealt with Tiempo plenty of times."

Midnight nodded.

"If she's a crack shot, why not kill him with the first shot?" Kyle put in, finally giving in to the desire to ask questions.

"Because she wouldn't want to kill him," Rhiannon said, her emerald eyes trained on Kyle, not sure how much he knew about her and Jason. "My sister wants Tiempo to pay for what he did to my husband. She wouldn't kill anyone else unless she was in danger herself."

Kyle nodded, assimilating what she'd said. "You said she wants him to pay—pay how?" he said evenly. He knew what he was asking, and wasn't sure whether she'd answer honestly either way.

"Actually, sir, I don't know for sure," Rhiannon said, looking right into his eyes. "I know she was very upset by my husband's death, and very unhappy that Tiempo got away with it." She shook her head. "I'm not sure how far she'd go to get revenge."

Kyle nodded slowly, accepting what she was saying and realizing she was telling him the truth. He looked at Midnight and saw that her mind was working already.

"What do you want me to do, Rhiannon?" Midnight asked.

Rhiannon didn't respond immediately. She swallowed a couple of times, then bit her lower lip in uncertainty. Finally she said, "I can't lose another member of my family to violence, Midnight. I want my sister alive, in whatever capacity that can be accomplished."

Midnight accepted that answer, nodding. "I will do everything I can."

"Thank you," Rhiannon said solemnly as she stood. Midnight reached out to hug her, already feeling a lump in her throat. Rhiannon left, and Midnight got on the phone.

"Cass, get Dave Dibbins as fast as you can and send him up, please," she said, already reaching up to massage her temple. Kyle watched, not saying anything. She hit the speaker again and dialed another number.

Spider answered on the second ring. "Nguyen."

"Spider, I need a favor."

"You got it," he replied, without waiting to hear what it was.

Midnight grinned. It was nice to have such loyalty on occasions like this. "I need Dave."

"Okay."

"I'm not sure how long I'll need him, but I need him to do something important for me."

"Midnight, you don't have to explain anything to me. You want him, he's yours. Just try to send him back undamaged—he's the best I have."

"I know he is, Spider—that's why I need him."

"Done."

"Thanks," Midnight said, smiling again and shaking her head at such unwavering allegiance.

"For you, anything," Spider said, his tone absolutely serious.

"As for you, my friend," Midnight replied with equal sincerity.

They hung up, and Midnight looked up to see Kyle watching her. "Hold that thought," she said, smiling and holding up one finger. Again she hit the speaker, dialing her secretary's extension. "Cass, can you please pull Stevie O'Neil's personnel file for me and bring it in. She'll be under resignations."

"Sure thing."

"Thanks," Midnight said, pleased with her ever-efficient secretary. She hung up again and turned back to Kyle. "Okay, what?"

Kyle just shook his head. "Nothing, I was just wondering…"

"Wondering what?"

"What you do to people to make them swear total devotion to you." His voice showed the admiration that he held for how she handled things.

Midnight shrugged off the compliment. "These people have

been with me a long time."

"And Rhiannon Templeton?"

"Don't start with me, Masterson," Midnight replied after a long pause.

Kyle laughed. There was a knock on the door and Cassandra bustled in, putting a file on Midnight's desk. "Sergeant Dibbins is outside."

"Thanks, Cass. Tell him to come on in," Midnight said.

"You wanted to see me?" Dave Dibbins asked from the doorway.

Midnight grinned at her longtime friend. Dave looked so much different than he had over fifteen years ago when they'd first met. Dave had been the leader of a gang; he'd been stealing money from his gang's drug profits and had been caught. Of course, Midnight's unit FORS had everything to do with that. It was Midnight's second-in-command, Joe Sinclair, who with the help of another member of FORS had held off Dave's gang when they wanted to kill their leader for his theft. It was also Joe that Dave Dibbins had turned to with his request to join FORS, since he was apparently out of the drug-dealing business.

Standing in her doorway, Dave Dibbins looked like a laidback rock star. He was tall and lean, wearing the most faded jeans and a navy blue shirt. He had sandy-blond hair that was cut in a long fade and shot through with lighter blond highlights gained from hours in the sun while surfing. He had sky blue eyes that showed only what he wanted people to see. His face always had a look of passivity, but Midnight knew that his mind worked constantly on the cases that loaded his desk.

In the seven years that he'd been a sergeant in the narcotics unit he had become the best narc she had. Dave had made cases no one else could make. He'd caught dealers no one else had ever been able to get near, much less make a case on. Midnight relied heavily on him to train all her new narcotics officers as well as for all the work he accomplished. Now she had one more mission for him.

"Hey, Dibbs," Midnight said, smiling as she motioned him into the office. "Thanks for coming."

Dave gave her a wry grin, lifting an eyebrow at her. "Midnight, you are the chief, ya know."

Midnight laughed and rolled her eyes. "Oh yeah, forgot," she said, waving her hand. "Dave, you probably remember Kyle Masterson, right?" She gestured to Kyle, who was still standing by one of the chairs at the conference table.

Dave walked over to Kyle, extending his hand and smiling broadly. "The train—yeah, I remember."

"The what?" Kyle asked, glancing over at Midnight, who immediately tried to hide her shock and amusement that someone had finally slipped and used the nickname Joe had given Kyle years before.

"Long story, Kyle," Midnight said, waving her hand to dismiss the whole thing. "Trust me, you don't want to know."

"Somehow," Kyle said, looking quizzically from Midnight to Dave, "I know that's not totally true. But I'll let it slide, for now."

Dave laughed, knowing he'd blown it but figuring it was him or someone else eventually—why not be a ground-breaker?

"So…" Dave said, sitting in a chair across from Midnight's desk and stretching his legs out in front of him comfortably. "To what do

97

I owe this honor?" His tone was casual, but his eyes were wary. Midnight wondered if she should check with Spider to see what trouble Dave had been up to lately. Dave knew that he wasn't guilty of anything that would incur Midnight's wrath, for which he counted himself lucky. He had a general idea of the hellfire that Midnight's husband, Rick, lived with on a daily basis. Not that he didn't envy the hell out of Rick for being lucky enough to have her.

"Well," Midnight said, leaning back casually as well and eyeing him speculatively. "Whatever it is, I'm sure I'll get the report eventually." Her gold-green eyes sparkled with humor as she saw Dave relax further, blowing his breath out in a sigh. Kyle took a seat at the conference table, watching the proceedings with interest.

"Okay, why *am* I here?" Dave asked.

"I need you to do me a favor," Midnight replied, her tone deceptively calm even as she stared directly into his eyes.

Dave's eyebrows furrowed for a moment, then smoothed as he said, "You got it."

Midnight grinned lopsidedly, figuring Kyle would see him as another one of her converts. She knew she might as well get used to his thinking on this, since this type of loyalty was evident in all the members of the original FORS. "And if I ask you to walk on water?" she couldn't resist asking, raising an eyebrow at Kyle.

Dave's look did not change. "I'm the man for the job."

Midnight's eyes fell to the gold cross Dave always wore. She'd thought for many years that it was a symbol of his faith. In fact, he had confided in her that it was a symbol of the life he'd left behind when he joined FORS. He'd bought it with his first big payoff from selling drugs when he was in the gang, and kept it to remind himself where he'd been. He never took it off.

"I know that," Midnight said as her eyes moved to meet his again. "But this mission is a little bit more important."

"Okay…" Dave replied in a measured tone.

He watched as Midnight reached out and picked up a manila folder that looked suspiciously like a personnel file. Maybe this was about his latest misstep—but upon closer inspection, Dave knew it wasn't his. His file was much fatter. He knew—he'd seen it.

Most of the stuff in his own personnel folder was commendations, award letters, and recommendations for promotions or special ops. There were, of course, a fair share of reports of minor incidents with suspects where his anger had gotten the better of him and he'd actually hit someone who really deserved it. In the end, all of the reports had been dismissed as minor, because Dave never struck an unarmed or handcuffed suspect. And he always had a reciprocating injury to show for his loss of control. There were also a number of injury reports in his file. He took his job seriously, and tended to go just a bit further to capture a suspect, even if it meant injury to himself. It was an exciting life.

Dave doggedly tried to catch the name on the folder's label, but Midnight was grinning at him as she shook her head. Then, to his surprise she slid the folder across the desk. Gingerly, Dave picked it up, and saw the name Stevie O'Neil. He trained his blue eyes back on Midnight.

"Uh-huh…" he said. He knew he was about to get a new assignment, he just didn't know how new. He assumed that Stevie O'Neil was a new trainee for narcotics; Dave was the resident field training officer for the unit. He already knew this was special, however, because he usually got his assignments from his lieutenant and best friend, Spider Nguyen.

"That isn't what you think, Dave," Midnight said, leaning back in her chair and putting an elegantly booted foot on the bottom drawer of her desk. As the chief, she had made some changes in her daily "uniform" of jeans, boots, and cotton Oxford shirts. Usually she wore impeccably cut chinos, long-sleeved silk blouses and more refined and stylish calf-skin boots. Even at thirty-seven, she looked beautiful and still a bit on the wild side, but when she donned the perfectly tailored jacket she wore to meetings, she fit in with the more professional-looking crowd. All in all, however, she was still pretty much the same woman that had fought on the mean streets of San Diego to beat back the onslaught of gangs in the city. Fought and won, in many cases.

"Okay," Dave said, his lips twitching in mild curiosity. "Then what is it?"

Midnight grinned; Dave always was her easygoing one. He took everything as it came.

"Well, that young lady no longer works for the department..." she began.

"You're transferring me to records retention?" Dave deadpanned, causing a chuckle from Kyle.

Midnight laughed, shaking her head. "No." Then her face grew serious as she looked back at him. "You see, we have there a former officer who may be going vigilante on me."

Dave stared back at Midnight for a long moment, his eyes narrowing as he pursed his lips in thought. He was definitely curious now. "And..." he prompted

"And..." Midnight echoed, her gold-green eyes staring directly back into his as she sat up, leaning forward in her intensity. "I want her back."

At the back of the room, Kyle was reeling slightly from the surprise Midnight had just dropped. He had thought maybe he'd cut the girl some kind of deal when they caught her, but wanting her back—was she crazy?

Dave's eyes reflected surprise too, even as his face remained passive. He looked down at the folder in his hands. Leaning back, he flipped it open, scanning through the information it contained as Midnight looked on.

Stevie O'Neil had been with the department for two years before she left. "To pursue other avenues" had been the reason listed on her exit interview. "Her probation reports were excellent," Dave said to no one in particular, reading on. "Her scores in the academy were surprisingly high in both marksmanship and arrest and control."

The purely physical side of him noted from the picture that she was a nice-looking woman with dark auburn hair, deep emerald green eyes, and porcelain skin. He flipped to her original application for the academy and noted the names listed as references. Dave glanced up to see that Midnight was watching him closely.

"Rhiannon and Jason Templeton?" Dave asked, his eyes reflecting that some understanding was dawning.

"Yep," Midnight said. "Her sister and her now-deceased brother-in-law."

"O'Neil, O'Neil..." Dave muttered, remembering the name from somewhere. Then he had it. He was a little stunned. "Was Frank

O'Neil their father?"

Midnight nodded, looking grave.

"Shit…" Dave breathed, shaking his head.

Midnight looked back at Kyle to explain this part of the puzzle. "Frank O'Neil was a patrol officer killed in the line of duty eleven years ago. He'd worked for the department for twenty years. He left a wife and two daughters behind."

"That's why you want her back," Dave said, with no question in his voice.

"She's family," Midnight replied.

Dave nodded, understanding perfectly what Midnight meant. Then he had another thought.

"She have anything to do with that textbook stitch that turned up last night?"

Midnight's lips tugged in a frown. "She might have, yes."

Dave nodded again, then canted his head to the side. "Media know the condition of the body?"

"Nope, just got the report."

Dave looked thoughtful for a moment. "And what does it say?"

"That lethal force was the final shot. That the victim was on the move till then."

"So if he was after her…" Dave began.

"She stopped the threat," Midnight said, finishing his thought.

Dave nodded. "Okay, so how do you want me to proceed?"

"I want you to make undercover contact with her."

"And if she recognizes me?"

"She probably will."

"And if she takes a shot at me?"

"Duck."

"Haha," Dave replied, grinning in spite of his sarcastic tone.

"If I'm right about her..." Midnight said, her eyes narrowing in thought. She shook her head. "She won't shoot a fellow officer."

"And if you're wrong?" Dave asked, and began to nod as Midnight grinned. "I know—duck!"

"In that file is all the info we have on her. I don't know what's current and what's not. We think she's working for Tiempo," she added, watching Dave closely.

Dave glanced up from the document in his hand, his face showing mild surprise. "If she is, our girl has done well, hasn't she?"

Midnight nodded.

Marco Tiempo was a drug dealer of some reputation. He'd killed off a lot of his competition. He was also the person the San Diego Police Department held directly responsible for the death of Jason Templeton.

"Hell," Midnight said, shrugging. "We may be doing Tiempo a favor here."

Dave nodded, his grin sardonic.

# CHAPTER 3

At two o'clock that afternoon, Kyle and Joe were on their way to Joe's house on the beach in La Jolla. Joe drove the new car he had bought a few weeks before—his "midlife crisis" car, as Randy liked to put it. It was a $135,000 Aston Martin V12 Vantage. Its sleek lines and ultra-powerful engine screamed rich man's toy. Joe's passion was the speed of the vehicle; he didn't care about the price tag, or the cliché that attached itself to a thirty-nine-year-old man with an expensive sports car.

Kyle looked around the interior of the car, noting the gauges and expensive leather upholstery. "Nice," he commented, aware that it was an understatement but not wanting to overdo it either.

Joe grinned. "Randy says I'll need the twenty-year-old girlfriend next."

"Will you?" Kyle asked, his grin wry.

Joe shrugged. "Randy's only thirty-three—that'll have to do."

"Is she a good shot?"

"The best," Joe said, rolling his eyes. "I trained her."

Kyle laughed. "Well, then she'll have to do."

"You've never seen my wife, have you?" Joe asked, giving Kyle a lopsided grin.

"Nope."

"Well, you'll see her tonight. If I have to settle with a woman, I'll stay in paradise with her."

"Love her that much, huh?" Kyle asked, knowing the answer—he could see it in Joe's eyes. "You could say that."

They were both silent for a while. Joe had heard about Kyle's wife, and didn't want to say something that might bring up bad feelings.

"So this house is how big?" Kyle asked after a long while.

"Five bedrooms."

"And you're asking how much?"

Joe rubbed at his chin with his forefinger. "How much are you paying in New York?"

"Twenty-five hundred."

"For what?"

"Three-bedroom apartment."

"Own or rent?"

"Own."

"And you're gonna let it out or something?"

"Yeah, I don't want to sell it just yet—the boys are still really attached to it," Kyle said, his tone deepening a bit. It was obvious the boys weren't the only ones still attached to it.

"And you can get that for it?"

"Easily," Kyle replied. Apparently Joe had no concept of New York real estate.

As Joe turned off the main road and headed up a driveway, he said, "Okay, how about fifteen hundred?"

Kyle started to answer, and then the house came into view. Midnight had been right; it was practically a mansion. It had columns and elongated windows. Two stories of beautiful home. It was at least four thousand square feet. He turned to Joe, remembering the price he had named. "Are you nuts?"

Joe grinned. "Why do you say that?"

Kyle glanced back at the house and made a gesture of incredulity. "It's a palace, compared to my apartment."

"This is California," Joe said simply.

"And it's just as expensive as New York, just spaced better."

Joe shrugged, turning to get out of the car. "It's paid off, and I don't need the money, Masters. I'm only charging you because Midnight told me to, so take it or leave it."

The two men faced each other over the hood of the Vantage. Kyle put his arms on the top of the car, looking once again at the house, then back at Joe. "Well, I may be some dumb flatfoot from New York," he said, grinning, "but I'm not that dumb. I'll take it, man. Thanks."

"You don't want to see the inside?" Joe asked, grinning too.

"Sure, why not?" Kyle said as they walked toward the front door.

An hour later, in Joe's car on the way back to the office, Kyle glanced over at him. "Can I ask you a question?"

"Shoot," Joe said, sounding like Midnight.

"Earlier, Dibbins called me 'the train'—you have any idea what that means?"

Joe laughed, shaking his head. "I can't believe he said that to you."

106

"So you do know what it means."

Joe grinned. "I should—I'm the one that started calling you that."

"Ah, I see." Kyle nodded. "And you started calling me that because...?"

Joe had the graciousness to look a little bit embarrassed. "Basically because every time you came to town, Midnight ended up looking like she'd been hit by a train."

"And I take it I was the train?" Kyle asked, grinning.

"Uh-huh," Joe said, smiling.

"Her husband heard this one too?" Kyle asked, his tone taking on a cautious note.

Joe looked thoughtful for a moment, then nodded. "Chances are real good he has."

"Great," Kyle said, sounding like he thought it was anything but.

Joe laughed. "Man, trust me, he's gonna have heard all about you before the day is out."

"That ought to be helpful."

"Look at it this way—there won't be anything left to hide, right?"

"I didn't have anything to hide in the first place," Kyle said confidently.

"Then there's nothing to worry about," Joe replied, sounding pleased.

Kyle looked over at Joe, his eyes narrowing. He had a feeling he'd just been tested, and had somehow passed that test. Joe dropped Kyle back at the department to pick up his rental car and then headed home.

Kyle went back to his hotel to try and relax for a while. He knew the evening was probably going to be a struggle, but also that he needed to make his peace with Rick Debenshire before he could really become part of this department. He felt as if the entire department was watching to see if he could do it or not. He lay on the bed, putting himself in Rick's shoes and trying to see how he would have felt if the roles were reversed. Kyle knew he'd be extremely cautious, and he'd be looking for signs of connivance.

He had no intention of trying anything with Midnight, but the important thing was to make sure Rick understood that. That was going to be the hard part. He couldn't honestly say that Midnight didn't hold some sort of intrigue for him. She did—she always had. Did he love her? No, he had never loved her. He'd always liked her a great deal. She was the kind of woman that stuck in a man's mind long after their relationship was over. One that always made a man wonder if he could have made a long relationship with her, if he could have been strong enough. Midnight was no wallflower; she had more fire than ten normal women. She didn't take anything lightly; she wasn't the wishy-washy, lovey-dovey type of woman. When Midnight Chevalier was younger, she had been as forthright and enthusiastic about sex as any man. Kyle admitted even to himself that when he thought of her, Midnight epitomized the wildness of his youth perfectly.

He'd grown up a lot since those days. Falling in love with a woman that wasn't interested helped a lot. He'd met Barbara when her cousin Mario was on trial for accessory to murder. He claimed he didn't do it; Barbara believed him, and had been at his trial every day. Kyle was responsible for the arrest, and so was usually present as well.

Barbara had come to him the first day and asked him why he thought her cousin was at all responsible for the death of this businessman when they already had in custody the man that had actually shot him. Kyle was taken with her dazzling blue eyes, her honey-gold hair; she had a nice body too, clad in a black Dior dress. So taken, in fact, it took him a minute to recall she'd asked a question.

"Your cousin ordered the hit on Mr. Aliayah," he had replied finally, his voice authoritative.

"What proof do you have?" Barbara had asked.

Kyle had grinned at her. God, she was naive! She had been twenty years old at the time, and a student at Harvard. He could tell she was young, and had led a very sheltered life. How anyone could not know that Mario Vendelia was one of the lowest lifeforms on Earth—Mario was a man who aspired to be a big man. Since he couldn't be a big man, he bullied anyone that got in his way. Aliayah had refused to deal with him. He had refused to do what Mario wanted, and Mario had had him killed. Unfortunately for Mario, he hadn't hired a very bright hitman, but one who had left evidence at the scene that was traced back. The hitman, a small-time loser, had been more than happy to give Mario up. Kyle had all the proof he needed. This young lady was about to get severely disillusioned.

"I have proof, Miss..." Kyle said, trailing off.

"Vicente," she supplied. "And I asked what proof."

"I'm aware of that, Ms. Vicente," he said, grinning. "But unless you have Deputy District Attorney in front of your name or I'm sitting on the witness stand, I don't have to tell you that."

Barbara narrowed her eyes at him. "You think you're clever, don't you?"

"Actually, I just think I'm right," Kyle replied, refusing to be taken so far with the girl that he'd allow her to get the better of him.

"Well, we'll just see about that, Officer."

"Actually, it's sergeant," Kyle replied, fixing his bright green eyes on hers.

"Sergeant," she repeated scornfully, then turned and walked away. He watched her go with a sardonic smile on his face.

Kyle watched her every day after that. He saw her talking to her cousin, obviously trying to give him encouragement. Mario would listen to her and pat her on the head like a good little pupil. Kyle could tell the guy had her snowed. Somehow it really irritated him; it bothered him to see how she looked up at him with such admiration. He knew she was in for a rude awakening, and soon.

The trial lasted a month. During that time Kyle watched as Barbara staunchly stood by her cousin's side. He saw how pale she became when the pictures of Aliayah's body were shown; his head had been all but blown off by the hitman's shotgun. She had obviously become faint, because she got up and walked out of the courtroom. Kyle found himself following. He caught up with her outside the door to the courthouse, leaning back with her head resting against the cold stones.

"Are you okay?" he asked.

She looked at him, her eyes accusing. "I'm sickened at the lengths the New York Police Department will go to to frame my cousin."

"You can't really think we're framing him," Kyle said disbelievingly.

"Yes, I can. You want to make a name for yourself, and this is your big chance."

Kyle laughed, leaning against the wall next to her. "Is that what he's told you?"

"He said you just want to take down a member of the family— you don't care how you do it."

"A little full of himself, isn't he?" Kyle said calmly.

"Why do you say that?" she asked, her eyes narrowing at the insult.

"Because he's about as small-time as 'the family' comes. He'd hardly be a big bust for me."

"You're saying he isn't?"

"Not hardly, little one," he replied, using the endearing phrase he'd been calling her in his mind. She was a tiny little thing; she stood five feet, two inches, and weighed maybe a hundred pounds. At six feet, three inches and 220 pounds, Kyle was a giant compared to her.

Barbara stared back at him, her blue eyes shining brightly with the fire of surety. "My cousin is not a criminal," she said, her voice strong with conviction.

"I'm afraid you're about to find out much differently," Kyle said, his voice softening, as he looked down at her.

And find out she did. When the witnesses came to the stand, one after another describing what kind of man Mario was, Kyle could see Barbara's faith in her cousin wavering. He found himself worrying about her. She seemed so delicate, so fragile, and he wasn't sure she could handle this kind of shattering disenchantment.

The day the jury came back with their verdict, Kyle made a

point of standing in the aisle near where Barbara sat. Her eyes traveled over to him a few times while the jury was questioned, and Kyle could see worry in them. Finally the judge asked the jury for their verdict, and Mario was pronounced guilty as charged. Barbara dropped her head in her hands, bending forward to rest her chest on her knees. Mario was cuffed and led from the courtroom. He didn't even bother to look back at his cousin. People filed out; no one bothered Barbara. It was apparent she was the only member of the family actually at the trial. Mario was very small-time; he didn't warrant the backing of the family.

Kyle walked over to Barbara, sitting down and watching her. It was obvious she was crying, but she was doing it very quietly. Kyle waited, hunched forward with his elbows on his knees, his hands dangling loosely. It took her a few minutes to notice him. When she did, she didn't lift her face to his; she merely murmured "Go away" through her hands. Kyle didn't reply; he just waited. "You're just dying to gloat, aren't you?" she said, still not looking up at him.

"No," he replied simply.

"What do you want?" she asked, sitting up to stare at him.

His reply died in his throat, strangled because seeing her lovely face tear-streaked and devastated had nearly choked him. He had to swallow a few times to get his voice to come out. "I'm sorry," he finally whispered.

Apparently that was too much for her to take, because she just crumpled against him, crying. Kyle was surprised, but his arms went around her protectively.

That night he took her to dinner. They talked and she told him about her cousin being her best friend when they were kids. That

Mario had been the one to stick up for her when the bigger kids would pick on her. He had been her knight in shining armor. She couldn't believe he would do something so horrible as order a man killed. She admitted that they hadn't been as close since they'd both gotten out of high school, that Mario did seem so much different now. Kyle found himself drawn in by her innocence and her loyalty to her friend, even if she had been wrong about him.

In the end, Kyle had fallen so completely for her that he'd been willing to do anything to get her to see him. He'd shown up at her apartment with flowers, and sat and talked with her for hours. It had been weeks before he'd even felt brave enough to kiss her, but things moved quickly after that. They'd been married a few months afterward, much to her family's dismay. He was "the cop," the outsider; he still was to many of them.

Losing her after fifteen years of marriage had been the hardest thing Kyle had ever had to go through. He just prayed that someday he would feel normal again. He was hoping this move to San Diego would do it. For him, it meant finally getting away from New York and everything that reminded him of Barbara. For his son Nick, he hoped the move would break him out of the cycle he was stuck in.

Thirteen-year-old Nicholas Masterson had been hanging out with his Uncle Tony a lot in the years since Barbara had died. That would have been understandable, since Tony was Barbara's oldest brother, but Tony was also a numbers man for "the family." Kyle was sure Tony was getting Nick interested in "the business," and Kyle didn't want his son even remotely involved in anything illegal. In the last year, Nick's attitude had become increasingly belligerent, and he'd developed an opinion of cops as "pigs." Nick and Kyle had come close to out and out blows a few times. Nick had grown into his height of six feet over the summer, and he seemed to believe that put him close to being even with Kyle on every level. Kyle consistently reminded him that he was by no means a man yet, and at the rate he was going he wouldn't live to be one either. Only time would tell if the move would serve the purposes he intended. That time would start tonight, with this meeting with Midnight's husband. He hoped it would go well.

Kyle was the first to arrive that evening. Mikeyla answered the door. She was surprised at how handsome this new Assistant Chief was. She'd heard her parents talking about him earlier in the evening.

"You must be Mikeyla," Kyle said, his smile open.

Mikeyla nodded. "Mom and Dad are in the kitchen." She let him in and led the way through the house.

Kyle caught a glimpse of Rick and Midnight's quick kiss as he followed Mikeyla into the kitchen. Midnight turned around and looked at him, smiling. She glanced back at Rick, who now stood behind her, watching Kyle over her head. Joe hadn't been kidding about the guy being good-looking.

*Midnight never did choose ugly guys, did she?* Rick thought wryly.

"Kyle Masterson, this is Rick Debenshire. Rick, this is Kyle," Midnight said, making the formal introduction as she stepped to the side.

Kyle walked forward, extending his hand to Rick without hesitation, his eyes on the younger man. Rick took the proffered hand, shaking it and nodding, as if Kyle had passed the first test. Rick turned and walked over to the refrigerator. Opening it, he reached in and pulled out two bottles of beer, holding one up to Kyle. "Beer?"

Kyle nodded, taking the bottle. After a long moment, Rick gestured with his head toward the deck outside. Kyle nodded and followed him out.

Rick leaned against the railing, looking out over the ocean. The sun was just setting, turning the whole world shades of pink, blue, and purple. Kyle stood watching both the sunset and Rick, not sure what was to come.

"So," Rick said finally. "You were with Midnight way back when."

"Yes, I was," Kyle replied calmly.

Rick turned toward him, his eyes searching his face. Kyle stood four inches taller than Rick, but it was obvious there were no inferiority issues in Rick's mind. After a long moment, he nodded again, looking thoughtful. "It was a long time ago."

It was Kyle's turn to nod. "Yes."

Rick nodded again and turned back to the railing. Both men were silent for a long time, lost in their own thoughts.

"Midnight told me about your wife," Rick said finally, his voice quiet and respectful. "I'm sorry."

Kyle instantly felt a lump rise in his throat at the tone of Rick's voice. He turned to look out over the ocean, trying to rein in his emotions before speaking again. He knew he was talking to someone who understood how it felt. He knew Rick's history, that not too long ago Rick had been in the hell Kyle was still in. Only Rick's nightmare had ended.

Finally he blew his breath out in a frustrated sigh. "I still miss her every day."

Rick glanced over at him, his eyes showing his understanding of Kyle's situation. "So some good friends wouldn't hurt," he said simply.

Kyle was momentarily surprised by Rick's statement, more so when the younger man extended his hand, staring straight into his eyes. As he clasped Rick's hand and nodded, Kyle realized he had just seen a glimpse of what Midnight loved about this man. He had expected to come here and soothe ruffled feathers and deal with jealous tirades. Instead Rick had offered him friendship. It was obvious that Rick Debenshire was quite confident about his place in his wife's heart; the thought made Kyle's own heart ache a little more.

When Rick and Kyle walked back in, Midnight watched them both closely. She caught Rick's grin and lifted eyebrow, as if he were asking, *What did you think I was going to do to the guy?* Rick walked over to her, kissing her lightly on the forehead just as the doorbell rang.

A few moments later, Joe walked in, his hand clasped in Randy's as he led her into the room. He walked right over to Kyle, shaking his hand and grinning as his glance slid from Kyle to Rick and back again. Then he turned to Randy, who was giving him a mockingly stern look. She'd already told him in the car not to cause problems, but she knew her husband well; she knew he was going to give Rick as much grief over this as possible. Randy was beginning to think Joe was taking lessons from his cousin Christian, who had a propensity for stirring up trouble in an otherwise serene situation.

"Kyle, this is my wife, Randy," Joe said, sliding his arm around her shoulders. "Randy," Joe said in a theatrically hushed tone, "be nice. This is the guy that could rescind that extended leave of absence you're on."

Randy elbowed Joe, making him laugh, as she extended her hand to Kyle and smiled warmly. "Please excuse my husband, Chief. He's a troublemaker."

Kyle laughed at that, shaking Randy's hand. "Yes, I've already dealt with him on this kind of thing. And please, call me Kyle."

Joe went to the refrigerator and leaned over the top of the door, giving Midnight a quick kiss on the lips. "When's dinner? I'm starved." He glanced back at Randy, gesturing to the bottles of beer in askance.

"No, no beer for me," Randy said. "But I will have what you're having, Midnight. Is that a merlot?" She gestured at the wine glass Midnight had just picked up.

A discussion ensued between the two women about the wine, while Joe and Rick bantered about some case that had gone south on them that day. Kyle watched it all, thinking it was amazing that these four were obviously so close and yet Midnight and Joe had indeed been a huge item at one point. Kyle even remembered finding himself a bit jealous of the blond Englishman's firm hold on her heart at some points in their relationship. Whenever Joe called, Midnight was there for him, even if it meant getting out of bed with Kyle there at three in the morning to sit and talk to Joe on the phone for hours. It was obvious Rick and Joe were good friends, and Joe's wife clearly had no problems with Midnight and Joe's relationship either.

Kyle was beginning to realize that being around this dynamic group might be an altogether healing experience for him. He knew that back in New York, with people who had histories like this, his fellow cops would be killing each other about now.

Susan Endicott made an engaging picture waiting at the airport gate. She wore a navy silk dress that flowed around her shapely calves as she paced nervously. Many men watched her with interest. In the last year she'd changed a great deal. Whereas she had previously been in the habit of looking unassuming and unremarkable, now she wore her long honey-blond hair in luxurious waves down her back, pulled softly off her face with a clip. She wore makeup in a subtle but attractive way, to highlight her deep blue eyes and high cheekbones. The dress nipped in attractively at her small waist and emphasized her very feminine shape, as well as her legs, which were enhanced further by her three-inch navy heels.

The changes in her were due completely to the attentions of one man. Christian Joseph Collins. A man who continued to confound her in his infinitely appealing way. Christian was startlingly handsome, with his jet black hair and light blue eyes set in an extremely handsome face. He was tall, standing six feet and two inches. He had shoulders that were broad without being overly so, and a body most women dreamed of. He was charismatic, intelligent, intense, and a very sensual man. Susan had been drawn to him from the first time she'd met him. He'd been very different a year before. He'd been cool and distant, but had warmed in Susan's presence, with her attention to him as a person rather than the handsome facade he used all too often.

Things between Susan and Christian had always been fire and ice. Susan had surprised herself with her response to him, but had grown much bolder in the years since Christian had literally taken her out of her own wedding ceremony. That was the kind of man

Christian was; he did things on impulse and never cared about what people thought about him or his actions. He was a very dynamic man, and being with him had made Susan come much farther out of the shell she'd kept herself in for many years. Being with a man like Christian gave her the confidence to try new things, and to be more open with the beauty he saw fit to comment on frequently. He was forever telling her how incredibly beautiful she was; it did enormous amounts of good things for her ego.

By the same token, Christian was not a commitment kind of person. As such, they had a rather odd relationship. He had told her he was in love with her, that if he ever married anyone she'd be the one. However, he could not and would not commit to being with only her. After her aborted wedding ceremony they had given a serious relationship a go, but within six months, Christian was edgy and almost impossible to deal with. He became moody and they fought a great deal. Finally he had told her he couldn't do "the relationship thing" anymore. At first she'd been hurt, feeling like she'd done something wrong. Christian had assured her that it was indeed him that could not handle things, and the blame rested with him only.

It had taken a couple of months of adjustment, but eventually they'd settled into the relationship they had now. Susan still wasn't sure where she really stood with him, but she did know that he was back to his former self, and he never hesitated to hold her, kiss her, make love to her, or tell her that he loved her. The fact was, Christian Collins was far too free-spirited to be easily caged. Susan wanted to have him all to herself with all her heart, but she also knew that being with him in any way possible was worth not possessing him totally at this point in their lives. It was still an adjustment, and she knew her family and friends didn't understand it, but she loved Christian, and knowing that he did love her was what she clung to with all her heart.

Christian Collins sat in his seat, his mind going over all the things he needed to get accomplished in the next two weeks before his next trip out of town. The inventory system he'd created for Midnight the year before had become a popular use of a new program called Microsoft Access. Midnight had been very pleased with the database he'd created for her, and had touted the program to the city council, who had in turn told other agencies about the program. Soon Midnight's office was filled with requests for her "computer guru's" assistance. Being the proponent of inter-agency cooperation that she was, Midnight was happy to loan Christian out to local agencies for their use.

Eventually it had become obvious that there was going to have to be some kind of contract agreement between Christian and many of the agencies, since their needs were much more than merely "help." Christian became a consultant for the San Diego Police Department. Midnight had gone so far as to send him through not only the best computer programming courses for Microsoft Access, but also through the police academy. Her logic was that he needed to "understand" cops to work for them. He officially had peace officer powers, and although he refused to actually carry a badge, he had on his person credentials identifying him as an officer and carried a concealed weapon within the State of California.

Sitting on the plane, flying back from a three-week-long stint in Seattle, Washington, he'd worked the entire time on his laptop. He'd pointedly ignored all the looks from the women around him, as well as the flight attendants' blatant attempts to flirt with him. Christian Collins was fully aware of his impact on women, and knew that if he was so inclined he could have his pick of any of the singles on the plane, maybe even a few of the married ones. He had his hands full, however. He had Susan, who, when he really cared to examine his feelings, was the one woman he loved besides his mother. She had stood by him in a nightmare time in his life over a year before, when he had been sure he was doomed. She'd given him love that he'd never been able to accept before, but with her, it had been different. He'd been willing to try a relationship with her, a committed relationship.

Unfortunately, it hadn't worked. Before long he found himself feeling trapped, and like a wild panther in a cage, he'd begun to pace and contemplate ways out. In the end, he knew if he allowed himself the way out he'd likely use, he'd hurt Susan immeasurably. He had just been straight with her, and told her that he couldn't handle being in a relationship anymore. Fact was, he was becoming restless and he needed to get out and cut loose again.

While Susan had changed a great deal in their time together, she'd also remained the same in a lot of ways. She was a very quiet, shy, conservative person. Unfortunately for Christian, that also extended to the bedroom, where he was used to a much wider variety. While he knew it was wrong to expect her to be totally uninhibited with him, she had actually become more inhibited after they'd gotten together officially. In the time before the wedding Christian had broken up, Susan had grown comfortable in his presence sexually. For some reason that confidence had fled when they were an actual couple. Suddenly, Christian had felt like he was with an unsure virgin again, and the feeling had made him uncomfortable and somehow angry at her for it. Like she'd sold him a bill of goods before they'd become a couple.

In the end, he'd known he would cheat on her to end their relationship, and the opportunity had readily presented itself in the form of her younger sister, Liz. Elizabeth Endicott was the antonym to Susan. She was outlandish and wild, and trouble from the word go. She was also young, just barely eighteen. But she'd already been kicked out of the best private schools in England, and was at that time "visiting" the States due to a recent scandal involving a high-ranking member of the aristocracy. She'd come to visit, and had once again laid eyes on Christian Collins; she'd seen him months before, when she'd been at her sister's wedding. She had made it known that not only did she want him, but that she didn't care that her sister had him at the time. Christian had, in the end, avoided the temptation, although she'd been blatant in her desire for him and things had come rather close. That was when he knew he needed to get out of the relationship with Susan.

He told her the truth—that he loved her, but that he couldn't handle such a hemmed-in way of feeling. Susan had been hurt—he knew she had—but she'd nodded with tears in her eyes and avoided him for three weeks. In the end, he had sought her out, goading her until she was angry enough to yell at him and call him all the names she'd been storing up in her head. He'd allowed her to scream and rage, eventually culminating in her slapping him. That was when he'd kissed her, although it had earned him another slap, after which he kissed her again. In the end, he'd made love to her, apologizing with his body in ways he never could with words. That had been the beginning of their odd relationship. Now they had a deep friendship that included sex. It was the best way to describe them. He slept with other people, and although she didn't really sleep with anyone else, she dated others. The relationship drove their families crazy, but it was what they had.

122

The plane taxied to the gate, and the passengers got up to leave. Christian received many admiring looks as he stood and stretched. It had been a long trip, and he was happy to be home. He pulled on the black leather coat that had been stowed above him, then picked up his leather laptop case and looped it over his shoulder. As he got off the plane, he winked rakishly at the stewardess, who smiled brilliantly at him. Then he headed up the gangway.

He spotted Susan easily and walked directly up to her. In one fluid movement he set his laptop down on the floor, slid his hand around the base of her neck, and pulled her to him. His lips claimed hers hungrily in a long, deep kiss, one watched with envy by many people around them.

As he kissed her, the world melted away for both of them. All Susan could think about was the scent of cologne mixed with leather and the feeling of his lips, his hands in her hair and at her waist. Christian could feel Susan trembling beneath his hands, and pulled her closer as if to envelope her in his warmth. He knew that what he was doing was in complete contrast to his need for space, but seeing her standing at the end of the runway looking so beautiful, he hadn't been able to help himself. Christian Collins wasn't known for denying himself something when he really wanted it. Susan was someone he couldn't seem to get enough of. When their lips parted, he hugged her close, knowing that her thoughts would be in turmoil. He was right.

"I missed you," he said, his lips against her forehead.

"I missed you too," she replied huskily, her voice muted because her face was buried against his blue shirt.

They made a striking couple. People in the terminal watched

them, staring outright at them, as if they were famous. After a long moment Christian reached for his laptop, keeping his arm around her shoulders, then led her toward the baggage claim. Susan snuggled against him, inhaling the scent of his Havana cologne.

"Oh, before I forget," she said, glancing up at him and thinking again how striking he was—it amazed her sometimes.

"What?" he asked as they reached the baggage area.

"Midnight has invited us to dinner this evening."

Christian glanced at his watch. "What time?"

Susan looked sheepish, realizing it was short notice. "Seven."

Christian pursed his lips, narrowing his light blue eyes. "Anyone else gonna be there, or is this another well-planned brow-beating?"

Susan couldn't help but giggle. Her Uncle Rick, although not hostile toward Christian anymore, still had a hard time with the idea that she had been removed from her wedding ceremony and hadn't been in another one with Christian shortly thereafter. Their current relationship was even more of a problem for Rick's sensibilities. There had been many "dinners" turned interrogations at her aunt and uncle's house. Susan couldn't blame Christian for his natural apprehension, but she did find it amusing.

"I think you're safe tonight," she assured him. "Joe and Randy will be there, as well as the new Assistant Chief. And you know Joe won't let my uncle harass you about us."

Christian looked thoughtful as the baggage conveyor belt started up. He said nothing as he waited for his bags, pulled them off the belt and turned to walk toward the escalator that took them toward the parking lot. Not until they were in the car did he glance at his watch again, and then look over at her.

"I guess we could head over," he said.

"Okay," Susan replied, glancing at him. He was grinning at her. "What?"

Christian shook his head, still smiling, then reached across the seat and placed his forefinger on her upper thigh, tracing it down the material of her dress to her knee. "I like this," he said, his tone low.

"Yes?" Susan asked, her voice trembling slightly.

A fire started in Christian's eyes as he nodded, looking directly into her eyes. "I'll like taking it off you even more." His voice was low and seductive, and Susan shivered in response.

Christian's grin widened as he started his car, which Susan had driven to the airport, and backed out of the parking space. Susan could never get used to his overt sexual nature. He was forever saying things that made her blush and shiver in anticipation at the same time. There had been so many times he'd surprised her. He didn't care what anyone thought of him, or what they saw him do. There had been many times in the past year when he'd purposely attempted to seduce her in public places. She was always too self-conscious to let anything actually happen, but that rarely stopped him trying. There had also been times when he'd actually gotten annoyed at her embarrassment, stating that she still treated him like one of her "other" boyfriends. Of course he thought of other men she dated as "pansies" because none of them apparently ever insisted that she sleep with them.

It was a fine line she walked in this relationship. Although they'd never really discussed it, Susan was fairly sure that if she slept with other men, Christian would no longer want her. He had never said as much, but it was obvious in his way that he considered her his territory sexually. Susan didn't really mind, since the only other sexual experience she'd had had been with her ex-fiancé/almost husband, Warren, and that had been nothing compared to the heat she experienced with Christian. She was fairly sure Christian was indeed the best man around in the lovemaking arena. Susan certainly didn't feel like she was being cheated of anything because she didn't sleep with anyone else. She did think, however, that Christian did feel that way, and that was why he slept with other women. In truth, she hadn't found a man that she desired even a tenth as much as she did Christian, so she didn't see the point in entering the sexual field with any of them. Certainly not if it would jeopardize her relationship with Christian, even if the double standard seemed outwardly unfair.

Thinking along those lines as Christian drove out of the parking lot, Susan glanced over at him. It was easy to see his self-assurance; it emanated from him like some kind of aura. She knew that was part of what attracted so many people to him. He made a person want to succeed in some small way with him, whether by winning his friendship, his admiration, his respect, or simply a night in his bed; no matter what it was, people were drawn to him. It made him very elusive and even harder to hold on to. Susan took consolation in the fact that he said he loved her like he loved no other woman. It was a good feeling, and helped to balance any other worries she had about her place in his life.

"So, what's been goin' on here?" he asked, breaking into her thoughts.

"Not much, life is calm here," Susan said, her voice holding a smile. She knew how he hated calm. "How was Seattle?"

He grinned. "Cold."

"How did the project go?"

Christian shrugged. "Still got another three weeks' worth of work to do."

"Three more weeks?"

"Yeah. I can probably do most of it 'round here, but I still have to go back to install it and run tests."

"How long are you home this time?" Susan knew she sounded like she was complaining but hated having him gone for such a long period of time.

"'Bout two weeks."

"And where is the next trip?"

"San Francisco," he replied easily.

"How long will you be gone then?" she asked, dismayed.

Christian glanced over at her, his look contemplative. "About a week."

Susan sighed quietly, though Christian caught the sound and grinned again. "Missed me, huh?"

Susan looked over at him, searching his face to try to determine if he was annoyed or just kidding her. Seeing that he was kidding, she smiled. "Yes, I did."

"Wanna show me how much?"

"What do you mean?"

Christian looked back at her for a long moment. Then his cynical mask dropped as he shook his head. "Never mind."

When they arrived at Midnight and Rick's he got out of the car and walked around to open her door. Susan could see that his cool facade was well in place. She knew she'd missed something and had a feeling she'd disappointed him again. Christian walked ahead, waiting for her at the front door before he rang the bell. Mikeyla answered. She smiled warmly at Susan, reaching out to hug her, then glanced up at Christian, never sure what to say to him. Even in her youth, Mikeyla knew that Christian was an unknown quantity.

Walking into the house, it was apparent the party was in the kitchen. Christian headed through and saw his cousin.

"Hey, man," Joe said, spotting Christian and Susan. He immediately reached into the refrigerator, where he'd basically taken up residence. Tossing Christian a beer, Joe looked at Susan. "You want anything?"

Susan just shook her head and walked over to hug Midnight and then Rick, her expression solemn.

Rick and Midnight exchanged a glance, then Rick looked over at Christian, who stared back at them passively. It was obvious something had happened, but this wasn't the time or place to get into it. Midnight stepped into the silence that followed.

"Kyle, this is Christian Collins. He's responsible for my inventory system."

Kyle sensed the undercurrent in the room easily. Even so, he smiled warmly at Christian and shook his hand. "I hear you're the man in demand these days."

"Yeah," Christian said tiredly, his English accent still thick. "Too much in demand lately."

"How did Seattle go?" Midnight asked, leaning back against Rick, who stood behind her with his arms around her waist.

"It went alright," Christian replied. "I'm thinking I need to get more lead time on some of these jobs though. So I can be better prepared for what I'm getting into."

"Well, we'll have to see what we can do about that," Midnight said. "Why don't you come by my office whenever you get out of bed tomorrow and we'll talk."

Christian nodded, glancing at Susan. At the rate things were going, he'd be getting up early, and from a cold, lonely bed.

During dinner they all talked about their views on law enforcement, how they thought things could be improved. Kyle and Christian agreed on the high-tech crimes issue; it was becoming a much bigger and more frequent problem than ever before. At one point Kyle turned to Randy. "You're on an extended leave from the department? Can I ask why?"

Randy nodded, smiling at Kyle. She already liked him; he was smart and openly friendly and really seemed to fit in with their group. "I'm going to school right now. I'm just a few classes away from my bachelor's degree in child psychology."

Kyle smiled. "That's great. How do you plan to use your degree?"

Randy glanced at Joe, who was sitting across from her. He grinned in response; they'd talked about this often enough. "Well, actually I want to set up a center for kids that get displaced from their homes during enforcement upheavals."

Kyle thought about it for a long minute, then nodded. "So when the parents get arrested and there's no one to take them, this center would?"

Randy smiled, happy that he understood the concept. "Yes, I

think it's far too traumatic for children to first see their parents arrested, and to then be marched off themselves to some cold, impersonal facility to be 'processed.'"

Kyle nodded, his mind working. "What would be different about your center?"

Randy considered her answer, appreciating the intelligent, direct way Kyle communicated. "It's my plan to have this center be a warm, loving, temporary environment for these kids. I would only have people working there that have a complete understanding of the process a child's mind goes through when they see their parents arrested, and how to handle that."

Kyle looked impressed. "Would your center help with a more permanent placement if the parent ends up incarcerated for a long period of time?"

"Certainly," Randy said, smiling. Kyle Masterson was indeed thorough. "It's my hope to have an up-to-date running list of good, pre-approved foster homes with profiles on each to match the right children with the right home. I don't think the child should be punished for the parents' inability to obey the law. I want them to have every chance of succeeding in spite of their parents' minor or major failures."

Kyle nodded again, then glanced at Joe. "She keep you up nights a lot?"

"You have no idea," Joe said, laughing as Randy made an indignant sound and shot her husband a mockingly vile look.

"Seriously, Randy," Kyle said. "I think it's an excellent idea, and one I hope you are able to put into action."

"Oh, she'll do it," Joe said seriously. "If it takes every penny I have, she'll do it."

There was silence at the table then, as Randy and Joe exchanged a deep, meaningful look. It was obvious to everyone that they'd discussed this many times.

"What about the other idea?" Joe asked Randy, his tone leading.

Randy narrowed her eyes at him, and he grinned back insolently.

"What other idea?" Midnight asked, her eyes going between the two.

When Randy didn't speak, Joe turned to Midnight "She has an idea for a mentoring program."

"Mentoring? Who would be mentoring? And who would they mentor?" Midnight asked, her mind obviously working already.

Joe again turned to Randy. She sighed and leaned her elbows on the table, looking down toward Midnight. "I had this idea that the department's officers and support staff could do the mentoring."

"And?" Midnight said, waiting for the rest.

"And," Randy began, giving Joe another narrowed look, "I was planning to present the idea to you formally in a week or so."

"Well, lay it out for me real quick," Midnight replied, used to making decisions at the drop of a hat.

"Okay, basically I thought we could take the juvenile hall referrals and match them up with some of our officers, perhaps cross-referencing particular types of offenses to an officer's specialty. It would benefit the youths because they would get to see that being a person that obeys the law can be "cool" as well as law-abiding and law-enforcing. The kids that would be part of this would have at least one juvenile hall booking. I've already made a contact there, a counselor who would be happy to refer kids he sees going the wrong direction to us."

"How much time would the officers have to dedicate to this?" Rick asked.

"At least three hours a week," Randy replied. "In order to make any type of impact on these kids, some time will be necessary. But that time can be anytime during the officers' off hours…" She trailed off as Rick looked over at Midnight expectantly.

Joe canted his head in Midnight's direction as well, and she started to grin. "Oh, no pressure here. I guess if we made this a departmental program, the officers could get credited a certain allotment of hours to do this as a public service."

Randy bit her lip, looking over at Joe, her eyes blazing with suppressed excitement.

"Do you already have a list?" Midnight asked, noting the excited light in Randy's eyes.

Randy looked a bit chagrined. "Well, I did take the liberty of asking my contact if he could give me a list for illustrative purposes."

"But these are kids he'd recommend for this program?" Midnight countered.

"Yes."

Midnight looked thoughtful for a moment, leaning back in her chair and steepling her fingers together, her eyes narrowing. Then she sat up.

"Be in my office tomorrow morning at ten, *with* your list. We'll iron out the details," she said, her voice all chief but her smile friendly.

Kyle turned to Susan and Christian, obviously intent on getting to know everyone at the table.

"So, Susan, what do you do?" he asked.

"I am the Sinclair children's nanny," Susan answered, sounding very proper.

Kyle narrowed his eyes, glancing between Rick and Susan. "And do I see a family resemblance here?"

Susan smiled, nodding.

"She's my niece," Rick supplied.

Kyle nodded, then looked at Christian quizzically. Christian chuckled. "Joe's my cousin."

Kyle shook his head, grinning and looked over at Midnight "You keep things all in the family around here, don't you?"

Midnight laughed. "Who can you trust but your own family?"

"You're stuck with us now too, Masterson," Rick put in, his look pointed.

Kyle inclined his head slightly at the significance of that comment. Rick was stating his acceptance of him publicly. Kyle knew that it meant a lot. Noting the exchange, Joe lifted his glass, and everyone followed suit.

"To our new Assistant Chief," Joe said, grinning.

"To someone that has a clue about hi-tech," Christian chimed in, giving Midnight a wink.

"To the man that is going to facilitate my seeing my wife more often," Rick said, smiling.

Midnight laughed, giving the men a mockingly sour look. "As long as you guys don't run him off the first day."

"Is the second okay?" Joe asked drily.

"Watch it, Sinclair," Midnight said, narrowing her eyes.

"Yeah, yeah," Joe said, waving his hand airily.

Midnight turned to Kyle. "The first thing I want you to do as Assistant Chief is get Joe in line."

"Patrol?" Kyle asked, his tone comical.

"At least—maybe even desk sergeant," Midnight replied.

"Hey now," Joe said, laughing.

"What about meter maid?" Rick put in.

Joe looked over at his lifelong friend, his eyes narrowed. "You're supposed to be on my side."

"Sorry," Rick said, looking anything but contrite.

They toasted, and the evening proceeded in an easy manner. Kyle left the Debenshire home feeling a sense of belonging starting in him. It felt good.

# CHAPTER 4

The following week, Dave had managed to work his way through the chain and arrange a meeting with Tiempo. He knew Stevie would be on hand, having garnered that she was Tiempo's security. Most drug dealers surrounded themselves with brawny bodyguards. Tiempo had chosen one that many men wished would guard their bodies horizontally for long periods of time. As Dave made his way into the palatial estate Tiempo owned high in the La Jolla hills, he noted there were other men lounging about the place, many of them armed. So Ms. O'Neil did have backup. When he was led into the library he got his first sight of Stevie O'Neil. She stood leaning against one of the windows, smoking a thin cigar. She wore all black. Her auburn hair fell well past her shoulders in a tousled, appealing way. Her green eyes were on him the moment he walked in; they widened ever so slightly, but no other emotion showed on her face.

"Mr. Tiempo will be with us in a moment," she said evenly. Her voice was just slightly husky.

Dave nodded, looking around him, his stance casual and unaffected by his surroundings. Many longtime drug dealers grew nervous when waiting for a man of Tiempo's reputation. He'd been known to grow angry at the slightest thing, and even to kill for the fun of it. In Dave's case, he would have everything to be nervous about, considering he was a cop and that Mr. Tiempo's security person almost assuredly knew just that and could tell Tiempo the moment he walked in. But no apprehension showed in Dave's manner; he might as well have been waiting for the maid to bring tea rather than for a notorious drug dealer.

After letting his eyes trail over the shelves of books and the room's leather furnishings, Dave allowed them to connect with Stevie's again. She was still watching him. After a few long moments he inclined his head, dropping his eyes momentarily in a sign of respect she was quite unaccustomed to. When his eyes came back to hers, he noted the surprise in them; his lips curled ever so slightly in a lopsided smile.

Tiempo walked in then, and Dave turned to him. They talked briefly about a shipment Tiempo expected the following week, and Dave wanting to score some higher-grade coke. Tiempo was, as usual, careful about how he discussed the shipment, especially since he had never dealt with Dave before.

After Dave left, Tiempo turned to Stevie and said, "Check him out."

Stevie nodded, and Tiempo left her alone again.

That night, Dave was already in bed, half asleep, when he heard the intercom to his front door buzz. Reaching above his head to the button, he depressed it. "Yeah?" he asked, his voice gravelly.

"Let's talk," came the reply. A female voice that Dave recognized.

"'kay," he said, pressing the button to unlock the door as he sat up and got out of bed, reaching for a shirt to put on over his sweatpants. He was still buttoning it as he walked out of his bedroom. Stevie stood in the living room, watching him come down the hall. Dave gestured for her to sit; she shook her head. Dave moved to perch on the arm of his couch, watching her. She wore the same clothes as earlier, but she'd pulled her hair back in a long braid with a red hair tie hanging at the end. Dave's eyes trained on the only spot of color.

Stevie's eyes dropped to the braid hanging halfway to her waist. She shrugged. "I hate all black," she said offhandedly.

Dave nodded, his eyes not leaving hers. He was waiting, his posture relaxed.

Stevie glanced around the room. His living room was made up of light elegance, with a very definite feel of the laidback person that lived there. His surf board stood in the corner by the entryway, as if ready to go whenever the mood took him, which it did most mornings. The furnishings were nice but uncomplicated, low-slung and sand-colored leather, unadorned tables, brass lamps with cream shades. His home seemed as uncomplicated as Dave appeared to be. But appearances could always be deceiving.

"So," Stevie began, her tone casual. "Should I be flattered or nervous?"

Dave's eyes reflected nothing. "Because?"

Stevie rolled her eyes to the ceiling, then looked back at him. "Because I have the city's best narc checkin' me out." Her tone remained casual, but it was clear she was quite serious.

The thought flickered through Dave's mind that he should have picked up his gun on the way out of his room. But nothing showed on his face as he answered her. "And I thought you were the one doing the checking out."

Stevie's eyes dropped to do a cursory check of his person. They lingered over his chest, which was for the most part bare, then trailed back up to his eyes. Dave was surprised to feel an instant response to that unspoken allusion, and didn't bother to hide the heat that sprang to his eyes. He was rewarded with her quick intake of breath, even as she glanced away. Dave grinned in spite of himself.

"So what does San Diego PD want?" Stevie asked when her composure returned moments later.

"You," Dave replied, his tone direct.

Again her eyes returned to his, searching as if trying to discern the meaning of what he'd just said. She saw nothing.

"I can't imagine why," she replied finally as she dropped into the chair behind her.

"No?" Dave asked conversationally. "You wouldn't happen to know about a guy that turned up dead in his apartment last week, would ya?"

"Lots of people turn up dead all around this city—what's that got to do with me?" Stevie shot back, her tone just as calm.

"Well, this one had a bad case of stitching. Seemed pretty textbook."

Stevie's expression didn't change, but her jaw tightened noticeably. "Damn shame."

"Yeah, tell me about it," Dave said, his eyes boring into hers, the disapproval in them clear.

Stevie didn't flinch or shrink from his reproof. It was clear to Dave that she was guilty of killing the guy. It was also clear that, as he and Midnight had suspected, she had had a reason and it was more than revenge.

There was a long moment of silence as they stared at each other, hunter and hunted—but it wasn't obvious who was who.

"So what's it going to take to get rid of you?" Stevie asked.

A slight smile played on Dave's lips. "You."

Stevie narrowed her eyes. She knew instinctively that he didn't mean it the way he'd said it. "What do I have to do?"

"Come back."

"What?" Stevie asked, dumbfounded by his answer and momentarily losing her cool. "Come back where?"

"To the department."

"For what? A shakedown?" Stevie replied, in a good imitation of many of the drug dealers he'd dealt with in the past.

"For your family."

"What the hell does my family have to do with this?" Stevie got to her feet, staring at him warily.

Dave gave her a look of reproach. "Your family has everything to do with this, O'Neil."

"No," Stevie said, shaking her head. She started to glance around, as if waiting for her sister and mother to appear out of nowhere.

Dave walked toward her, searching her eyes. "It does, Stevie. We know it does."

"We?"

Dave's eyes held hers. "Your sister, me, the chief…" he replied, his voice softening.

"And she wants you to take me down." Stevie's voice held just the slightest tremor. It was obvious she was referring to the Chief of

Police.

Dave reached out involuntarily, smoothing his thumb over her cheek, wanting to take the wariness out of her eyes. "She wants me to bring you back, Stevie. To the family."

Stevie's brows furrowed momentarily. Then it became apparent that understanding had dawned. To his surprise, she started to shake her head as she moved away from him. His hand on her arm stopped her. "Stevie, if I can't bring you back, I'll have to take you down. I don't want to have to do that."

She pinned him with a look. "Then don't," she said bitingly.

"I don't have a choice."

"You have a fucking choice, dammit," she snapped, her cool lost in the face of his admission.

"No, I don't," he said softly, his hand still on her arm. "Give me one."

"What do you mean?" she asked, again thrown off by his demeanor.

"Give me a choice—help me."

"How?" she asked, surprised by his intensity. Why did he care what happened to her?

"Make a deal with me."

"What kind of deal?"

"A deal of give and take."

"Give and take? Who does the giving?" she asked, her tone taking on the cynical note of someone who'd grown used to one-sided deals.

"I do."

"And I'll bet all the taking too."

"Nope, you'd have to do the taking," Dave said, staring into her eyes. She couldn't detect any sexual advance from him, so what were they bargaining for?

"Okay," she said finally, stepping back and brushing his hand off her arm. "Let's put our cards on the table here. What will you give me?"

"Two weeks."

"Two weeks? Of what?" she asked, wondering if she was ever going to catch up in this conversation.

"Of my experience, knowledge, and expertise."

"And what do I have to take?" she said, trying to cover the fact that she still didn't know what he was offering.

"You have to take the outcome for better or worse."

"Goddamn it, Dibbins, just fucking say what you mean!" she yelled, her anger boiling to the surface. She felt like a fool in the presence of someone obviously used to playing games of innuendo and half-truths.

Dave grinned openly at her outburst. "Okay, here's the deal. I will help you. I'll clear my desk of all my other cases for two weeks. I will work with you on this, to take this bastard down. I will dedicate all of my time to it. But," he said, holding up his index finger, "at the end of two weeks, regardless of whether we have enough to bust him, you come back to the department with me and never look back. Do we have a deal?"

Stevie stared back at him for a full minute, trying to assimilate all he had just said. "You'll help me?" she asked, making sure she'd fully understood.

"I'll help you."

"You'll work on nothing but Tiempo for two weeks?"

"I'll eat, drink, and sleep Tiempo for two weeks."

"And you'll help me take him down?"

"If it's within my power to do it, yes."

"Can you do it?"

"I can damn sure try."

"And I come back to the department?"

"Yes."

"As what? An inmate?"

Dave grinned at that, shaking his head slowly. "An officer."

"You can do that?"

"I can do that."

"But why?" she asked, her disbelief evident.

"Because that's what Midnight wants."

Stevie looked back at him, then finally nodded, as if still trying to accept what he was telling her but willing to trust him for the moment.

"Sergeant, I think you have yourself a deal," she said after a long pause.

"Cool," he replied simply, grinning at her engagingly.

Stevie narrowed her eyes. She'd have to be careful with this one.

Donovan Curtis stood in his kitchen, chopping vegetables. He was wearing faded blue jeans and a black cotton shirt, open at the throat. His sleeves were rolled up over tanned, well-toned forearms, and he had a dishtowel thrown carelessly over his shoulder. Locks of sandy-brown hair fell over his forehead as he chopped. He sported a neatly trimmed goatee. He was barefoot, but his lean, tall frame was the picture of modern masculinity. The radio was on in the living room, just a few feet from the kitchen, so he didn't hear the front door open.

When Erin Shandley laid eyes on him for the first time she was sure her heart stopped, and she didn't think it had anything to do with the surprise of finding someone in the house when she expected it to be empty. When Donovan's head snapped up, a frown on his lips, all she could think was what incredibly beautiful eyes he had, a teal blue that seemed to glow.

"Hi," she stammered, realizing how awkward a situation this was.

Donovan canted his head to the side, a grin starting on his lips. "Hello…" he said, trailing off with an invitation for her to explain what she was doing in his house.

"You must be Donovan," Erin said, still standing in the doorway to the kitchen as if rooted to the spot.

"I'm Donovan," he said matter-of-factly as he set his knife down and turned to her, reaching up for the towel on his shoulder to wipe his hands. "And who would you be?" he asked, his grin widening.

"Oh, duh," Erin said, rolling her eyes at her own stupidity. "I'm Erin Shandley. I'm a friend of Jeanie's."

She stepped forward, extending her hand. He took it, smiling down at her. "Nice to meet you, Erin. And my fiancée is where?"

"She dropped me off—she had to go pick something up. She said she'd be right back," Erin rattled off, nervous in his presence. She couldn't stop staring up at him. Jesus! Jeanie was a lucky girl!

Donovan nodded and went back over to the cutting board. Erin noticed then that there was a pot boiling on the stove, and the aroma of chicken came to her as she inhaled. When she turned back to Donovan, he was looking at her.

"Jeanie said you cook," she said lamely.

He laughed. "Did she also tell you that she doesn't?" His grin told her that it was probably an ongoing joke between the two of them.

"Well, she said you do most of the cooking," Erin said, chewing on her bottom lip nervously.

"Yeah," he said, laughing again. "Because last time I let her cook, she almost ruined one of my best saucepans."

Erin laughed, thinking that did sound like Jeanie. She watched as Donovan picked up a glass of wine and took a drink, glancing at her over the rim of the glass.

Gesturing to her with the glass, he asked, "Do you want some wine?" Then he canted his head to the side, giving her a measuring look. "Or are you old enough?"

Erin gave him a wide smile. She heard that a lot. "Yes, I'm old enough, but just barely." She wrinkled her nose comically. "I've never tasted wine, though, so I don't know…"

"What have you tasted?" he asked, leaning against the refrigerator.

"Champagne, and a beer once," she replied, making a face. "Beer is gross."

Donovan laughed, liking her youthful candor. "You just haven't tasted the right kind yet." He held his glass out to her. "Would you like to try this?"

Erin was surprised. She had never been in the presence of a guy this good-looking before, and she certainly had never had a man like Donovan be as nice to her as this. They didn't even make men that looked like Donovan in Iowa.

Tentatively, she reached out and took the glass. Donovan watched her with a warm grin on his face. When she hesitated, he said, "It's just old grapes—it can't kill you."

She laughed at his description, then took a sip. It was definitely different, and definitely an acquired taste, but she found that she liked it.

She handed the glass back to him, nodding. "I like it. It's really different from what I've tasted before, but it's good."

"Do you want one of your own?" he asked, already reaching for one of the crystal wine glasses suspended from the bottom of his kitchen cabinets.

"Sure," she said, thinking, *Can I just keep drinking from yours?* She knew she was being bad. This was Jeanie's man, and she was having all these thoughts. She almost giggled to herself, thinking she was such a kid.

Donovan poured her a glass of wine and handed it to her. Taking another drink of his and then refilling his glass, he glanced over at her. "So do you work for the department?"

Erin sipped her wine. "I work in the secretarial pool."

Donovan nodded. "I thought you seemed a little young to be an officer."

"Just twenty-one a month ago," she said, biting her lip.

Donovan caught that and canted his head to the side again. "Do I make you nervous?"

Erin couldn't stop her mouth from falling open at the directness of his question. She closed it hastily as she felt a blush creep up her cheeks. She averted her eyes as she nodded.

"Why?" he asked, his look puzzled.

"Um," she stammered, not sure what to say, then blurted out her answer anyway. "Because I'm not used to gorgeous guys being nice to me." She rolled her eyes, putting her forehead against the cabinet next to her. "God! I can't believe I just said that!"

Donovan laughed; the sound was warm and rich. He shook his head, still smiling. "Don't worry about it."

"Oh yeah," she said, rolling her head from side to side, her forehead still pressed against the wood. "So you say now—later you're gonna think, what a dork!"

Again Donovan laughed. "Sorry, I'm not a 'what a dork' kinda guy."

She rolled her head to the side, looking up at him. "No?"

"No."

"Whew!" she said, grinning as she straightened up. "Another social disaster averted. Where's my wine?" Reaching for her glass, she pretended to take a long drink. Donovan grinned. He already liked her; she was very unaffected.

Erin was pretty in a very fresh way. She was more cute than

beautiful, with blond hair and creamy skin, and big, bright blue eyes that reminded you of wide-eyed innocence. Today she looked particularly young; her hair was pulled back in a ponytail, and she wore only light makeup. Her outfit was a pale blue straight skirt and a navy blouse, with navy flats.

They chatted a few more minutes about what he was cooking, and made some small talk about the weather while Donovan went back to chopping. A little while later Jeanie came in.

"Hey!" she said, smiling widely at Donovan. "I didn't expect to see you here!"

"I do live here," he pointed out, even as he leaned down to kiss her softly on the lips.

Jeanie reached around, smacking him playfully on the butt as she laughed, twitching her nose. "I know you live here, brat. You're just never here anymore!" she said, and in the same breath, "God, I hate that goatee. When do you get to shave it?"

Donovan gave her a look of mock affront. "I happen to like the goatee," he said, smoothing his fingers down the sides of it.

"It's scratchy," Jeanie said, wrinkling her nose again.

"Wah," Donovan said, grinning as he poured her a glass of wine. Then he looked over at Erin. "What do you think?"

"About what?" Erin hedged.

Jeanie turned, leaning against the counter between Erin and Donovan as she waited for the answer.

"About the goatee," Donovan clarified.

"Um…" Erin grinned solicitously, then bit her lip as her eyes darted between Donovan and Jeanie. "I kinda like it."

"Ugh!" Jeanie said, throwing up her hands, while Donovan beamed. She shot him a dirty look. "Well, I *don't* like it, and you have to *live* with me!"

"Oh, I dunno about that..." Donovan said, looking thoughtfully at his wine glass then quirking his eyebrow at Erin.

"Shut up!" Jeanie said, laughing as she smacked him on the butt again. Donovan and Erin laughed. After a long moment, Jeanie glanced between the two of them. "So I take it you two met?"

"We had no choice, Jay," Donovan said, giving her a caustic look, his grin still evident.

"Sorry, I didn't know you'd be home," she said, gesturing futilely. "Why are you home, anyway?" she asked, sipping her wine.

"Got time off—thought I'd come home to my girl," Donovan said, smiling down at her.

"You left that fancy undercover apartment to come home to me," Jeanie said wistfully, even as she grinned. "What a guy."

"If you want me to leave..." He put his wine glass down and took a few steps toward the front door.

Jeanie grabbed him by the belt, pulling him back. "Hold on there, buddy! You're not going anywhere."

Donovan grinned at Erin. "I love it when she gets rough."

Erin laughed.

Donovan turned around, grabbing Jeanie up by the waist and lifting her off her feet, sitting her down on the counter so that she was face to face with him. Jeanie laughed, putting her arms around his neck and pulling him close. Donovan leaned in, his lips hovering near hers, looking into her eyes. "I love you."

"I love you too, Donovan," Jeanie said, kissing him softly, then dropped her head to his shoulder, nuzzling his neck with her lips. Donovan hugged her to him, closing his eyes. He was enjoying the feel of her again.

Erin tried to ignore the exchange, but couldn't help but watch, as if this were her favorite romantic movie. Donovan and Jeanie really were a great-looking couple—Jeanie with her long chestnut hair, her beautiful face set with dark, long-lashed eyes, and her perfect, petite body and great tan. And then there was Donovan, who was just gorgeous, and obviously so sweet.

Jeanie and she had talked about Donovan. Jeanie had told Erin how Donovan had been her first lover, and how wonderful he'd been. She'd told Erin about Donovan being shot, and how they'd broken up because Jeanie couldn't handle how serious things were. Then about the car bomb in Mexico, when Jeanie had heard a San Diego PD officer had been killed but didn't know if it was Donovan or Midnight Chevalier. Later, of course, Jeanie had told her about how Donovan had proposed on their trip up the coast. It was one of the most romantic things Erin had ever heard.

Now, meeting Donovan, she could see why Jeanie's eyes shined so bright when she talked about him. It was apparent they were very close.

Erin hoped someday to find someone like Donovan. Her first brush with "love" had left a great deal to be desired. At least she had Bobby to show for it. Bobby was her five-year-old son, and the reason she'd been able to go on so many times in the last five years.

Growing up in Iowa had left a lot to be desired in terms of excitement. So when Tyler Bodine had blown into town on his motor-cycle, it had seemed like some great adventure to flirt with him. He had seemed so handsome, with his blond hair and brown eyes. He was five feet, ten inches, and muscled from working construction. Being a virgin at fifteen, she had no idea that messing with a nine-teen-year-old man was a bad idea. She realized that a few hours later when he all but raped her in the barn out behind her parents' house. It wasn't really rape, because she didn't really mind until he actually entered her, and it hurt so much she thought she was going to die. Then she cried and pleaded with him to stop, but he just said, "Well, the damage is done now—might as well finish."

She realized much later that she should have known then what kind of man he was, but she didn't. Afterward he was nice, and apol-ogized for hurting her. "It always hurts the first time," he said. "The next time won't hurt so much." Well, the next time did hurt just as much, and the time after that, and the time after that.

Tyler was working at a nearby farm, helping to build a cattle pen and a barn. The man he was working for had known Erin her entire life. He'd seen what was going on between the young man working for him and "little Erin," as he had thought of her. Mr. Handy had seen fit to inform Erin's parents of what he thought was happening. They had questioned Erin, but she told them they were just seeing each other, that nothing sexual was going on. The fact that she'd lied to them became evident four months later when she cried in their arms, telling them she was pregnant. Erin's father had gone after Ty-ler with a shotgun.

It had been the classic shotgun wedding, Erin in her ill-fitting Sunday dress and Tyler in his best jeans and a white-collared shirt loaned to him by Erin's father; it was two sizes too big and had a stain on the pocket. They'd moved into her parents' small mother-in-law cottage, and things had been okay. Tyler had become even more of a stranger after that. He'd worked long hours at the Handy place, and finished the job a month before the baby was due. Tyler traded his motorcycle for a truck and packed up the few things they had, along with Erin, and they left town. Erin's parents had been distraught, but Tyler had been adamant. "I'm not staying in this one-fucking-horse town."

Erin was determined to make her marriage with Tyler work. She thought she loved him; after all, he was her first. Tyler told her he loved her—usually when he made love to her at night in the dark, but she was sure he meant it. The baby's birth had occurred when they were passing through a town; he dropped her at the emergency room and came back to pick her up two days later when she was released, barely glancing at the baby and not even asking how she was.

The birth had been terrifying. It had hurt so much, and she'd been so afraid and alone. The nurses were mean to her, telling her she should have taken a prenatal class so she'd know what to do. Since they didn't have any insurance, the hospital wouldn't give her any medication to help ease the pain. She'd screamed over and over again, begging them to get Tyler for her. She had cried when the baby was born, and she'd named him Bobby after her father, Robert.

A week later, Tyler found work in Wichita, Kansas, and they got an apartment. It was small, but Erin set about trying to make it a nice home for them. She found some material to make curtains, and tried to find furniture at the secondhand store. She walked or took the bus to wherever she could, taking Bobby with her in a handmade carrier that she wrapped around herself. It was during that time that she became a loving mother in every way. Even though she was a child herself, her baby's safety, health, and happiness became paramount.

Tyler took to being out at all hours of the night, leaving Erin and Bobby alone. Whenever Erin would question Tyler, he would say he was picking up extra work so they could find a better apartment with some "real" furniture. When he was home, he criticized her cooking, her decorations, and the way she handled Bobby. If Bobby cried for more than a minute, Tyler yelled at her to shut him the hell up, then proceeded to tell her what a lousy mother she was, that if she was smarter she'd know what to do to keep her baby happy. But since she wasn't... he'd always leave that part off, letting her imagine what he meant.

The beatings started a year and a half after they were married. Tyler had come home drunk. He had gotten paid that night, and had spent half his paycheck buying rounds at the bar. When he handed Erin half the meager sum he usually gave her for buying groceries, she asked where the rest was. "Gotta cut back," Tyler slurred.

"That sure didn't apply at the bar tonight, did it?" Erin snapped, in a rare show of anger.

Tyler backhanded her. "I make the fucking money, I can spend the fucking money—you got that, bitch?" he yelled.

Erin had been stunned. She'd never in her life been hit in the face. But Tyler wasn't done. He'd gone on to hit her again and again, telling her that she better not ever question him again. After that, he beat her whenever he was in a bad mood, or whenever she had the nerve to question him.

It had taken her three years to finally set aside enough money to get away from him. She had been terrified that night six months ago, when she took what money he had left from his paycheck out of his wallet as he lay passed out on the couch and grabbed the small suitcase and raggedy backpack in which she'd stored as much clothing and food for herself and Bobby as she could. She had managed to save a measly five hundred dollars, and she had another five hundred from what was left of Tyler's check. She bought them bus tickets under fake names and headed for California.

Once there she found herself a job as a waitress, and found three roommates who were college students. One of the girls, thankfully, was studying to be a daycare provider, and went to school nights, so she offered to watch Bobby while Erin worked. A month later she found out about some night courses she could take to learn to work on a word processor, and spent her last two hundred dollars to enroll. In four months she had her certification for office skills, and went looking for a job. She got lucky on her third interview, with the San Diego Police Department. She'd been working there for a week when she met a very harried officer coming in the door one day with an armload of papers. Erin offered to help her, and Jeanie accepted gratefully. They'd become fast friends. Now she'd met Jeanie's other half. Life was definitely getting interesting.

The day after his meeting with Stevie, Dave walked into Midnight's office to report his progress. Midnight was pleased to hear that the meeting had gone well. Dave was a bit sheepish to mention that he'd offered to drop his other cases for two weeks without clearing it with her or Spider first. Midnight waved his discomfort aside.

"Dave, you did what you needed to do. Don't sweat it." Midnight already knew the argument she was going to get from Spider, but was ready for it all the same. "So, do you think you can do it?" she said, voicing the same question Stevie had asked the night before.

Dave leaned back against the wall, shrugging casually. "I'm gonna do my best, but either way we get her back, right?"

Midnight didn't reply at first, searching his eyes. "Yeah, you're right," she said. Then, after a long pause, "What do you think of her?"

Dave's lips tugged in a wry grin. "What do you want me to think?" He knew where Midnight's thoughts were going.

"I just want your opinion," she replied mildly.

"Uh-huh..." Dave said, his grin still in place.

"Sergeant Dibbins, don't give me that bullshit grin. Just tell me what you think of her," Midnight said, doing her best to sound official but ruining it with a grin of her own.

"I think she's a very intense young lady who will be quite interesting to work with."

Midnight narrowed her eyes at him for a moment, aware she was being stonewalled but also realizing that in not answering her directly, he *was* answering her. She smiled. "You just be careful."

"I always am," Dave replied smoothly, giving her a casual salute as he turned to leave the office.

Midnight still looked thoughtful when Rick walked in a few minutes later.

"What did I miss?" he asked casually as he leaned against her desk.

"Dave just reported in on my errant officer."

"Ah, how'd the meeting go?"

"It went well, except he offered to work with her on this for two weeks while ignoring all his other cases."

Rick rubbed the bridge of his nose with his index finger, eyeing her speculatively. "Did you authorize him to do that?"

"No, but if it works..."

Rick canted his head to the side, giving her a measuring look. "This means a lot," he said softly. "Why?"

Midnight looked back at her husband of almost twelve years, ever astounded at his intuition. "Because she's family."

"Devereaux was family," he pointed out, referring to a bad cop they'd busted three years before.

"Devereaux was out for himself and his greed," Midnight replied stridently. "Stevie is looking for justice, because..." She trailed off, and Rick's eyes narrowed.

"Because what, Night?" he asked gently.

Midnight took a deep breath, her chin coming up a bit, as if she were accepting what she was about to say. "Because I let her down." Her voice was strong, but it was apparent to Rick that the situation was affecting her deeply.

"Night..." he began, shaking his head.

"No, Rick, don't," she said, shaking her head too. "Don't say that it's not true, because it is. Her brother-in-law was killed and my department couldn't make a case against the man that did it. I let her down, so she went to finish the job."

"That's bullshit, Midnight," Rick said, his tone short; he hated her demeaning herself because someone else failed to make a case. "We can't win them all—you know that. And you know that you can't control everything in this department. You're the only one that went to bat for Templeton when the press was saying he'd been at fault in the accident. You're the one that made sure it was investigated thoroughly. You're the one that got his name cleared. You, Midnight, no one else. You can't blame it on yourself if that bastard Tiempo was too fucking slick to get caught for this."

Midnight looked back at him for a long moment. His eyes searched her face, pleading with her to listen to him. Finally she blew her breath out in a long sigh, nodding.

"You're right, I know you're right. But I can't let her get herself killed for this, Rick."

"I know," he replied simply, reaching out to touch her cheek softly, then brushed a lock of her hair back from her face and leaned down to kiss her on the lips. "I love you," he said, as if trying to mend her with his words.

"I know," she said with a grin, echoing his earlier words.

Rick sat back against the desk again. "So he thinks he can make the case?"

"He said he's gonna try."

Rick smiled. "Usually means he'll do it."

"Yup," Midnight replied, smiling too. "So," she said, changing the subject again, "was this an official call?"

"Actually, it was." Rick grinned. "I'm goin' on a warrant with Manny tonight—just wanted to let ya know."

"What's Manny got goin' on?"

"He's got an inside on the Dos Fuegos."

"Hmm… really?" Midnight's attention was piqued.

"Yeah, it's a girl that dated the leader. I guess he did her pretty bad, and she wants revenge."

"Revenge is too quickly sated. What else has he got?"

"Well, he says she's pretty serious, and has a lot of info that we can use." Rick checked his watch. "In fact, I'm supposed to go meet her downstairs like now—I'd better go." He stood up. "You okay?"

"I'm always okay," Midnight replied, grinning up at him. He still looked incredible after all these years. Midnight stood too, glancing over to make sure he'd closed her door when he'd walked in. She slid her hand over his chest and up to his neck. He lowered his head, kissing her lips softly, but with just enough desire to make her tingle, as she always did with him. His hands at her waist gave her a gentle squeeze.

"I'll see you tonight," he said with a promising smile.

"Count on it," she replied, staring up into his eyes.

"Ohh…" he said, his voice a light groan as he grinned.

Making his way back down to the FORS offices, Rick thought about his wife. He and Midnight had been together for a long time. They shared everything, including fair-sized tempers and stubborn streaks. They'd been through hell together, and had weathered it. He knew to his very core that Midnight was the one woman he was meant to be with. There had been little doubt of that since shortly after he'd met her eleven years before. Midnight had all the fire and passion that he himself had. She was able to match him in intensity and drive, and she challenged him in every way. He'd never before met a woman that could do that, even though he'd had many in his life before Midnight. Most had simply thrown themselves at him, willing to let him do anything to them as long as he paid attention to them. Then there were the women that thought they could play the hard-to-get game. They'd tried it, and he'd walked. None of them interested him long enough to chase.

But Midnight had been more involved with his best friend when they'd met, and she certainly hadn't been the type to throw herself at any man. He'd seen fire and intensity in her that interested him. Eventually, he'd also seen a vulnerability that had brought out feelings of protectiveness he'd never had for any woman before. It was that combination of hardened cop and helpless waif that caught him so unawares. He'd never regretted it for a minute since. He loved his wife with every ounce of his being, and he was secure in the knowledge that she felt the exact same way about him.

Stepping off the elevator, he walked toward his office. Manny was already there. Manny had been a member of FORS for going on nine years, and he frequently baited Rick about Midnight; he had a crush on her, as did many men in the department. Rick saw that he was talking to a young woman. When he walked into his office, he smiled at her; her eyes were on him immediately. She was very pretty, in a hot, all dark eyes and long, dark hair way. No wonder Manny wanted to work closely with this one, Rick thought wryly.

"Hey, Manny, what's happenin'?" Rick asked. He clapped the younger man on the shoulder.

Manny turned around and smiled. "You're late, boss," he drawled.

"Yeah, yeah, so shoot me."

"Gladly." Manny laughed. "Look, Rick, this is Angelica Muñoz. Angelica, this is my LT, Rick Debenshire."

Rick extended his hand automatically, already noting the heat in the young woman's eyes. *What's goin' on here?* he thought, even as Angelica extended her hand. Her look was direct, her dark eyes fairly smoldering. "It's good to meet you, Angelica."

"Yes, Rick, it is." Angelica said, her voice low and as smoky as her eyes. Warning bells went off in Rick's head. He glanced over at Manny and saw that he was looking between Angelica and him, his expression indicating surprise at her sudden intensity.

Rick nodded, grinning lopsidedly, his blue eyes narrowing just slightly as he let her hand go.

Two days after meeting Dave Dibbins, Stevie found herself in his classic 1970 Dodge Charger, with its navy blue leather interior. The inside of the car smelled like the man driving it, a mixture of leather, salt water, and his cologne, which had a fresh but rich smell to it. Stevie watched Dave as he drove. She noted that he was as relaxed at the wheel of his car as he had seemed in Tiempo's library two days before, even if he was on his way to a meeting that could have any kind of result. Stevie couldn't fathom this man's ease; she knew she was twisted in a hundred different knots, and she was careful not to show it when she was around Tiempo or his men, but sitting in Dave's car, she was shaking. She adjusted the vent to blow into her face, feeling the need for more air.

Dave caught the movement and noted her trembling. His hand moved from the steering wheel to cover hers, resting in her lap; they'd stopped at a light. When Stevie raised her eyes to his, he was looking directly at her. He gave her a small grin. "It'll be cool," he said calmly.

Stevie stared back at him for a long moment, wanting to ask how he knew that but realizing that she was dealing with someone who'd been doing this stuff for years, not the mere year and half she had. Finally she nodded, feeling him give her another squeeze before the warmth of his hand left hers.

Giving herself a mental shake, Stevie looked outside, watching the cars around them. A dark-haired man in a Porsche Boxster pulled up next to Dave's car on the driver's side. The Porsche's engine revved as the man behind the wheel glanced challengingly over at Dave. Dave's left arm was extended, his wrist resting on the steering wheel, his right hand on the gear shift. He glanced over his left shoulder at the guy in the Porsche, catching the other man staring at Stevie. Dave twisted his lips in a disapproving smirk and looked away. Seconds later the light changed, and the Porsche roared off. Dave continued to drive at his normal speed. After a few minutes Stevie couldn't help but comment.

"Okay, I don't get it."

"Don't get what?" Dave asked, his voice smooth and low.

"I can feel the power of this engine—that guy was challenging you, and I know this car could have taken his. Why didn't you go for it?"

Dave glanced over at her, then back at the street. "What was the point?"

"To kick his ass."

"What would I have accomplished?"

"I don't know," Stevie said, letting her breath out in a sigh. "Just to do it. To win."

Dave looked thoughtful for a moment, then shrugged. "I'm not going to throw a rod or shear a gear for some punk in a Porsche. I know I can beat him—chances are good he did too. What was the point in proving it?"

Stevie just stared at him for a long moment, then shook her head. "You're not like most guys I know."

Dave inclined his head. "I'll take that as a compliment."

Stevie noticed the grin on his lips. She laughed in spite of herself. "Maybe you should." She gave him a direct look. "Do you get nervous?"

Dave didn't answer for moment, then nodded. "Sure I do."

"Are you nervous now?"

"No."

"Why not?" she asked, surprised.

"What do I have to be nervous about?"

"Well," Stevie began, confounded by his mellow attitude. This was police work—it was supposed to be tense and nerve-wracking, wasn't it? "How do you know that Tiempo hasn't figured you out?"

"Has he?" Dave replied calmly.

"No, not that I know of, but—"

"Then what's to worry about?"

Stevie made a frustrated sound in the back of her throat, rolling her eyes. "How do you know you can trust me?"

"Can I?" he asked, glancing over at her, his sky blue eyes seemingly looking straight into her. "Trust you?"

Stevie was taken aback by his direct look, as well as the question. It took her a moment to answer. "Yes, you can."

He smiled, and it reached his eyes. "Then what's to worry

about?"

"Ugh!" Stevie said, throwing up her hands but laughing at the same time. "How do you know you can trust Tiempo? How do you know he's not going to kill you just because he doesn't like the way you look?"

"I don't," Dave said calmly.

"Well?" Stevie said, seizing on his answer. "Doesn't *that* make you nervous?"

"No."

"Why the hell not?" she asked, her voice rising in frustration at not being able to figure him out.

He glanced at her, his eyes holding hers for a long moment. Then he turned back to the road. The silence stretched for a full minute. Just when Stevie was sure he wasn't going to answer, he started speaking.

"I believe that when you're born, your death is predetermined. If I'm meant to die at the hands of some drug dealer like Tiempo while doing my job, then I am. I can't change it, so there's no point worrying about it, because being nervous can get me hurt. There's no point in damaging myself any further than necessary, right?" His voice was calm, and Stevie knew she couldn't argue with that kind of logic. It did give her a very definite insight into this man, who was, to her, a walking enigma. *But,* she thought, *maybe that's what makes him the best narc in the country.*

At the same time, Dave was assessing the young woman sitting beside him. He could sense her impatience, and wasn't sure if he should attribute that to her personality or the current situation. She was close to settling a longstanding score, and that could be making her edgy. Dave was inclined to believe that Stevie O'Neil was a constant furor of activity, though; she seemed to have harnessed some sort of power source, and was holding it just under her skin. He wondered how good a hold she had on that power, though.

He found out later that day.


Tiempo, Dave, Stevie, and a couple of Tiempo's bodyguards were talking over lunch at the pool at the Hotel Del Coronado. The breeze coming off the ocean was light, and the day was warm without being oppressive. Dave sat across from Tiempo, with Stevie to his right. She was straight-backed, one leg out in front of her, her forearms resting lightly on the arms of her chair. She seemed relaxed, her face serene. She looked more like a beautiful debutante than a bodyguard. The two other bodyguards lounged against a nearby wall, two feet from the table.

Dave and Tiempo were discussing the merits of the latest football team when a man walked toward them. There was nothing menacing about him; he seemed to be looking away from them, as if searching for someone else. He stopped at the table and looked at Tiempo, smiling as if to an old friend.

"Ah, Tiempo, my friend. It has been a long time, no?" he said jovially.

Tiempo laughed, sitting back to look up at him. "La Guardé, how are you?"

"I'm just fine, my friend." The man reached up to scratch his protruding stomach. "And how are you?" he asked as his eyes trailed over to Stevie, an interested light in them instantly. She looked back at him calmly, her expression giving nothing away.

"Fine, of course, fine. Business is good, no?" Tiempo asked, his tone changing slightly.

Even as Dave caught the challenge in that tone, the man standing above Tiempo slipped the hand scratching his belly under his jacket in a lightning-fast move. Dave was standing to pull his weapon when he caught a flash of rich red hair. With his hand on his gun, Dave saw that not only had Stevie vaulted out of her chair, but she was even now holding a particularly lethal-looking gun to the man's gut. She whispered to him in a calm voice, "I don't think you want to do that."

She was purposely standing between Tiempo and the man, as any good bodyguard would be. She had the moves down—Dave had to give her that.

La Guardé had quickly dropped his hand, and he nodded, his eyes narrowing at Stevie. He glanced at the two other bodyguards, who were now standing behind Dave, threat evident in their stances.

Dave sat down with an air of relief, then grinned over at Tiempo. "For a minute there, amigo, I thought I was going to have to save you."

Tiempo grinned, patting Stevie patronizingly on the rear as she moved the man away from them. "Ah, but you can see I have good protection, no?"

"Yes, I can see that," Dave said, with an admiring glance at Stevie. He caught the jealous glint in Tiempo's eyes and quickly changed the subject back to the football they'd been discussing previously. The rest of their business was concluded an hour later. Stevie left the restaurant with Tiempo and his men.

Early that evening, Stevie arrived at Dave's house again. He let her in. She was wearing black, her hair loose this time. Dave motioned for her to sit, and she flopped onto the couch, glancing up at him as he perched on the arm above her.

"Do we have enough on him yet?" she asked, her tone showing her frustration and annoyance.

"Did he make another pass at you?" Dave asked calmly.

Stevie looked up at him sharply, her jaw tightening. "What makes you say that?"

"Are you saying he hasn't made a pass at you?"

"Hundreds of them," Stevie replied shortly, dropping her eyes from his.

"And today he made another one," Dave said, as if completing her sentence. He studied her face. "And this time he didn't want to take no for an answer." His eyes narrowed even as he said the words.

Stevie looked up at him again, clearly surprised that he seemed to know. Finally, she blew her breath out in a frustrated sigh, shaking her head. "No, he didn't."

Dave nodded, as if accepting that he'd been right. "This is getting dangerous now." It was a statement, and Stevie could see his mind churning. His blue eyes pierced hers then. "Do you want out?"

She was taken aback by the question, and she could see that he was serious. But Dave knew her answer even before she gave it, because her jaw tightened, like a physical manifestation of her tightening resolve. "No."

Dave grinned, giving her a nod of respect. They went on to discuss the business dealings he was arranging with Tiempo, when they'd arrange the buy, and how Dave intended to take Tiempo down once and for all. Three hours later, Stevie left.

Dave was half asleep when the intercom for his front door sounded. Reaching up sleepily, he depressed the button. "Yeah?"

"Dibbs, it's me," came Stevie's voice. Dave recognized the tension in it immediately, as well as the fact that she'd called him Dibbs. He knew there was trouble.

"Hey," he said smoothly. "Come on in." He pressed the unlock button even as he made sure his firearm was secure under his pillow. Sitting up and drawing on a shirt, he waited for her. He wasn't altogether surprised when Tiempo pushed her into the room, with two of his men behind them.

"What's goin' on?" Dave asked, looking dumbfounded, his eyes lingering on Stevie almost sensually. He already had an idea of what this was about; he was going to play it to the hilt.

"Well," Stevie said, her eyes locking with Dave's, "Tiempo saw me leaving here earlier, and he's a little put out. He thinks there's something going on." Her smile was knowing.

Dave pretended to drag his eyes away from Stevie's to look at Tiempo, then put on an expression of chagrin. "Hey, man, I didn't know she was your piece."

"What are you talking about?" Tiempo practically spat. "She works for me. I want to know what the fuck is going on."

Again Dave let his eyes trail over to Stevie's, a grin playing at his lips. "Just what's natural between a man and a woman..."

"Bullshit. She said she didn't know you before the other day," Tiempo said stridently. He didn't like being played.

"She didn't," Dave said, his grin wide. "We got to know each other the other night when she came to *check me out.*"

"Puta!" Tiempo spat, shoving Stevie toward Dave. "I don't believe it!"

Stevie caught herself before she could fall with surprising agility, moving to sit on the bed next to Dave. "What, you want some kind of proof?" she said, her tone scornful, even taunting.

Tiempo's eyes burned as he looked back at Stevie, his anger almost tangible. He thought he was being played by two cons; he wasn't convinced they were sexually involved. "Yes, I do," he muttered threateningly.

Stevie's mouth dropped open in shock, then turned into a sneer as she looked back at Tiempo in disgust. "I will not be ordered to prove something just because your male ego can't take the—"

Her voice cut off as Dave's hand closed around a handful of her hair, pulling her around as his lips covered hers in a kiss that started out fierce then melted into hungry passion. He grasped her waist, dragging her body close to his, as his lips made a sensual exploration of hers, licking seductively at her lips, coaxing a moan from her. Stevie molded herself to his body, forgetting everyone in the room. He held her close, pressing her against his chest, her hands sliding over his arms and up around his neck, into his hair, to pull him closer, closer. Losing herself in the kiss, in the strong, sensual feeling of his lips against hers, his tongue hot and wet, plunging into her mouth and withdrawing, mimicking the act of joining their bodies, making her moan again at the thought.

The sudden absence of his lips left her gasping for breath, her face pressed against his neck, as Dave looked up at Tiempo, slightly short of breath himself. Stevie could feel his heart pounding under her hand, which rested on his chest. She heard him talking and tuned in to what he was saying.

"...women just can't shut up long enough to deal with things, you know?" Dave's voice held humor, but was husky, showing the effects of the kiss he'd just given her. Was he faking it? Stevie found herself wondering as she pressed her lips against his neck, pretending for Tiempo's sake but also wanting to affect him as he had so easily affected her. She felt Dave glance down at her, his neck muscles flexing at the movement. She could almost picture his lewd grin as he said, "Now, if you gentleman will leave, so we can finish what we started..."

Tiempo and his men made a hasty retreat. It was obvious that Tiempo wasn't happy about this turn of events. Better that than thinking Stevie and Dave were playing him.

The silence in the room seemed to expand in the moments that followed Tiempo's exit. Stevie found she couldn't lift her head to look up at Dave; it was like she was frozen. After a few moments, she felt him pull away, his left hand at her waist as he leaned back to look down at her.

"Hey," he said softly

She lifted her head, not sure what she'd see on his face. She saw concern.

"Are you okay?" he asked, his voice still slightly husky. He had only leaned back a few inches when she lifted her head. Her lips were very close to his chin; if he lowered his head just an inch their lips would meet again. She found she couldn't look away as she nodded slightly.

"Do you…" she stammered, trying to find a way to lighten the mood. "Do you kiss all your women like that?"

A grin tugged at his lips as he looked down into her eyes. "Are you complaining?" His voice held humor, even as she saw the heat still burning in his eyes.

"Well, no," she said, willing him to lower his head, wanting him to so much. "I just thought that if this was just for show…" She let her voice trail off as she wet her lips with her tongue. His eyes followed the movement as he tilted his chin down ever so slightly to do so.

"Well, it was for show," he said, his voice dropping to a deep whisper. "But it was the real thing." On the last, his lips lowered to within a hair's breadth of hers. She could feel his breath on her lips.

"But they're gone now," she whispered, her breath coming quicker.

"Yes, they are," he replied, his lips brushing hers.

Stevie shivered at the effect he was having on her senses. She'd had no idea he could be so sensual. "You could kiss me again anyway," she said, throwing all pretense and caution to the wind.

Dave didn't answer for a long moment, drawing back slightly to look searchingly into her eyes. Stevie could feel his answer coming before he even started to speak, and became determined to change it before he could finish.

"I could, but—" was all he got out before her lips pressed against his, her tongue slipping between them to lick his lips as he had hers. Dave knew he was lost then, and gave in to the desire he'd been harboring since the first time he'd met her. Stevie found herself engulfed in his passion, and in moments was swept up in it with him.

Afterward, Stevie was sure she'd never get her heart to stop pounding. Her body was still shuddering in little aftershocks of what he'd made her feel. As she lay against him, she began to think he was like some kind of drug; she'd heard that certain drugs could enhance one's orgasm, but she was sure she'd just experienced that without needing chemicals. She'd always had a very adventurous sex life. She'd grown up with the belief that she would take everything in life that she could get. Incredible sex was one of the things she didn't hesitate to pursue. Dave Dibbins had certainly delivered in that arena.

Propping herself up on one elbow, she looked down at him. He was lying on his back, his left arm under her and wrapped around her waist, keeping her close. His other hand rested on his chest. She lay on her side, her body pressed along the length of his. Her auburn hair swept over his shoulder as she leaned over him, falling across her face. His eyes were closed, but he opened them when he felt her hair on his chest. They regarded each other for a long moment, then a grin tugged at his lips.

"Lost that battle, didn't I?" he said lightly.

"Definitely," she said, grinning down at him. "But I have to say, you did so rather admirably."

He quirked an eyebrow at her. "Admirably?" he repeated, as if testing the sound of the word. "I don't think I've heard that one before." His grin was infectious then, and Stevie laughed, dropping her head to his shoulder to kiss his skin.

When she pulled back she looked at his shoulder and noted the thin scar there. She traced her nail over it. "What's this from?"

Dave glanced down. "Gunshot at a raid," he answered easily.

Stevie widened her eyes at him. "Shot in the line of duty," she murmured, lowering her mouth again to his shoulder, kissing the scar then trailing up to his neck.

He made a contented "mmm" sound in the back of his throat.

Again she pulled away, looking down at his cross. "Religious?" she asked. That didn't fit what little she thought she knew about him.

He grinned. "Nope. I bought that cross with my first real drug money."

"Really, now?" Stevie said, looking appropriately surprised.

Dave shrugged. "A long time ago I ran a gang that sold drugs. I wised up with some help and straightened myself out. Now I do this. The cross is a reminder of where I came from."

Stevie gave him a measured look. She remembered hearing that he'd been part of the renowned gang task force started by Midnight Chevalier. She realized she'd always assumed he'd been law enforcement the whole time. A new dimension to Sergeant Dave Dibbins, the country's best narc.

He reached up to brush her hair back, and she saw the tattoo on his arm. Again she was surprised. She moved closer to him so that she could see it better. The tattoo was a Celtic cross outlined in black, with red lines within the borders. Vertically down the center of the cross, in an Old English–looking font was the word *Apostles*. Under the cross, in bold, graffiti-like script outlined in black and filled in with blue and yellow, was *I. B. Bad Boys*.

"Your gang?" she asked as she traced her finger over the letters.

Dave nodded.

"I. B. Bad Boys?"

He shrugged. "That's what we were."

"You were a bad boy?" Stevie asked, grinning.

His expression was impassive, but there was a mischievous glint in his eyes as he said, "Still am."

"Yes?" she said, staring into his eyes.

"Oh yes," he replied, pulling her down to him, and his lips took possession of hers again. He made love to her, just as intensely as before, but he took his time this time. Hours later he lay half over her, his left leg and arm thrown over her possessively.

A shrill ring roused them from sleep. Dave sat up and reached over to his nightstand for his cell phone.

"This is my undercover line, so don't say anything, okay?" he said, glancing at Stevie as he pushed the button.

She lay watching him as he talked, fascinated by his ever-changing persona.

"Dibbs," he answered. A pause. "Yeah?" Another pause, his eyes flicking to hers. "No—no, that wasn't the deal." His finger tapped his leg in agitation even as his voice remained calm. "He said ten—twelve wasn't the deal." Anger sparked in his eyes, his hand clenching in a fist. "The product is shit, I won't pay twelve for it," he spat. Then it was as if something clicked in his head, and he closed his eyes. His chest expanded as he took a deep breath through his nose, then blew it out silently through parted lips and moved his neck around as if working out a kink. He unclenched his fist, extending his long fingers as if stretching them. She could almost feel him calm down.

He opened his eyes, training them on a point across the room but not seeing anything there. When he spoke again his voice oozed casual arrogance. "Hey, look, if he wants to charge twelve he can just find another buyer. I hear Miami's nice this time of year." Another long pause, a grin tugging at his lips. "Yeah, ten-five might be doable. I'll let you know." A few polite "goodbye"s and "I'll call you"s and he hung up. He reached over, putting the phone back on the nightstand, then lay down next to Stevie, noticing as he did that she was still watching him avidly.

"What?" he asked, grinning at her.

"Damn..." she said, shaking her head.

He looked perplexed. "What?"

"What was that?"

Dave glanced over at the phone then back at her. "That was me almost losing a deal I've been setting up for over six months now."

"You actually lose deals?" Stevie asked disbelievingly.

Dave gave her a puzzled grin. "Some."

"But not that one."

"Not that one."

Her eyes searched his face for a long moment. "Do you realize what a mass of contradictions you are, Dave Dibbins? I just don't get you."

Instead of answering her, he leaned over and kissed her again. His lips moved from hers to her cheek, then to her ear, where he whispered, "I get me." She shivered as his teeth grazed her earlobe, and then his lips made their way down her neck. Soon after that she forgot everything but the way he made her body feel. Neither of them got much sleep that night.

# CHAPTER 5

The morning after her meeting with Chief Chevalier, Rhiannon Templeton got into her office at the regular time of 7:30 a.m. She was surprised to find Christian Collins already hard at work at his computer. While Christian didn't work for her, he worked with her handling property, although his main responsibility was the maintenance of the inventory system and more recently the consulting work for other departments. On this particular morning, however, she noted he was busily working on entering property information into the computer system—something that was normally her job.

San Diego Police Department was increasing its budget every year. This directly affected Rhiannon's job, in that more property was being purchased, which meant she was required to track more and more equipment. Midnight Chevalier-Debenshire had wisely split the property job into two sections, creating an extra position. One position handled evidence, cataloging it, monitoring the chain of custody, and so on. Rhiannon had ended up with the daunting task of handling the fixed assets for the department, both expendable items like car batteries, film, ammunition, flex cuffs, and the like, and non-expendables, like cars, guns, computers, batons, and flashlights.

Christian had designed the inventory system she worked with, and so he was invaluable to her as a problem solver. She'd been surprised at first when she'd met him. He was strikingly handsome—he seemed like he should be in movies or something, not some computer person in a police department. As it turned out, Christian was very down to earth. Even though he was fully aware of his looks and the impact they had on people, he wasn't conceited. He exuded a confidence that was magnetic, but Rhiannon could never detected any kind of egotistical nature in him. In the end, she found she couldn't help but like him.

Since Jason's death, Rhiannon had changed a great deal. Whereas she had been a very outgoing, open, happy person when her husband was alive, she was closed off and introverted now. She spent a lot of time alone, in silence. She didn't even listen to the radio anymore, because she always found herself listening to the classic rock stations her husband had liked so much, hearing songs that ripped through her heart with a flood of memories. She rarely, if ever, saw friends from her past, because they held too many memories for her as well. Very few people caught glimpses of the woman Rhiannon Templeton had been three years before—but Christian Collins was one of those few.

"What are you doing here so early?" she asked, sitting down at her desk and reaching over to turn on her own computer.

"Working," Christian said, grinning.

"You do that?" Rhiannon replied with a smile.

"Sometimes. When the mood takes me."

Rhiannon glanced over at the stack of paperwork sitting next to him at the terminal. "And your mood told you to work on my stuff today?"

Christian grinned sheepishly. "You looked swamped."

"I am swamped!" Rhiannon said, rolling her eyes. "But that's not your job, Blue—it's mine."

"I'm property too, and you needed help."

"Yes, but—"

"No buts," Christian cut in smoothly. "Don't worry about it— I'm all caught up."

Rhiannon narrowed her eyes. She knew that his workload, although totally different from hers, was just as heavy. Finally she shook her head, realizing she wouldn't get him to admit that he was just helping her to help her. "Well, whatever—thank you," she said, then asked, "What time did you get here?"

"Six." He glanced at her, sure he knew what she was asking.

"That early, huh?" she said, wrinkling her nose sympathetically.

"Yeah," Christian replied, his eyes narrowing slightly.

He and Susan had not slept together the night before, as he had suspected they wouldn't. When they'd gotten back to the house after dinner at Midnight's, there had been a minor emergency with one of the children, and Susan had stayed up at the house to help. Christian had proceeded to his room down at the carriage house at the edge of Joe and Randy's property. He'd taken a shower and then lain down on his bed. He'd fallen asleep and had never heard Susan come in. He hadn't seen the way she'd looked down at him, wanting to wake him but afraid to for fear he'd tell her to go away. In the end she'd turned and left. Christian had awoken at 5:30 and, burying his disappointment that she hadn't come to him, got up, got dressed, and come to work to push aside the building anger.

Later that morning, Christian knocked lightly on Midnight's door. A usual, he heard her say, "Come."

176

Walking in, he looked at the Chief of Police, the one woman he had wanted since he'd met her but could never have. It was a source of amusing dismay for him. Christian Collins had been able to get any woman he'd wanted for years, but Midnight Chevalier was unattainable, and not because she was another man's wife, but because she didn't want him. Christian knew it was because she was in love with Rick, but it had become a wry joke between him and the chief. He'd frequently ask, "Want me yet?" With a grin and a shake of her head, she'd reply, "Not yet." Midnight had become the infinite challenge, albeit not a serious one; even Christian Collins had to respect a love as deep and abiding as Midnight and Rick's.

When Midnight was believed dead, Christian had been suspected of being in cahoots with the men that had ordered her murder. In truth he had been trying to infiltrate their plan to stop them, when no one else could get near them. At Midnight's funeral, Rick Debenshire had literally attacked him, believing Christian was one of Midnight's murderers. The words "She trusted you!" and the anguish behind those words had echoed in Christian's head for months afterward, even though Midnight had been found alive and the men responsible for trying to kill her had been brought to justice or killed, an act orchestrated through Christian's connection to them. It was still a source of many nightmares. The days when they'd believed he was part of the ring that had killed Midnight had been days in hell for him.

Now, he couldn't help but flash back to those times. It amazed him that a woman like her could take all that she had been handed in life and still come back fighting.

"Hi," Midnight said, glancing up from a report. She looked at her watch, then grinned. "Not too early, huh?"

Christian gave her a sour look as he sat down in a chair in front of her desk. "I got in at six."

"Oh," Midnight replied, looking a little crestfallen. "I don't suppose you want to talk about it, huh?"

"About what?" Christian deadpanned.

Midnight looked back at him for a long moment, obviously debating how much she wanted to interfere with him and Susan. Susan was Rick's niece, and very dear to both him and Midnight. It was hard, trying to maintain a level of uninvolvement with employees when they happened to also be people she loved. In this instance, Midnight knew that what was happening between Christian and Susan was something that only time could sort out for them, so she decided to leave it alone if he didn't want to talk about it.

"Moving right along," she said, grinning. They discussed the lead time he wanted for his inventory projects, and other matters pertaining to briefing the clients before he actually went to the site for the work. An hour later they were wrapping up the details. "Anything else?" Midnight asked, glancing up from the pad she'd been writing notes on.

"Actually," Christian said, his expression thoughtful, "yes, there is."

"Okay," Midnight replied, sitting back in her chair.

Christian paused for a moment, gathering his thoughts. "Rhiannon needs help, Midnight. She's getting buried down there."

Midnight looked perplexed. "She hasn't said anything to me, and she hasn't missed a deadline yet."

"I know she hasn't," Christian said, his lip curling in distaste.

"And she won't miss a deadline for you, even if she has to take the work home and stay up all night doing it."

Midnight looked back at him for a long moment, a question clear on her face. Christian answered it for her before she could even formulate it.

"She is devoted to you, Midnight. You are the woman that gave her dead husband back his dignity. As far as she's concerned, she owes you a lot, and she repays it doing the job you gave her."

Midnight was stunned. Sitting back in her chair, she tossed her pen on her desk and blew her breath out in a deep sigh. She turned back to Christian, her look self-castigating. "Guess I should have figured that out, huh?"

"You can't know everything, Midnight," Christian replied, ever loyal himself. "This department has been expanding by leaps and bounds for years. I don't think even you realized how big a job it was you were handing her. But with that grant money you got last year, you hired seventy new officers—they come with a whole complement of equipment. That means a lot more work. And now that you got that eighteen million…" He trailed off as Midnight started to nod.

"Yeah, I know," she said. "Okay, what do you think she needs? How many people?"

"First of all, she needs to get that inventory taken," he said, referring to the departmental inventory that had to be done to locate all of the equipment that showed on their records.

"I want someone on that with her anyway. I don't need her getting a lot of flak," Midnight said.

She was fairly sure Rhiannon had received a lot of antagonism from officers who saw her as the person who had taken the late

Devereaux's job. There'd been a lot of muttering about a cop being killed, and about how the person associated with that dirty cop—who had conveniently been the one to kill him—had gotten off scot-free. The fact that he was the cousin of Joe Sinclair, a well-known, well-respected captain in the department who also happened to be Midnight's best friend, didn't help matters much. Midnight had tried to keep rumors and hurt feelings in check, but one could never totally manage that in a department as large as hers. She was worried that in doing the departmental inventory, Rhiannon would be face to face with many of her nay-sayers. She was afraid that would prove to be too much strain on a woman who was already under a lot of personal pressure.

After a few moments' thought, Midnight said, "I think I'll have Kyle work on this when he gets here. It'll be a good way to meet and deal with everyone in the department on a more official basis."

Christian nodded, then gave her a crooked smile. "Did I hear the rumor about him right?"

Midnight narrowed her eyes at him. "Don't even start with me, Collins."

Christian laughed. "I'll take that as a yes." He gave her a serious look then, staring right into her eyes even as his grin started. "Lucky guy."

"Yeah, yeah," Midnight said, waving away his comment and rolling her eyes.

"Rick didn't seem too upset."

"Why should he be?"

"He's got you now."

"My point exactly."

"But if I were Rick, I wouldn't like it."

"He doesn't have to like it—he just has to trust me."

"And he does," Christian said, his tone not the least bit questioning.

"Yes, he does."

"Smart guy."

"Very," Midnight replied, grinning at their exchange. Christian Collins had a very quick wit, and she enjoyed bantering with him sometimes.

"Smart enough to land you," Christian said, getting to his feet. "So you'll get Rhiannon some help in the meantime? I mean, I don't figure an Assistant Chief will get his hands too dirty."

"Don't underestimate Kyle, Blue. He's a hard worker—he's going to be a good asset to this place," Midnight said, standing up too. "I'll get her someone else to help out in the meantime though, yes. Okay?"

Christian nodded, looking satisfied. "Thanks, Midnight."


Things with Tiempo were progressing at a frustratingly slow pace. Stevie was at her wits' end by the middle of the second week Dave had dedicated to the case. She knew she was getting close to losing Tiempo once again, and she couldn't bear the thought.

She tried to push Dave to get down to business with Tiempo one evening, after yet another day of no commitment by Tiempo to deliver. She buzzed the intercom and waited for him to answer. He opened his front door wearing faded jeans and an unbuttoned navy blue Hawaiian shirt. Seeing that it was her, he stepped back and gestured for her to come inside. He detected instantly that this was not a social visit. Since that first time, they hadn't been together sexually. Dave hadn't pushed the relationship, accepting that she would set the pace.

Dave walked over to his living room couch and sat down, watching her as she started to pace. She didn't speak for a long time; he simply waited. Finally she turned to him, coming over and sitting down next to him, turning sideways to face him.

"Why aren't you pushing this deal with Tiempo?" she asked, her voice holding the anger and desperation she was trying not to show.

Dave took a long pause before answering. When he spoke his voice was calm and assured. "You can't push dealers, Stevie, or they push back. Then you end up either dead or with your cover blown. That won't help us much."

His calm answer frustrated her more. Her green eyes flashed with her effort to control her anger.

"You just don't care either way, do you?" she said. "Either way you get what you were sent for, right? Who the hell cares anyway, right?" She looked away from him.

"I care," he replied simply, his voice still calm.

"Bullshit!" she yelled. "All you care about is doing what Chief Chevalier told you to do. This isn't a case to you—it's a fucking game, and you're not even playing it right."

"Stevie, this is no game."

"Like hell it's not!" She was letting her anger loose now, not caring what she said. "You and Tiempo are playing cat and mouse. And in three days you get to walk away and I get screwed. You get to go back and tell your chief you did everything you could, which was nothing, and I get stuck with nothing for a year and a half of my fucking life! No one gives a shit that my brother-in-law is dead, that my sister may as well have died with him. That every day I feel like my life is missing something because that bastard Tiempo couldn't just take his lumps the day they went to arrest him." She stopped long enough to take a ragged breath, then yelled, "Goddamn you!"

"Stevie…" Dave began, his voice soothing.

"No!" she screamed, clenching her fists. "Don't tell me how I need to be patient. I can't be anymore. I'm losing this—I'm losing everything I worked for this last year and a half, all because I made a deal with you. I won't do it—I won't. If we can't bust him then you can walk out and I'll stay on him until I take him down, one way or the other."

"I can't let you do that," he replied. His voice was serious, though his posture was still relaxed.

"Then you can try to bust me," she spat, her anger uncontrollable now.

"I won't try, Stevie—I will," he said, his voice quiet, not even slightly tense, his body language alone screaming confidence in its nonchalance. "I'll do what it takes to get you out of this alive. One way or the other."

"You bastard!" she screamed, lashing out, meaning only to slap him but forgetting that her fist was still clenched.

Before she even knew what was happening, her fist was caught and she was taken to the floor with her arm twisted up behind her back. She could feel his knee at the small of her back, his weight holding her down. His other hand pressed against the middle of her back. She had been taken down like a criminal, and she suddenly realized that even though he'd seemed totally relaxed, he had been ready for her assault. She'd never had a chance to hurt him. Then it hit her that she was ready to attack the one person that might be able to arrest Tiempo and give her back her life. That understanding led quickly to shame. Suddenly all she wanted to do was get away. She struggled against his hold.

"Stevie," he said sternly, right next to her ear as he leaned down over her. "Calm the hell down."

"Let me up," she grated out, trying to use her legs to push back against him. She didn't like the feeling of helplessness at all.

"Don't make me hurt you."

He sounded like a cop talking to a criminal resisting arrest. She was a criminal, after all, wasn't she? She'd killed a man; she'd been working for a drug dealer. If they didn't take Tiempo down by the end of the week and she carried out her threat to continue with him, this could be real someday. All these thoughts ran through Stevie's head, and finally it hit her. She had become one of them. She was a criminal. How would her father feel about that? How would Jason? It was the last two thoughts that made her cry out. The subsequent anguish she had held back for so long, for the losses she'd sustained, flooded her mind. The tears started then. Tears of anger, pain, sadness, and helplessness.

To her surprise she felt herself released, and suddenly Dave was pulling her into his arms, holding her against his chest. She buried her face in his shirt and allowed herself to cry for the first time since she'd set herself on a course to take Tiempo down. It seemed like hours. Dave was silent the entire time. He held her, at times stroking her back.

When she'd finished crying she leaned against him, feeling exhausted. Still he said nothing. *He probably thinks I'm nuts,* Stevie thought, but she couldn't bring herself to look up at him. She was ashamed for what she'd tried to do, for being so nasty and then actually trying to strike him. Then, to make matters worse, to have not only burst into tears like some silly schoolgirl but to have had the man be gallant enough to try to comfort her as she did so.

Stevie let her mind drift over all this as she leaned against him, feeling drained. She'd been tense for the past few days, hardly sleeping at night as she worried about what would happen by the end of the week, or not happen.

Suddenly she felt herself being picked up as he moved to stand, and she realized she'd actually been drifting off to sleep. Dave held her cradled in his arms, and she kept her face buried against his shoulder, her arms around his neck. He carried her to his bedroom and laid her on his bed. When she looked up, his back was to her as he lit the end of a stick of incense, blowing on it until the tip glowed and fragrant smoke trailed up. The room was semi-dark, the only light coming from the hallway.

He turned to her, not saying a word as he lay down next to her. Staunchly refusing to meet his gaze, she trained her eyes on his shirt as he turned onto his side. He reached over and pulled her back into his arms. Stevie found herself drawn into his warmth, enjoying the feeling of acceptance that his actions reflected. She lay in his arms, the back of her head resting against the hollow of his shoulder, her face against his neck. She fell asleep that way.

As she slept, Dave lay staring at his ceiling, reflecting on the night's occurrences. He knew she was getting edgy over losing Tiempo. He knew that her anger was just a manifestation of that nervous energy. What bothered him was the way she'd lost all control of her temper. It had made him realize that he needed to get her out of this situation regardless of the outcome at the end of the week. If she was this edgy, this desperate to get Tiempo, it would start to show soon, and Tiempo would pick up on it. If Tiempo was even slightly suspicious of her, he'd kill her; Dave knew he would. He also knew that he'd hurt her immeasurably before he killed her, because it was apparent Tiempo was interested in her as more than a bodyguard. Men like Tiempo didn't react to rejection well. Combine her rejection of him with any suspected duplicity, and Stevie would suffer greatly. Dave had seen the result of women's suspected disloyalty. It was brutal, and many times fatal. He had no intention of allowing that to happen to Stevie O'Neil. She'd been through too much to allow an end to her life simply because she couldn't control her temper.

Stevie woke the next morning to the feel of Dave's lips on her cheek. She opened her eyes and noted he was standing next to the bed. He was wearing an open shirt and shorts over a short wetsuit.

"I'll be back," he said, and left the room.

Stevie turned over, looking at the clock. It was still fairly dark in the room, so it wasn't fully day yet. The clock said 6:00 a.m. Groaning at the stiffness in her neck from obviously having slept in Dave's arms all night, she turned back over. Glancing down, she noted she was still wearing her shoes. She got up slowly and kicked them off, then removed the rest of her clothes, tossing them onto a chair. She slid under the covers and went back to sleep. It was three hours later when she heard the shower start.

When Dave came out of his bathroom ten minutes later, she was sitting up, the covers pulled up over her. Her legs were pulled up to her chest, her arms wrapped around them, her chin on her knees.

Dave was wearing faded jeans with no shirt, his hair still damp from the shower. He sat down on the bed, and Stevie found herself admiring his chest once again. When she looked up, it was to note his blue eyes watching her. She immediately found herself biting her lower lip as she waited for the reproach she was sure was about to come. She steeled herself for it, determined to take anything he said, knowing how wrong she'd been the night before.

"Do you want coffee?" he asked, his voice as smooth and calm as ever.

Stevie was stunned for a moment. He wasn't going to say anything? She nodded dumbly.

Dave got up. "I'll be back in a minute."

He left the room and Stevie got up to throw on her jeans and at least her shirt. She figured he'd want to talk about the night before over coffee; she didn't want to be naked when they did. She was sitting Indian-style on the bed when he walked in with a mug of coffee and handed it to her.

"You're not having any?" she asked, surprised.

"Already had three cups," he said, grinning as he sat down on the bed again. His eyes surveyed her as she took a sip. "You feeling better?"

Stevie hesitated, not sure how to answer. She wanted to apologize, but wasn't sure whether anything she said would help. Again she found herself nodding.

Dave nodded in response. "We're having lunch with Tiempo today. I'll see what I can do to get him to set a time for delivery."

He said it so simply that it took a moment for Stevie to realize he'd just given in to what she'd been demanding last night. She thought about what he'd said about pushing drug dealers.

"Isn't that dangerous?" she asked, aware that she was saying the exact opposite of what she'd said the night before, and curious as to whether he'd call her on it.

Dave shrugged. "Can be, but I know how to do it." He said it so casually, his eyes sliding from her as he did, that she knew instantly that he was downplaying the gesture.

"Dave…" she began, shaking her head.

"Look," he said. "Take a shower, do whatever you need to. I'll be back in about two hours. Be ready to go."

With that he stood up. He walked over to his dresser and pulled on a black T-shirt, then went to his closet and took out a steel-gray shirt before sitting down to put on his shoes. Stevie watched as he secured his gun at the small of his back. She was still watching him when he turned around, running his hands through his hair to smooth it. He came over to her, leaning down and kissing her softly on the lips.

"I'll be back by eleven," he said, and walked out of the room again.

Stevie couldn't believe it. Not only had he not chastised her for being stupid the night before, but he was even planning to put himself in danger to give her what she had said she wanted. Only now she was afraid that she'd asked too much.

As they were finishing up lunch, Dave leaned forward, his expression serious.

"So when are we going to do some business, Tiempo?" he asked, his voice cajoling.

Tiempo looked at him for a long moment, as if trying to figure out what Dave meant, then nodded. "Ah, sí, business," he said, an undercurrent to his voice. "There is just one little problem."

"What's that?" Dave asked, sitting back calmly.

Seemingly out of nowhere, Tiempo produced a gun and put the muzzle to Dave's forehead. "You see," he said, his voice still deceptively smooth, "I don't know if I can trust you yet."

Stevie felt all the blood leave her face, but she couldn't react. She was just waiting for the sound of the gun going off. She knew if she heard it she'd kill Tiempo herself. Her hand was near her own gun, but she didn't draw it. Looking over at Dave, she expected to see fear. Once again, she was stunned.

With a gun to his head, Dave Dibbins still remained calm. His face was passive, and his eyes were on Tiempo, but there was no fear in them. He hadn't moved, or even tensed a muscle. It was obvious, too, that Tiempo was surprised by Dave's lack of reaction, because the gun wavered.

"Why do you not react, my friend?" Tiempo asked, his curiosity obviously overriding his need to play the tough guy.

"Are you going to shoot me?" Dave asked idly.

"I might," Tiempo said, his tone a sneer.

Dave pursed his lips. "Do I have any control over whether you do or not?"

"No," Tiempo answered, smiling evilly, thinking Dave was going to beg now.

Dave shrugged. "Then what's the point in getting upset?"

Tiempo looked stunned, his mouth dropping open as he stared back at Dave. Finally, after a few tense moments, he lowered the gun, shaking his head in amazement. "You are insane, my friend."

Dave grinned, shrugging again. "Nope, I just don't worry about things I can't change."

Stevie was sure she was going to pass out from the relief flooding her veins, but to her credit she hid it well. She merely appeared relieved that her boss hadn't killed another person, not that she'd been terrified for that person.

When Tiempo turned to order some champagne from the waiting butler, Dave glanced at Stevie. He could see the relief on her face, and quirked his lips in a quick grin.

Later, as Stevie was escorting Dave out, Tiempo called her back to him. Dave walked out to his car and waited. Stevie came out a few minutes later.

"Drive," she said as she got in on the passenger side, her tone all business now.

Dave got in and started the car, glancing over at her. "Where to?"

"Hotel Intercontinental. Tiempo wants to make the deal there tomorrow at one."

Dave noted the controlled look on her face and nodded. Ten minutes later, they pulled up in front of the hotel.

"Go make the arrangements," Dave said. "I'll meet you down

190

there." He pointed at the bay next to the hotel. Stevie nodded and got out of the car.

Twenty minutes later, Stevie walked up to his car, but he wasn't in it. She scanned the area and saw him running at breakneck speed along the water's edge. Walking down the grassy area of the bay park, she headed toward the spot she knew he would reach, given his direction. Sitting down on a stone picnic table, she waited for him. He stopped a foot from her, gasping for breath, and bent forward, his hands on his knees. Stevie sat watching him for a full five minutes before she spoke, waiting for him to catch his breath.

"You okay?" she asked finally.

Dave nodded, sitting on the bench in front of her. "Arrangements made?"

"Yeah. You sure you're okay?"

"For a guy who just about got his head blown off, yeah, I'm fine," Dave said, his grin starting.

"I have to tell you, Dibbins, you're amazing," Stevie said, shaking her head. "I've seen Tiempo do that to other men, and watched them reduced to groveling puddles." She shook her head again. "I don't know how you do it, how you keep from being afraid."

"Who said I wasn't afraid?"

"You didn't look it in the slightest."

He shrugged. "I was scared, but if he was actually going to kill me, I wasn't going to give the asshole the satisfaction of showing fear."

"Yeah, but you could have told him you're a cop, or something to prevent him from shooting you."

"You think so?" Dave asked, giving her a sidelong glance. "He does that as a test, to see what people will do. He gets off on the fear they show—it's a power trip. He also has the chance to see if they'll admit to anything interesting. Like being a cop. He would have killed me for sure then. I had nothing to gain by showing him any of my cards. So I showed him nothing."

"Wow…" Stevie said, unable to fathom how this man's mind worked or how he could keep such a tight leash on his emotions when the need called for it.

She'd learned in the academy that fear caused a huge adrenaline rush, the fight or flight reaction. The fact that not one muscle had twitched to show that rush was amazing. He had controlled his own adrenaline. She looked at him then, narrowing her eyes as if studying him.

"That," she said, nodding over her shoulder, back toward the beach, "was the release, wasn't it?"

"Release?" he asked, giving her a calculated look, like a teacher with a pupil.

"Yeah, of the adrenaline rush you got when Tiempo pulled the gun. You managed to control it long enough to get down here and run your ass off."

Dave inclined his head. "Gotta let it go or it'll eat you up."

Once again Stevie found herself surprised. Was there never going to be an end to what this man could do?

They discussed the meet after that, and Dave took her back to Tiempo's house.

Jeanie, Donovan, and Erin were in the bar 10-7. Donovan had a few days off from his case, since his suspect had gone to Miami for a week. Much to Jeanie's irritation, the woman had actually invited Donovan to go along "to play." Donovan had turned her down, citing a lot of connections he needed to make. Jeanie had heard that she was a real man-eater, and she didn't want her getting her claws on him. He laughed it off when she got irritated about the woman's advances, but eventually Donovan stopped telling her about them. When he'd brought up the offer to go to Miami, it was the first time in a long while that he'd mentioned any flirtation by his suspect.

Erin and Jeanie had been hanging out at the house when Donovan walked in that evening. They were watching a movie, so they didn't notice him right away when he came down the hallway. He'd stood leaning again the hall wall, watching them. Erin glanced up, and grinned as he put his finger to his lips to keep her from saying anything. He walked over to just behind where Jeanie sat on the couch, obviously engrossed in the love scene in the movie. Leaning down, Donovan kissed her neck, making her jump. When she glanced up, he laughed and kissed her on the lips.

He'd suggested that they all go out for a few drinks, saying that he needed to take the edge off. Both girls thought the idea sounded great. So two hours later, here they were in 10-7. Donovan had definitely taken the edge off, since Jeanie had volunteered to drive them all home that night. She was also pointing out all the available cops to Erin, embarrassing her thoroughly. Donovan was laughing, greeting friends and moving on to beer after a few shots. He'd even coaxed Erin into having a shot with him, the lethal Stars at Night. Jeanie told Erin the story of how the first time she'd gone out with Donovan as "friends," he'd let her try his drink. She then went into how one of

Donovan's friends had been getting way too friendly, and Donovan had ended up decking him.

"He hit his friend for you?" Erin asked. She glanced at Donovan, who was shaking his head and rolling his eyes as he took another drink of his beer.

"You did too!" Jeanie said, hitting him on the shoulder.

"Did you?" Erin asked, grinning at him from across the small table.

"Okay," Donovan said, setting his beer down. "Maybe."

"That is so romantic!" Erin said, her voice melancholy.

"Maybe?" Jeanie countered "You decked his ass," she continued, grinning widely. "Knocked him clean out too."

"Wow!" Erin said. "One punch?"

"He probably passed out," Donovan put in wryly, never one to brag.

"He did not—you put him out," Jeanie said.

"We don't know that," Donovan said, the beginnings of a grin on his lips.

Jeanie smiled. "My ass we don't."

Donovan looked back at her. "Your ass, huh?"

"Yeah," Jeanie countered haughtily.

In reply, Donovan leaned over and kissed her. It lasted an extra few moments as they apparently forgot themselves. Then Jeanie pushed him away, rubbing her chin. "Those damned whiskers have got to go, Curtis."

"Oh stop," Donovan said, running his fingers over the goatee.

"You're just too sensitive."

"Me?"

"Yeah, you—such sensitive skin," he replied, raising an eyebrow.

"Bullshit. Any woman would complain about those whiskers—they're rough and scratchy."

"They are not," Donovan said, grinning again.

Jeanie put her hands on her hips, giving him a deadpan look. "When's the last time you kissed your own face, Curtis?"

Donovan pursed his lips, canting his head to the side. "Guess I didn't think of it that way. But still, lots of guys have goatees and women who kiss them."

"Yeah, but I'll bet the women complain about scratchy faces," Jeanie said, laughing now.

"Bullshit," Donovan said, taking a long swig of his beer. "I can prove it."

"How?"

Donovan gestured around him. "There's a bar full of women here. I'll kiss one and we'll see if she complains about scratchy whiskers."

"My ass you will," Jeanie replied, narrowing her eyes at him, but a grin played at her lips.

"Why?" Donovan asked, sitting up straighter. "Afraid I'll prove you wrong?"

"No, I'm afraid if you kiss one, they'll fall in love and I'll lose you forever."

Donovan laughed, throwing his head back. Erin and Jeanie laughed too, in response to his lively mood.

"So how do I disprove this theory of yours?" he asked, leaning forward on the table.

"You can't—that's the point," Jeanie said, giving him a "so there" look.

Again Donovan pursed his lips in thought. Then he stood up, leaning over the table. Putting his hand to the back of Erin's head, he leaned down and kissed her lips. The kiss lasted only a few moments, but Erin was sure she'd stopped breathing. Within seconds Donovan was sitting back down and giving her a quizzical look.

"So?" he asked, looking straight at her.

It took Erin a few moments to find her voice. She had to swallow twice to calm her senses. She looked at Jeanie and noted that her friend did not look happy at what Donovan had just done; she was staring at him, her mouth hanging open. Donovan didn't notice Jeanie's stare; he was looking at Erin, waiting for his answer.

"Um," Erin began, finding her voice. "I…" But she couldn't even begin to finish.

Jeanie got up from the table and walked away.

Donovan's eyes went to her then. "Jay?" he said, obviously surprised by her action. Jeanie didn't look back, only shaking her head as she headed for the bathroom. Erin got up and followed her, not sure what she was going to say but definitely not wanting to stay at the table with Donovan.

The kiss had unnerved her. She knew she was attracted to Donovan, had been from day one. But his kiss had made every sense in her body sing. She knew it was a horrible thing to be attracted to her friend's fiancé, but she couldn't seem to help it. Erin was actually glad that Donovan wasn't around much at this point, because she knew she'd have problems coping with her fascination with him.

Erin found Jeanie in the bathroom, leaning against the wall.

"Hey," Erin said softly.

"Hey."

Erin moved to lean next to Jeanie. After a few long moments of silence she said, "You okay?"

Jeanie was quiet for a few seconds longer, then blew her breath out in a sigh. "Yeah, I was just surprised he did that."

Erin nodded, not sure what to say. "He has had a lot to drink."

Jeanie glanced over at her, her look considering. "I know he has," she said, not sounding convinced that that was why he'd kissed the other girl.

"He was just trying to prove his point," Erin added, doing her best to make everything better.

Jeanie didn't say anything for a long moment, then looked over at her. "Did he prove his point?"

Erin bit her lower lip. Finally she nodded, almost miserably.

"Oh shit!" Jeanie said, laughing and shaking her head.

Erin laughed too, relieved that Jeanie wasn't mad.

"God, don't tell him. I'll never get him to shave that thing off!" Jeanie said, then turned to the mirror to check her makeup.

"What if he asks again?" Erin said, turning to the mirror too.

Jeanie grinned. "Tell him you need to deliberate on it for, like,

197

the next two years."

"Shame on you!" Erin said, laughing.

"Hey, I don't have to like losing, do I?"

"No, you don't have to like it." Erin smiled. "You better get back out there, or he's going to get worried."

"Ya think?" Jeanie said. Grabbing Erin's hand, she tugged her out of the bathroom and back toward the table. Erin smiled, glad that she had maybe helped her friends. Her thoughts still lingered on the kiss as Jeanie walked over to Donovan.

Jeanie shoved the table back a couple of inches and straddled his lap, facing him. Putting her arms around him, she leaned down and kissed him. Donovan's hands slid up her back, one going to the back of her head as they kissed. Jeanie caressed his neck, moving her fingers through his hair. People around them starting whistling and making catcalls. Jeanie and Donovan laughed when they realized they were the object of everyone's attention, and Jeanie buried her face in Donovan's neck. He grinned, looking over at Erin, who stood a few feet away. He gave her a cavalier wink, and she smiled at him. It was a fun night.

# CHAPTER 6

As she'd promised, Midnight had allowed Randy to begin her mentoring program. Randy spent hours figuring out scheduling and working with the officers taking part in it. She wasn't home many nights. Joe was ever supportive of her efforts so didn't complain about being on his own a lot for dinner. When she got home, she'd usually find him asleep on the couch with a report lying on his chest. She'd wake him and take him down to their room to put him to bed. She'd come in a little while later after straightening up the house and looking in on the children. There was some guilt there, knowing she wasn't spending enough time with any of them. She told herself that as soon as she got the project off the ground, she could go back to spending evenings at home again. Randy knew that Joe understood what she was doing, and she loved him more for his unending support.

Many nights when she crawled into bed next to him, he would be asleep. On this particular evening, he was awake when she got into bed. He held out his arm to her, and she snuggled against his side, his arm going over her protectively.

"So, how's it going?" he asked, his English accent still clear even after many years in the States.

Randy glanced up and saw that he was looking down at her. She took a moment to kiss his chest, then said, "It's going good. I should have everything running smoothly in a few more weeks."

Joe nodded. "Good. Everyone working out okay?" He knew she'd had some reservations about some of the officers who'd volunteered for the program.

"Well," Randy began, levering herself up on her elbow to look down at him, "I talked to Midnight about Terry and Janzen."

"Yeah, and?" Joe prompted.

"Well, she agreed that they were both probably doing it to get the admin time more than for the program itself, but she said to let them give it a shot, and she'd watch their time personally."

Joe looked thoughtful. "That should work, right?"

"Yeah." Randy shook her head. "I don't know how she does it— I really don't."

"What do you mean?"

"I mean, I don't know how Midnight keeps track of everything. She takes on way more than any normal human being can handle, and nothing gets by her."

Joe grinned, his eyes twinkling in the darkness. "She's been doing this shit for years, babe. She's used to it."

Randy just nodded.

"But you got it all worked out?"

"Yes, all worked out."

"Good." He reached out, touching her under the chin and guiding her face down to his. Their lips met as he kissed her softly. Her hand slid over his chest and he groaned at the contact. Randy shivered in response, still thrilled that even after all these years he still responded that way to her touch. They kissed for a long time, his hands touching her, caressing her, and Randy doing the same to him.

"Joe, please…" she breathed eventually, her body aching for him, her hands grasping at him to pull him ever closer. Joe grinned against her lips, knowing he was driving her crazy and enjoying himself thoroughly in doing so.

When his body finally entered her, she moaned loudly, but it was lost against his lips. They made love, enjoying the closeness that comes from being together for years, knowing what the other wanted, giving and taking, and reveling in the excitement of being together.

Afterward, Randy lay in his arms, happy and sated. She could hear Joe's heartbeat, since her head lay on his chest. She'd noticed that he'd coughed a few times while they were making love, but she'd figured she'd wait till afterward to ask him about it. She knew that a lot of the time his cough was a prelude to catching pneumonia, an illness he'd been prone to since childhood. It was a fleeting thought as she drifted to sleep, lulled by the warmth of his body against hers and the feeling of complete fulfillment. *I'll ask him in the morning,* she thought, and fell asleep.

The next morning he was up and gone before she even woke. He left a note to say that he had a search warrant and was going in with Rick's team. She told herself she'd ask him about the cough that afternoon, but time got away from her again. Their lives were so busy these days, it was astounding.

Tiempo paced the floor in the rented penthouse suite of the Hotel Intercontinental. The view of San Diego was spectacular, but he didn't notice. Dave Dibbins was late for his deal.

Stevie leaned against a nearby wall, her arms crossed in front of her chest, looking bored. She was hiding the fear rising in her well.

She couldn't figure out where Dave was; he'd dropped her off at her house at 11:30 that morning and told her he'd see her at 1:00, but he wasn't there. It was 1:15, and Tiempo was getting very edgy.

There was a knock at the door. Stevie pushed off from the wall and walked over to check the peephole. It was Dave, and he looked back at her as if he could see her through the hole. He seemed perfectly calm, as usual. Stevie tamped down on her irritation. What was he doing? Was he really crazy? No one kept Tiempo waiting. She opened the door, giving him an "Are you nuts?" look as he walked by her.

"Tiempo," Dave said, strolling over to the other man. "Sorry I'm late—had a last-minute call from another connection."

"You are shopping around still?" Tiempo asked disbelievingly.

"Never miss an opportunity," Dave replied evenly. "Now, I've been offered three keys for three hundred. Can you match that?"

"For three hundred? You lie!" Tiempo yelled, shaking his head. "You push me too far, señor."

"Hey, you don't want to deal, we won't deal, but I need my product and I'm not paying five hundred for it when I can get it for three."

"Bah! It is crap if you can get it for three. Probably cut with baking soda. My stuff is pure."

Dave looked thoughtful for a moment, then said, "If your stuff is good, then I'll pay four for it."

"No! We had a deal. Three keys for five hundred thousand."

"I don't see the product here," Dave said, glancing around.

"It's here," Tiempo said, snapping his fingers at Stevie. She reached into a closet and withdrew a valise.

"I'll test it and we'll see how good it is," Dave said, sounding skeptical.

He proceeded to produce a butterfly knife, expertly flipping the blade into place. He stuck it into a block he pulled out of the bag and withdrew some powder. Producing a small kit from his pocket, he tested the cocaine, dropping the powder into a vial of liquid and shaking it. The results showed that it was indeed high grade.

"Okay, I'll pay four for it," Dave said, his tone still very serious.

"The deal was five, pendejo," Tiempo gritted out, his anger mounting. Stevie raised her head warily, recognizing Tiempo's fury. Her senses were working overtime; she was trying not to tip Dave's hand, but desperate to keep this from going bad. She couldn't handle any more deaths in her life.

"Well, I'm changing the deal," Dave said, staring into Tiempo's almost-black eyes.

"You pendejo!" Tiempo spat, reaching for his pistol. Stevie drew her weapon, only to find that Dave had amazingly produced his own gun in that time and had it pointed at Tiempo's head.

"Not this time, Tiempo," Dave said, his voice deadly calm.

Tiempo held his hands out to his side, narrowing his eyes at Dave in thwarted anger. "You will die for this."

Dave grinned, not looking concerned. "I think you're a lot of talk, Tiempo."

"Oh, you think so, do you?"

"Yeah, I do. I mean, who have you really killed?" Dave said conversationally.

"I have killed many."

"Yeah, like who?" Dave sat down, keeping his eye on Tiempo the whole time. "Anyone important?" His voice said he didn't think Tiempo could have killed anyone that mattered.

"I am going to kill you," Tiempo said, his anger stepping up another level.

"It's a capital offense, you know," Dave said, his tone still conversational.

"What?" Tiempo said, looking at Dave like he was crazy.

"Killing a cop."

"What cop?"

Dave grinned benevolently as he produced his badge and said, "This one."

"You won't be the first."

"Oh, really?" Dave replied mildly, his skepticism clear. "You've killed a cop before?"

"Just one, but I almost got his partner too." Tiempo was obviously ready to brag right now because he was sure Stevie would somehow get him out of this.

"When did this supposedly happen?" Dave asked, looking bored.

"Four years ago. He tried to make the mistake you're making now."

"And what mistake is that?"

"He tried to arrest me," Tiempo said, spinning to face Stevie and yelling, "Shoot him, now!" With that he dropped to the floor, expecting a hail of gunfire. When nothing happened, he looked up in surprise.

Stevie stood gazing impassively down at him.

"What are you doing?" Tiempo screamed.

"She's doing the smart thing, Tiempo," Dave supplied as he stepped over and grabbed a handful of the other man's shirt to haul him up off the floor.

The door to the suite was thrown open and in walked Joe and Rick, guns in hand but held down to the floor. Rhiannon Templeton came in behind them, followed by Midnight. Kyle Masterson strolled in last and leaned against the back wall, merely observing the proceedings.

Dave turned Tiempo around to face Rhiannon.

"Tiempo," Dave said mildly, "you might remember Rhiannon Templeton."

Tiempo's eyes narrowed at her.

"I'm the partner you almost got," Rhiannon said. Her voice could have cut ice. "The one you got was my husband." Her emerald green eyes burned into Tiempo.

"And my brother-in-law," Stevie chimed in.

Tiempo's head snapped around. "You?" he said, his voice so choked it was almost pleasurable to hear it.

Stevie walked over to stand next to Rhiannon, and it became very apparent the two were sisters. "Yeah, Tiempo, me," she said.

"You bitch!" he screamed, suddenly realizing he'd been played, and that everything he'd thought was secure was no longer so.

"Hurts when everything you know is ripped out from under you, doesn't it?" Rhiannon said, sounding a lot like the narc she used to be. Everyone in the room heard it.

Dave leaned down to whisper in Tiempo's ear. "You're over."

Tiempo didn't reply, just stared back at Stevie with intense hatred.

"She's no cop," Tiempo said, grasping at straws now. "She's not wearing a badge."

"Oh, yeah, that's right—I almost forgot," Midnight said with a baleful smile.

Tiempo's eyes widened as Midnight produced a badge from her pocket and tossed it to Stevie, who caught it deftly and clipped it to her belt.

Stevie stared back at him, and finally said what she'd held in for so long. "Marco Tiempo, you are under arrest for narcotics trafficking and the attempted murder of a peace officer. You have the right to remain silent..."

And so it went. Stevie finally got to take down Marco Tiempo. Unfortunately, at that moment she couldn't arrest him for the murder of her brother-in-law, but she knew she could produce records for Midnight and the DA that would prove he was dealing at the time he had been killed in an accident while pursuing a fleeing Marco Tiempo, which would show that he was evading arrest at the time of the incident.

Marco Tiempo was going to jail for a very long time, and Stevie finally felt some vindication.

Joe and Rick took custody of Tiempo, handing him off to some officers just outside the room. Rhiannon hugged Stevie, whispering, "We'll talk later." She followed Tiempo and his escort out.

Midnight turned to Stevie, her look appraising. Stevie suddenly felt like the scum of the earth she had become, and was basically expecting to be the next person led away in cuffs.

"You did quite well for yourself, O'Neil," Midnight said, her tone all chief.

"Thank you, Chief," was all Stevie could manage. She'd always idolized Midnight Chevalier as the person she wanted to be when she grew up. She still did, and now she felt like a lowlife.

Midnight was silent for a moment, looking straight into Stevie's eyes. "Your father would have been proud," she said, very seriously. "I want to see you in my office at nine a.m. the day after tomorrow."

"Yes, ma'am," Stevie managed around the sudden lump in her throat, trying desperately to hold back the tears caused by the mention of her father.

"And Stevie?"

"Yes, ma'am?"

"Call me Midnight."

With that, Midnight turned and walked out of the suite, leaving Stevie standing there feeling stunned. She stared down at her hands for a long moment. They were shaking.

When she glanced up, she noticed Rick Debenshire looking at her, a lopsided grin on his lips.

"You impressed her," he said, canting his head to the side. "That's not an easy thing to do, ya know."

Stevie grinned rakishly, her soul already beginning the mending process. "Gotta get lucky sometime, right?"

Rick threw his head back and laughed, nodding in agreement. Stevie noticed that Joe Sinclair was smiling too, and nodding in what looked like approval. *Wow*, she thought. *This is what it's like to be approved of by the Gang.*

The "Gang" was how everyone in the department referred to Midnight's inner sanctum of friends, comprised mostly of the original core members of FORS and extended family. Everyone in the department was jealous of the Gang, and would kill to be accepted as one of them. It wasn't so much the idea of promotions, because not everyone in the Gang was of a high rank, but there was a level of accepted excellence involved with being part of the group. Every person in the Gang was the best of the best at what they did. Just like the most popular kids in high school, everyone wanted to be one of them.

"Hey," Dave said, his voice bringing her out of her ruminations. "You still with me?"

She turned to him, her eyes meeting his. "Yes."

His eyes were searching hers, as if trying to discern something. "You okay?"

Stevie took a deep breath, blowing it out in a long, relieved sigh, then nodded. "Yeah, I'm okay. This was much easier than I expected it to be."

Dave grinned. "Yeah. Fun, huh?"

Stevie laughed. "So much fun."

"So, now what?"

"Oh," she said, sighing dramatically, "think I'll go get my nails done, have a massage…" She started to laugh. "I don't have the faintest notion."

"Well, how about you start by having dinner with me at my place tonight?" he said, his grin engaging.

She smiled back. "I think I can manage that."

Later that day, she had a talk with her sister. Stevie was in the apartment Tiempo had paid for, packing the few things she had there. Rhiannon was still stunned over the fact that Tiempo had finally been arrested and would eventually face charges related to Jason's death. She was also very intent on making her sister understand how much she had risked in accomplishing this task.

"Stevie, don't you realize that getting yourself killed wouldn't have brought Jason back?"

Stevie sighed deeply. "Yes, Rhi, I realize that."

Rhiannon leaned forward over the clothes they were folding and putting into boxes and hugged her little sister close. "I love that you cared enough about Jason to do this, Stevie, but you have to understand how much you mean to me." There were tears in Rhiannon's eyes. "You and Mom are all I have left. I couldn't handle losing you too."

"I know," Stevie said, not sure how to explain that she had had to do something. It had been a deep, burning need, one that she had known would never go away. Jason had been the big brother she had never had. He'd been so nice to her, always treating her like his own sister. She had loved him so much, and losing him like that had been like losing their father all over again. Stevie wouldn't let Tiempo get away with it—she couldn't. The bastard that had gunned their father down had gotten away with it; they'd never found out who'd done it. There was no way Tiempo would go free, not while Stevie could do something about it—and she had.

"Where are you going to stay?" Rhiannon asked after a long silence.

Stevie shrugged. "I don't know yet. Just know I need to get out of here, before Tiempo's associates find out what happened today."

"True, they're a little funny about cops working them over," Rhiannon said with a sly grin, sounding for a second like her old self. She looked at her sister for a long moment. "Why don't you come stay with me?"

Stevie seemed surprised by the invitation. She shook her head slowly. "I dunno, Rhi. It's been a long time since we've shared the same space…"

Rhiannon laughed, looking around her. "Yeah, and I can see you're still a slob."

"See?" Stevie said, grinning in spite of herself. "You'd go crazy with me there messing up your perfect little world."

Rhiannon sobered for a moment. "Maybe I need someone to mess up my perfect little world."

Stevie's lips tightened in consternation. She knew her sister had no actual life, that she existed in a haze of memory and work. She didn't date, she didn't go out—she just worked and stayed away from people. Maybe it would be a good thing to move in with her.

"Okay," Stevie said. She grinned at her sister. "Just remember you asked for it."

That night, Stevie showed up at Dave's for dinner. He opened the door and gestured for her to enter. She followed him back to his kitchen and stood watching him finish up cooking. He'd made spaghetti, telling her that was about the only thing he knew how to cook. They sat down to eat. He had an oak kitchen table, with matching chairs that had deep blue cushions on them. Everything about his home seemed natural and very much him. Stevie couldn't get over how different he was from what she had always imagined he'd be like.

Dave caught her looking at him again and asked, "What?"

"I just…" she began, not sure how to put her thoughts into words without sounding stupid. "You're very different from what someone would imagine a narc to be."

"What do people imagine narcs to be like?" Dave asked, sitting back.

Stevie grinned, feeling like a silly kid all of a sudden. "I just mean, you're so ultra-calm, so into earthy things… I don't know, just different."

Dave nodded, then pinned her with a look. "Is it a bad kind of different?"

"No!" Stevie assured him, grinning at her own outburst. "You just seem, I don't know, so… sweet."

"Sweet?" Dave sounded both surprised and perplexed.

"Yeah," Stevie said, her voice softening. "Like the other night, when I got out of hand. Instead of giving me the ass-whipping I really deserved, you took care of me, and in the end put your own life on the line to give me what I wanted. Sweet doesn't really cover all that— more like fantastic."

Dave seemed to be assessing what she'd said, his brows furrowed in thought. Then he looked up at her again, his sky blue eyes staring right into hers, and stunned her with his next statement.

"That's what family does, Stevie."

"Family?"

"Yeah," he replied softly. "You are part of our family. Midnight wanted you back in, and after I met you, so did I. You risk your life for family." His comments were made so simply that Stevie was quiet a long few moments, absorbing what he was saying.

"Wow," was all she could manage when she found her voice again.

Dave grinned at her, understanding what she was feeling. He'd felt it too, many years before, when he'd become part of something much bigger than himself. When he'd joined FORS and suddenly had people willing to die for him, ordinary Dave Dibbins was no longer alone or ordinary. Suddenly he had people who would back him up, no matter what the fight. It was scary and incredible all rolled into one. And it had come as a shock, and Stevie was going through that shock right now.

It took her a few minutes to gather her composure, but Dave had to give her credit; she regrouped faster than anyone he knew.

She took a long drink of her wine. "You know, it would have been nice to know what your plan was today."

"What do you mean?" Dave asked, surprised by her change in topic.

"I mean, showing up late like that. I was worried sick."

"That," he said, grinning, "was not on purpose. We were having problems with the wire and I didn't want anything to go wrong."

"So the 'other deal' was just a fast makeup?"

"Yup."

"Damn, you're fast on your feet, Dibbins," she said, shaking her head in amazement. "So that whole thing wasn't planned?"

Dave shrugged. "Nope, pretty much seat-of-the-pants time."

"Do you do that a lot?"

"Only when things get screwed up in a hurry," he replied, laughing.

"So, when he went for his gun…?"

"Oh, I wasn't risking that again—that's when I'd had it."

"So that's when you changed the plan."

"No, Tiempo changed the plan," Dave pointed out. "I just made it work for us."

Stevie shook her head again, not sure that she'd ever be as good as Dave but hoping she'd get a chance to find out.

"You know," Dave said, "it would have been helpful to know it was just going to be you, me, and him."

"I didn't know it till the last minute. He dismissed everyone else, said I was all the protection he'd need." Stevie grinned as she stated the last.

"Oops," Dave said, grinning back.

They continued dinner in companionable conversation, eventually moving into the living room. The more Stevie talked to him, the more she realized how completely in control of himself he was. And the more she wanted to make him lose his control. To that end, she moved forward on the couch and kissed him. It was a deep, hungry kiss that held all of the relief that she had stored inside. Dave's hands moved to her back, drawing her closer, pulling her over to his lap. The kiss lasted for a long few minutes, during which they both became breathless.

"I need you," Stevie said when she pulled away for a moment, her voice a breathy gasp.

Dave nodded, standing up and pulling her with him. He kissed her again before turning to lead her down the hall to his room. They removed each other's clothes, and he sat down on the bed; she stood in front of him, leaning down the few inches to keep contact with his lips. He held her back, caressing her. Her hands on his shoulders pushed him back onto the bed. He pulled her down with him, then with surprising strength held her against him as he moved them both up, her body over his.

Stevie kissed him again, her tongue sliding between his lips, probing his mouth hungrily. His kisses were as hot and hungry as hers. Stevie pulled back to look down at him.

"I want to do this to you," she said huskily.

Dave looked back at her, staring up into her eyes as if trying to read her meaning there. He apparently understood what she meant, because he nodded, closing his eyes slowly as if to prepare himself.

Stevie kissed his lips again, then proceeded to move along his neck, his collar bone, his chest. Touching him, tasting him, making him moan and shudder, his hands grasping at her. He finally lost the control he'd held on to so tightly and begged her to make love to him. When she did they were both more than ready. He said her name over and over again as her body slid down over his, and she cried out at the contact and the heat. They reached a quick and fervent climax.

They lay together afterward, not talking, just catching their breath and drifting. She still lay with her body over his, her face buried against his neck. She moved her lips to his ear, kissing it softly and whispering, "Thank you."

Dave knew what she meant, and he knew it had nothing to do with the sex. She was thanking him for helping her. He turned his head, leaning down slightly and kissing her lips softly. "You're welcome," he whispered against them. They drifted off a few minutes later and slept soundly through the night.


The next morning, Stevie felt Dave kiss her on the cheek as he left. She turned over, glancing at the clock. 5:30 a.m., his surfing time. She shook her head, unable to fathom how he could get up so early even if it was for recreation. She was still asleep when he got back at 7:30. He showered and climbed into bed with her. Stevie snuggled up next to him. He smelled like soap and aftershave.

"Mmm…" she said as she snuggled against his neck.

Dave grinned, leaning down to kiss her forehead. She moved her head back so he could kiss her lips. He slid his hand around the back of her head, his other arm going around her waist to pull her close. They kissed then, eventually making love. They spent the better part of the morning in bed.

After eventually getting up and having coffee, they lazed about for a while, and then Stevie left to go over to Rhiannon's to organize her stuff. She had dinner with Rhiannon that night. It was a quiet evening. They talked a little bit, but both were lost in their own thoughts. Stevie wasn't sure what the meeting with Midnight would produce. Part of her was still terrified that Midnight would arrest her. She'd told Dave that earlier in the day. He'd laughed and reminded her that if Midnight had wanted to have her arrested, she'd had ample opportunity. Stevie couldn't argue with that logic, but it still worried her. Rhiannon was reliving her last days with her husband, and trying to put her demons to rest.

*Rhiannon was twenty-one when she started with the police department. She was her father's daughter, very gung-ho, having graduated from the academy with top honors. Her father had been shot in the line of duty when she was fourteen; she intended to serve his memory well. Her first day, she showed up to work with her uniform pressed, her shoes shined, her badge proudly displayed. She went to roll call and was assigned her field training officer, her FTO.*

*She'd been warned by many of her dad's friends that her FTO might be a major hard-ass on her, especially since she'd been a cop's kid. She'd worried herself sick the night before her first day—what if her FTO hated that women were becoming cops? What if he didn't like her? And worse, what if she failed probation?*

*When she walked up to him, calling him "sir," he was talking to someone—a woman. She was smiling up at him in obvious infatuation. When he turned around to look at his newest trainee, he grinned. "Don't call me sir," he said, his blue eyes warm. "Makes me feel like an old man."*

*"I, uh…" Rhiannon had stammered, stunned. "Yes, sir."*

*He smiled broadly. "Call me Jason and we'll get along just fine."*

*"Yes, s—I mean, Jason."*

*At thirty, Jason Templeton was an all-American quarterback* type, with a muscular but not bulky body, blond hair cut short, and blue eyes set in a handsome, square-jawed face. Rhiannon had been around police officers her entire life, but Jason Templeton set her back a few paces. His smile was open, his manner friendly. She wasn't sure exactly how to react, so she retreated to what she'd been taught her entire life. She gave him respectful silence and endeavored to learn everything he had to teach her.

Jason was an excellent teacher. When she did something wrong, he pointed it out to her in a way that allowed her to keep her dignity. She'd heard of trainees who actually cried at the end of a shift because their FTOs were so hard on them. Jason wasn't that type of man. He was stern when the time called for it, during situations that could put her in physical danger. He would instruct without barking orders, but would be very concise when the situation warranted it.

Within a month she felt she had learned so much more than she'd ever thought possible. She was grateful to him for his way of teaching. She also understood why so many of her fellow graduates from the police academy envied her luck at getting him for an FTO. He was good, the best, and she had drawn the lucky number. She didn't realize that the chief of the department had personally arranged it so she would have the best FTO. The chief had been partners with her father, Frank O'Neil, when they both started out on patrol. He had been devastated to lose him. When Frank's oldest daughter had applied, the chief was determined she'd have the best opportunities he could give her. That was Jason Templeton.

Jason had no idea why he'd been assigned to the young woman he was training. He did know that she was an excellent pupil. He had, of course, heard who her father was, and what had happened to him—murdered by a cop-killer while on patrol. Jason had to hand it to

Rhiannon—she never mentioned her father or attempted to gain sympathy in any way. She worked hard, and it was obvious she was dedicated to becoming the best cop she could possibly be. He wondered, however, if she ever loosened up. It was apparent to him that she studied all the time. Whenever they'd pull someone over, she knew the correct penal code to write them up, including the level at which she could use her judgment. She was polite, calm, professional at all times—and she was emotionless. From what he could detect, she had no life outside the department. She didn't meet with friends after her shift, and she didn't talk about anything other than police work.

Jason had come from a background of police officers. He knew how important it was to cut loose and enjoy oneself when not on duty. He had seen what happened to officers that lived for the job—they died for the job. Some became alcoholics, others became hermits, still others got into abusive relationships because they couldn't put the job away. Jason had learned very early on that when you were off duty, you needed to let the job go.

In the past month, he had taught Rhiannon a lot about their work. Now it was time to teach her about letting it go. One morning after their shift, he surprised her by asking her to breakfast.

"I..." she said, stammering as she tried to come up with an answer. "I don't know..."

"Come on, O'Neil, it's breakfast—it's not against regulations or anything," Jason said with his usual smile.

Rhiannon grinned self-consciously. She knew what a hard-ass she sounded. "Okay, okay," she said, holding up a hand in surrender. "I'll meet you out here in fifteen minutes." She gestured to the hallway outside the locker rooms.

"Deal," Jason said, turning and going into the men's.

Fifteen minutes later, Rhiannon was waiting for Jason when he walked out. He wasn't sure if he was disappointed or amused that while she was wearing street clothes, she still wore no makeup and her hair was still up in the usual severe bun. She didn't do civilian life too well, did she?

"Let's go," he said, gesturing for her to precede him.

They walked out to the parking lot, and he led her to his vehicle. His pride and joy—his baby, as he liked to think of it. It was a classic '56 Chevy, restored with his own two hands—350 small-block engine, racing tires, blue-dot tail lights, chromed-out engine and exhaust, thunder-black paint with the blue-black flames fanning from the hood down either side of the car. All-original black leather interior and a suicide knob on the stick. He had put many years of blood, sweat, and tears, as well as a number of paychecks, into this car.

To his utter relief, Rhiannon O'Neil was suitably impressed. She ran her hand along the fender, walking from front to back, leaned down to check the exhaust pipes, noted the rims, the tires. She glanced up at him as he watched her examine his car and smiled.

"Very nice, Officer Templeton. Fifty-six?"

"Yes, ma'am," he said proudly.

"Original paint?"

"All but one fender."

She looked closely at the paint job again. "Can't detect it—good match," she said approvingly. "Interior?"

"Original."

"Engine?"

"Some modifications. I like speed," he said with a smile.

She grinned. "Go figure, Officer."

With that he opened the passenger door for her with a flourish, inexplicably happy that she appreciated his car. When he got in and started it, he watched her cant her head to the side, listening to the sound of the engine. She nodded, again looking impressed.

"Nice rumbler," she said, smiling.

They made the short drive to the restaurant. All the while she looked around at the interior of the car. Her hand slid over the flawless dash in obvious reverence. She watched as he shifted, noting the suicide knob and the smoothness of the change. She was indeed impressed.

"So," he said when they were seated in a booth, "how do you know so much about classic cars?"

Rhiannon shrugged as she looked at the menu. "My dad loved them—used to take us to car shows all the time."

He grinned. "And I see you learned a thing or two."

Rhiannon looked up at him, and for the first time he noticed the absolute green of her eyes. They were like perfect emeralds. They always worked together at night, so he rarely saw her in broad daylight, and this morning the sun was shining through the windows of the café and he could see her eyes very clearly. He was stunned for a moment, so much so that he missed what she said.

"I'm sorry," he said, giving himself a mental shake. "What did you say?"

"I said, my dad left me his Mustang. It's a sixty-seven and a half."

Jason whistled appreciatively. "I'd like to see it sometime."

*"You can see it when we get back. I drive it every day."*

*"Will wonders never cease," he shot back with a smile.*

They ordered their breakfast, and when the waitress walked away, Rhiannon looked him straight in the eye.

*"So, Jason, what are we doing here?"* Her tone was so matter-of-fact that he almost choked on the coffee he'd just sipped.

He gave a little cough, blinking as if she'd just insulted him. *"I, uh…"* he said, realizing quickly that he was stammering like she did when he cornered her. *"I wanted to talk to you about your social life,"* he said, being more blunt than he'd meant to in his haste to take back his composure.

*"What social life?"* she asked, surprised.

*"That, Officer O'Neil, is my point."*

*"I don't get your meaning,"* she replied, sitting up straighter. He thought she did indeed get his meaning and she didn't like it.

He narrowed his eyes at her. *"What do you do when you go home in the mornings?"*

*"Why?"* she asked defensively.

*"Just tell me."*

*"I don't go home in the mornings."*

His brows furrowed. *"Where do you go?"*

*"I go to the gym,"* she said, then shrugged. *"It's less crowded then, and I'm able to work out in peace."*

*"So you work out,"* he clarified. *"For how long?"*

*"Two hours,"* she said, looking mystified at his line of questioning.

"Okay, then what?"

She was silent for a few moments as if hesitant to answer.

"O'Neil?" he prompted.

She sighed. "I go home, polish my boots, clean my leather gear, check my weapon and clean it, then do review."

"Review?"

"Yes. I review the sections of the knowledge domains that we hit on during our patrol."

Jason nodded slowly, thinking, Jesus, she's worse than I thought! "So you do cop stuff."

Rhiannon looked at him like he'd lost his mind. "Templeton, I am a cop."

"I know that, O'Neil," Jason replied, his patience slipping a bit at her deadpan comment. "But before you became a cop, you used to be human."

"I am human!" she snapped.

"No, you're a walking, talking penal code in a uniform."

Rhiannon scowled at him, but said nothing for a long few moments. "Are you saying that I'm not doing my job well?" Her tone was even, but her eyes told a whole other story. In them he saw what he could only define as sheer terror.

It was Jason's turn to sigh, and he shook his head. "No, O'Neil, that's not what I'm saying."

Rhiannon swallowed against the lump in her throat. "Then what are you saying?" she asked, her voice suddenly not as strong as it had been before.

*Again he breathed a sigh of frustration. This wasn't how he'd planned to approach this. "Look, in this job we have a lot of stress— you know that."*

*Rhiannon nodded, but said nothing, becoming once again the avid pupil. Her hands were folded neatly in front of her on the table and she was sitting up straight, staring him right in the eye as he spoke.*

*"We're on duty 24/7. It takes a lot out of us. We're not like regular people at regular jobs."*

*Again Rhiannon nodded.*

*"We see more terrible things in one day than most people see in a lifetime. And it takes a toll on us emotionally and sometimes physically."*

*Jason paused, seeing that her mind was working and realizing she was trying to come up with an answer before he finished speaking. Without stopping to think, he reached out and touched her hands. "Rhiannon, you need to learn when to stop being a cop for a little while."*

*Her expression changed when he touched her hands, then again when she heard the words he'd said. He saw confusion cross her features, then dismay. He knew she thought she was somehow failing as a trainee.*

*"Rhiannon, listen," he said, his tone more intent now. "You're a fantastic cop. One of the best I've trained so far. But you can't be this all the time. You have to take some time out for you."*

*She blinked a few times, obviously trying to come to terms with what he was saying, then nodded slowly.*

*Their food arrived, and he took his hands away. She promptly dropped hers into her lap. They didn't speak the rest of their time in the restaurant. Jason wasn't sure if he'd gotten through or if he'd just hurt her feelings immeasurably. He hoped for the former.*

*On the drive back she was silent, staring out the window. He left her to her own thoughts, not wanting to compound any damage he might have done. When they got back to the department, she got out of the car before he could get out to open the door for her. She leaned down, looking back in at him through the open passenger door.*

*"Thank you," was all she said before closing the door. Jason watched her walk into the building, not sure what to think. After a few long moments he drove away, heading for his loft downtown. He spent a number of hours that day thinking about his trainee, wondering over and over again if he'd done the right thing. Maybe he was pushing too hard; maybe she did have a life outside the department and he was assuming too much. Was it wrong for her to want to be the best cop she could be? No, but it was wrong for her to give up living to be one.*


*That day was a turning point in their relationship. The following day, once in their patrol car, she sat behind the wheel, staring straight ahead for a few long moments.*

*"O'Neil?" Jason said, not sure what was wrong.*

*She turned her head to look at him. "You're saying I need to loosen up," she said simply, making him realize she'd thought about this all day long.*

*"I'm saying you need to cut loose every now and then, or you're going to make yourself old long before your time," Jason said seriously.*

*Rhiannon nodded, then turned to face forward. After a minute she shrugged, nodding again. "Okay."*

*Nothing more was said that night about the conversation the morning before, but Jason noticed the next day that Rhiannon was suddenly more open and sociable. She started making conversation with him, laughing when suspects came on to her, even joking with him about all his "girlfriends." She confided later that her father had always told her that being a police officer was serious business, not to be taken lightly. That their responsibility was great, and that they needed to treat everything with professionalism. It had been ingrained in her from childhood.*

*"O'Neil, no offense, but your father was from the old school, and that's why so many of the cops from the old school are divorced alcoholics. They had no outlet for the stress they were under every day."*

*Rhiannon nodded, understanding what he was saying. Remembering the depressions her father would go through, when he only wanted to be alone. It was difficult to face the reality that her father had had his flaws; she'd always been afraid to admit them, even to herself. After all, he was her daddy and she'd loved him dearly.*

*"Loving him meant you accepted his flaws," Jason said one morning at breakfast when she brought up her previous obtuseness. "It doesn't mean he didn't have any. And you're not sullying his memory by realizing what his faults were and making sure you don't make the same mistakes."*

*Rhiannon grinned. "How'd you get so wise, Templeton?"*

*Jason grinned back at her. "A whole family full of cops."*

*He told her about his family: his father, who was ex-highway patrol; his mother, who was a dispatcher; his brother, who worked for the sheriff's department in Kansas somewhere. His uncles, who were both*

Federal Department of Justice. Even his aunt, who was a customs agent.

Jason found that Rhiannon had a very definite quality about her. On the one hand, she was a good cop; she did her job well, and tried to learn as much as she could. On the other hand, she had this vulnerability that lay just under the surface, which she rarely showed him. Something made him want her to share that side with him. She was very intelligent, so their conversations were always lively. She'd also learned quickly that she was "allowed" to disagree with him, so when she didn't agree with something he said, she argued. She never, however, disagreed with him on the job. She trusted his knowledge on everything pertaining to police work. So while he found it great that she questioned things about his views on politics, life, and love, it was a big compliment to him that she trusted his abilities as a training officer so thoroughly.

Three weeks after they'd gotten to this new level in their partnership, Rhiannon came down with the flu. She called off shift two days in a row, which for her was monumental. After the second day, Jason decided to check up on her, to make sure she was okay.

She answered the door to her apartment in a bathrobe, with her hair up in a towel. She looked surprised to see him.

"Jason," she said. "What are you doing here?" It was obvious from the sound of her voice that she was congested, and her face was pale.

"Came to check on you—see if you needed anything," he said, not wanting her to think he was checking up on her in terms of her calling off sick.

"Do you want to come in?" she asked, standing back and opening

226

*the door wider.*

*"Sure," he said, and walked inside.*

*Rhiannon went over to the couch, where it was obvious she'd been lying. There was a pillow and blanket, a coffee mug with a tea bag label hanging out of it, and tissues.*

*"All set up, I see," he said, gesturing to the couch and coffee table.*

*"Yeah," she said softly. "Do you want to sit down?" she asked, moving her blanket out of the way.*

*He nodded, sitting down a couple of feet away from her.*

*"Are you feeling any better?" he asked solicitously.*

*She grimaced. "Not really. I thought a shower might help," she said, gesturing to the towel on her head. "But it didn't really."*

*"Do you need anything? Medicine, hot soup, anything?" he asked, sounding like a concerned parent.*

*"Company?" Rhiannon said hesitantly.*

*"I can do that," Jason said, grinning.*

*They sat and talked for a little bit. He caught her up on what had been happening while she was out. They watched some TV for a while. When it was obvious she was getting tired, he told her he was going to get going. She walked him to the door.*

*He turned around and looked down at her. "Get some rest, and make sure you dry that hair before you do. If you get a chill you'll get more sick."*

*"Okay," she said simply, looking like the obedient child.*

*"I'll come check on you before shift tonight. Don't even think of coming back tonight, you hear me?"*

"Yes, sir," she said, the beginnings of a grin on her lips.

"Don't 'yes, sir' me, young lady—just do what you're told," he said with a laugh. "I'll see you tonight." He gave her a long look, then turned and walked out the door.

That evening he showed up with hot soup in hand. She thanked him for his thoughtfulness. He noted her hair was in its usual bun and wondered idly if he'd ever see it down.

"Isn't that uncomfortable?" he asked, pointing to her hair.

"What?" she said, reaching back to touch the bun. "This? No, not really. It's easier than getting all tangled up in it when I sleep. And with my fever and all, it's so hot when it's down."

"Okay..." he said, trailing off as he shook his head. He never understood women's thinking.

Rhiannon grinned. "Trust me on this, Templeton."

They talked about how she was doing, and when she thought she'd be back. She tried to say she'd be back the next night; he told her she'd be back the night after that if she was still feeling better.

When Rhiannon didn't say anything, Jason gave her a stern look. "This is when you say 'yes, sir.'"

Rhiannon looked rebellious. He narrowed his eyes. She sighed. "Okay—yes, sir."

"Good girl."

"Very patronizing, Sergeant," she countered.

"Was it?"

"Yes, unless I'm a dog."

"You're not a dog."

"No."

"Then you aren't a good girl?" he asked, grinning.

"I've been an angel since the day I was born."

"See? I was right."

"Ugh!" she said, throwing up her hands.

Jason laughed. "You'll never win, O'Neil. Face it."

"We'll see."

"Uh-huh," he replied, giving her a suspicious look. "I'm gonna take off. You get some more rest."

"Yes, sir," she replied obediently.

"You're learning," he said, chucking her under the chin as he grinned down at her.

"I've been taught by the best."

"Yes, you have," he replied, smiling now.

He left, only to return the following morning with tea and croissants, her usual breakfast. That evening he came back with soup again, and again the following morning with breakfast. Rhiannon was endlessly amused and warmed by the fact that her FTO was such a big softy. She told him that the third morning he was over.

"Soft? Me?" he replied. "No, I just want you back to full strength so I don't have to keep doing your job and mine." His tone was stern, and for a moment he managed a straight face, only to ruin the effect with his ever-affable grin.

"Yeah... big, tough guy," Rhiannon said with a nod, looking far from convinced. "Well, I'll be on tonight, so you don't have to worry anymore."

*"Good," he said sharply. Then he broke into a grin again. "I'm gettin' lonely."*

*"Ahh..." Rhiannon said, laughing.*

*"Yeah, shut up," Jason grumbled.*

*He left a short time later, and Rhiannon again reflected on her luck. How much luckier could she have gotten? An FTO that was a good teacher as well as a hell of a nice guy.*

*Rhiannon showed up on shift that night, but it was very obvious she still wasn't feeling 100 percent. Jason told her to go back home, but she refused, citing that she didn't have that much sick leave on the books and she couldn't afford to be off payroll. He couldn't argue with that, so he conceded. He refused to let her drive that evening; he also thanked God that it was the middle of the week, so it was generally quiet on their shift. By the end of the night, it was obvious she was fighting to stay awake.*

*"Do you have meds with you?" he asked, glancing over at her while they completed paperwork on the few calls they'd handled in the last two hours.*

*"Yes, but I can't take them yet."*

*"Why?"*

*"Because they make me sleepy, and I have to drive home."*

*"When were you planning to take them?"*

*"Right before I leave the office."*

*"They could still hit you before you get home," he pointed out. "Especially considering how tired you've been tonight."*

*Rhiannon shrugged. "Then I guess I'll wait till I get home."*

*"I have a better idea."*

*"What?"*

*"I live downtown. Why don't you just crash at my place and then you can go home later tonight, since we're off for the next two days."*

*"I don't want to impose, Jason," she said, feeling like the world's biggest pain in the butt.*

*"O'Neil, the imposition would be if you managed to get yourself killed on the way home," he said sternly. "All that good training gone to waste—and think about the paperwork I'd have to do."*

*Rhiannon grinned. "I know, I know—you hate paperwork."*

*"I hate losing good trainees more," he said seriously.*

*Rhiannon looked back at him for a long time. She sighed. "Okay, you win. I'll crash at your place this morning."*

*"Good."*

*After they got off shift, she followed him the three short minutes from the department to his loft in the Gaslamp Quarter. Walking in, she noticed that he seemed to favor casual and comfortable furniture over style. His couch was a sectional, large, overstuffed, and covered in a simple navy material. There was a matching recliner and foot stool. His coffee table was simple but nice in oak; his kitchen table and chairs were oak as well.*

*"Do you want anything to eat before you take your meds?" he asked.*

*"No, I'm fine."*

*He walked into his kitchen area and got her a glass of water while she pulled the medicine in its little packet out of her purse. He handed* her the glass and she swallowed the pills. Then he showed her to his bedroom.

"You can take the bed. I'll sleep out there on the couch."

"Jason, I don't want to put you out."

"Hey," he said, grinning again. "How do you know the couch isn't more comfortable than my bed?"

"Is it?"

"I'll take the fifth on that one," he said, laughing. "Seriously, though, this way you'll have some privacy, okay?"

"Okay," she said, too tired to argue anymore. She was surprised to note that his room was clean and his bed was made. "You're a good boy, Templeton. You make your bed before you go to work and everything?"

Jason shook his head. "Are you kidding? I have a lady that comes in every other day to clean. I'm basically a slob."

She laughed. "Oh, so I got the lucky day?"

"Yep," he said. He left the room, and she took off her shoes and jeans and got under the covers. It felt strange, being in his room, in his bed. She looked around. There weren't any pictures on the walls, but she saw his uniforms hanging in the closet on the side that was open, and he had a few pictures of what had to be his family on his dresser. She made a mental note to look at the pictures later if she got a chance. She already felt herself drifting off to sleep. Turning her head, she realized she must be on the side of the bed he usually slept on, because the pillow smelled like his cologne. She inhaled deeply and felt a warm tingle flow through her. For once she didn't stop to analyze what that meant, just let herself drift off.

*She woke to the sound of his voice softly calling her name. When she opened her eyes, he was sitting on the side of the bed. She had no way of knowing he'd been sitting there for about ten minutes, just watching her sleep. It was dim in the room, indicating daylight was fading. She noticed that he was dressed in different clothes.*

*She sat up, missing the stunned look on his face as she rubbed her eyes. "What time is it?"*

*"Five thirty," he said, his voice sounding a little strange.*

*She lowered her hands and looked at him, seeing that he wasn't looking at her face but her shoulder. She glanced down and realized that her hair had come loose while she'd slept. It now lay in waves over her shoulders and halfway to her waist. She grinned.*

*"Jesus Christ, O'Neil," he said, his tone a bit awed. "You have hair."*

*Rhiannon laughed softly. "You didn't think I had hair?"*

*"Well, I knew you had hair, but I didn't realize just how much."*

*"Now you see why I pull it up so much. It's really a hindrance. I've been thinking of getting it cut ever since the academy."*

*"Don't you dare," he said seriously, then looked abashed at having said what he'd been thinking without checking it first. "Uh…" he stammered, but Rhiannon laughed.*

*"That's exactly what my dad would have said. That's why I've always kept it long. He always said, 'Females were meant to have long hair!' Upon reflection it is a bit sexist, but…" She shrugged.*

*There was a long moment of silence, then Jason took a deep breath and sighed, looking up at the ceiling.*

*"I think we have a problem, O'Neil," he said, his voice serious*

233

*again.*

*"We do?" she asked, surprised.*

*He glanced at her, his eyes moving to her hair, then down from her shoulders over her legs, which were exposed, since she'd kicked the covers off while she'd slept. His gaze swept back up to her face. "Yes, we do."*

*Rhiannon suddenly looked confused and worried. "What's the problem?" Had she done something wrong? Had she gotten too comfortable in his presence? Had she said something she shouldn't?*

*Jason looked directly into her eyes. "The problem is that I want you," he said simply.*

*So simply in fact that it took her a long moment to catch on to what he'd said, and before she could respond his lips were on hers. She was stunned at first, but realized suddenly that her body was responding strongly. His hand was at her waist, his other touching her face, sliding through her hair. Within moments she was kissing him back— there was no more hesitation. When her hands slid up his chest and her arms encircled his neck, both his arms went around her, pulling her closer, the kiss deepening dramatically, as if he'd been holding himself back until then.*

*After a few minutes, he laid her back on the bed, still kissing her. His hand was at her cheek, cupping her face, his thumb stroking her skin. After a few moments, his hands slid down to her neck, and inside her shirt to touch her bare shoulder. She grasped at his back at the feeling of his hand on her bare skin. Jason reached up and pulled his shirt off over his head, tossing it aside, wanting to feel her hands on him too. She obliged that desire by running her hands over his back; her nails— always kept trimmed but never too short—grazed his skin, making him* shiver. When it was obvious he wasn't going to go any farther than she indicated she wanted him to, she reached between them and unbuttoned her shirt. She'd gotten two buttons undone when his hands moved to finish the job.

His appreciative low whistle greeted the first sight of her body. He had figured that all that time at the gym would have taken away any signs of femininity, but he'd been wrong. Her body was well toned, but very definitely feminine. Rhiannon was delighting in the sight of his body as well. He was well muscled, more so than she'd thought he'd be; his clothes hid a lot.

He took it slowly, caressing every inch of her skin, seeming to take pleasure in awakening every sense she had. She writhed with pleasure, doing her best to touch him in the same way, but knowing that she was far too inexperienced at this to be as effective as he was. She had in fact had only one other lover, an inept one at that. Jason knew exactly what he was doing, and she was sure she was going to go crazy if he didn't consummate this new level of their relationship soon.

"Jason, please..." she finally begged, her voice a husky whisper against his ear.

She heard him take a sharp breath, not realizing that he was having to rein in his own desire to keep from losing control; hearing her voice like that, so close, had sent an almost electric pulse along his nerves, screaming for release.

Once he was in control of his passion, he did as she wanted. They made love, and he brought them to a climax together. His mouth was near her ear as he reached his release, saying her name over and over again, shortening it to what sounded like "Rannon" in the final moment.

*They didn't talk about what they were doing, this relationship they had. They talked about everything else, but Rhiannon was terrified that someone would find out and he'd get into trouble. She was, after all, his trainee. Because she was afraid to point it out and lose him, she didn't say anything, hoping that would keep anything from happening. They spent every morning after work at his loft, making love and talking about everything from Vietnam to cars, from weather to music.*

*One morning after their shift was over, he met her outside the department.*

*"I have something I need to go and do this morning," he said. "I'll meet you at the loft in about an hour, okay?"*

*Rhiannon nodded. She had her own key to his loft; he'd given it to her that first day they'd made love. He leaned down and kissed her quickly on the lips, then turned and went to his car.*

*True to his word, he was at the loft an hour later. Rhiannon was sitting at the kitchen table, wearing only her shirt and socks. Her legs were tucked under her as she drank tea and read the paper. Jason walked over and leaned against the table, next to where she was sitting. When Rhiannon looked up, she saw that his face was serious.*

*"What's up?" she asked, worried.*

*"Nothing," he said calmly. "I was just looking at you—is that okay?" he asked with a grin.*

*"Yeah, it's okay," she replied, giving him a sour look, then smiled.*

*He took her hand, pulling her out of the chair and up against him. He leaned down and kissed her softly, then led her over to the couch. He sat, and she lay down with her head in his lap, something they often* did in the mornings. They talked for a few minutes, about work as usual, reviewing the night's shift. Then they moved on to other topics.

During the course of the conversation they started talking about how being a cop made them so different from other people. How cops tended to have only other cops as friends.

"Cops understand other cops," Rhiannon said, shrugging. "That's what my dad always said, and I think it's true. Don't you?"

Jason shrugged. "It is true for the most part, but it can be a bad thing too."

"How?" she asked, sitting up and facing him.

Not wanting to lose physical contact with her, he reached out and pulled her onto his lap. She sat straddling him.

"I just think when you limit yourself to other cops, you end up only talking about work all the time, and it can become more negative than positive."

Rhiannon looked thoughtful for a moment. "Maybe. But you also don't run into the conflicts you can with people who aren't cops."

"Like what?"

"Like people who don't believe drugs should be illegal, or that drinking and driving is okay, or whatever other laws people don't like. It becomes a hindrance for a cop, because we have a conflict between doing our job and having friends."

Jason thought about that, appreciating the fact that she looked at everything, not just accepting someone else's opinion. He nodded. "You could be right. So what about marriage?" he asked. "Do you think cops should marry other cops?"

"I think it's easier."

*"Easier? How?"*

*"Well, other cops understand the odd hours, the stress, the stuff we go through."*

*"So, you'd marry a cop?"*

*"Yes."*

*He grinned. "Wanna marry me?"*

*Rhiannon laughed. "If you're lucky," she said, smiling broadly.*

*He reached into his jacket, smiling. "Maybe this will give me luck," he said, and pulled out a small box. He handed it to her.*

*Rhiannon's smile faded, her eyes widening as she looked from the box to his face. "Jason..." she said, trailing off as he opened the box. Nestled inside was a diamond ring. He was definitely not playing around here.*

*"I love you, Rhiannon, and I want you here with me all the time." He kissed her softly on the lips. "Marry me."*

*She stared back into his eyes. He could see she was trying to come to grips with what he was saying. He prayed silently that he hadn't overestimated her feelings for him. All he knew was that he wanted to be with her all the time; when she wasn't around he couldn't stop thinking about her. She had captured his heart so quickly and so thoroughly, he thought he'd die if he couldn't have her as his forever.*

*"Rhian?" he said, his voice soft but holding a note of worry.*

*She blinked a few times, shaking her head as if to clear it. "Jason. Jason, God, I'm sorry," she said, making him feel suddenly sick. So much so that he almost missed what she said after that. "Yes, I want to marry you. I'm sorry, I was just so surprised that you felt like I do, I never dreamed that I could be that lucky."*

"Lucky?" he managed to stammer, even as his heart soared.

"Yes, that you love me too."

"You do?" he said, realizing that he sounded like an idiot and not caring one bit.

Rhiannon looked at him for a long moment, a tender little smile on her face. "Yes, Jason Templeton. I love you, and I would be honored to be your wife."

Jason pulled her into his arms, hugging her so tight she couldn't breathe. She laughed, realizing that her dreams had indeed just come true. She knew she'd been in love with him from the time he came to see her when she was sick. She had seen in him the gentleness and caring that was so rare in men, especially men in their profession. It had taken her aback to realize she was in love with him, and she had told herself sternly that she needed to keep things professional. It hadn't worked, but she hadn't been the one to give in. Now to find out that he loved her, that he wanted to marry her, was just beyond comprehension. She was happier than she'd ever thought possible.

That day, she took Jason to meet her mother and her younger sister, Stevie. They went to her mother's house first. She was very pleasant to Jason. She wasn't overly enthusiastic about Rhiannon marrying another police officer, but Rhiannon understood that. MaryAnne O'Neil had lost her husband of nineteen years because he was a police officer; she didn't wish that same fate on her daughters.

They left her mother's house and drove over to the high school to meet Stevie when she got out of class. They waited out front, leaning against Jason's car. Jason found that he couldn't stop grinning like an idiot, and whenever he looked down at Rhiannon she was doing the same. It was pretty fun, this being in love thing.

Stevie came out of the school and spotted the cool black '56 Chevy with the flames right away, then noticed that it was her sister and some really nice-looking cop-type standing next to it. She walked over, for all intents and purposes looking like the classic rebel, with her faded jeans, black T-shirt, jean jacket, and tennis shoes. Her hair, a couple of shades lighter than Rhiannon's deep auburn, was pulled back in a long braid. She looked the car over as she said, "Heya, Rhi." Then she looked directly at Jason. "Who're you?"

Jason glanced at Rhiannon and grinned. "Cop's kids," he said, then turned back to Stevie and extended his hand. "I'm Jason Templeton."

Stevie looked at his hand and nodded, making no move to take it. "You're her FTO," she said matter-of-factly.

"Yes, I am," he replied, dropping his hand and moving it to scratch at the small of his back, where his off-duty weapon rested.

"So why are you here now?" Stevie asked, her ever-suspicious mind not missing a thing.

"Stevie!" Rhiannon snapped. "Don't be such a snot, okay?"

Stevie grinned, enjoying that she'd made her sister lose her patience. Rhiannon was always the sweet, angelic sister; Stevie strove to be the exact opposite.

"So..." Stevie said, moving to look the car over more thoroughly, running her hand along the body, talking casually over her shoulder. "You two are a thing, huh?"

"A thing?" Rhiannon repeated, wondering why she'd thought this would be a good idea.

"Yeah," Stevie said, looking inside the open passenger window.

"You know, fucking and all that."

"You kiss Mom with that mouth?" Rhiannon said, embarrassed that her sister was being so rude.

"I kiss lots of people with this mouth," Stevie countered. She straightened, smiling up at Jason. "So, you staying or just passing through?"

"I'm staying," Jason said, not put off one bit by Stevie's audacious behavior.

Stevie looked thoughtful for a moment, nodding as if making some sort of decision within her own mind. She extended her hand.

"I'm Stevie, and you're pretty much stuck with me too."

Jason took her hand and smiled down at the younger O'Neil sister. This girl was going to be trouble for any guy that tried to deal with her. He was glad he'd apparently passed whatever test she'd been giving him.

From that day forward, Stevie and Jason were like brother and sister. He was forever rescuing her from some trouble she was in, a job previously handled by her older sister. They'd get calls in the middle of the night from MaryAnne, worried because Stevie hadn't come home; it was Jason that would find her and take her back to her mother's house, or back to his and Rhiannon's home if she was drunk, because Rhiannon was adamant about their mother not seeing her youngest daughter inebriated. Jason would be the final say on whether a guy Stevie was dating was a slime or not; if Jason didn't like him, he didn't get very far. Stevie put her faith in Jason's judgment. He became the father she'd lost and the older brother she'd never had.

If Jason had disapproved of something Stevie was doing, she

*would stop doing it. But because he'd admired her spirit, he was careful to never say anything negative unless what she was doing was going to cause her harm.*

Stevie had been almost as devastated when Jason was killed as Rhiannon had been. But Stevie had taken her anguish and turned it into a rage that she'd controlled and focused on getting revenge for her brother-in-law's killer. The fact that she finally had made it easier to breathe. That night Stevie lay in her bed, thinking about what had come to pass. She fell asleep hoping that next she could manage to get her sister to live again.

That same night, Rick and Midnight were sleeping when the phone rang. Rick groaned, reaching out automatically to pick it up.

"'lo," he said, barely awake.

"Señor Debenshire?" queried a heavily accented voice.

"Yes?" Rick replied, coming further awake as his sixth sense started to tingle.

"Is Señora Debenshire in?"

"She's right here," Rick said. He knew this was not going to be a good phone call, sure that he recognized the voice of the Mexican police chief. He nudged Midnight gently. "Night, it's for you."

Midnight turned over, taking the phone.

She spoke for a few minutes while Rick waited anxiously, then reached over and hung up.

"What?" he asked, his nerves already on edge.

Midnight took a deep breath, blowing it out slowly. He wasn't going to like what she was about to tell him. "Julio Martinez escaped from the Mexican prison tonight."

Rick was sure his heart stopped. "He what?" Rick was praying he hadn't heard right. That he hadn't just heard that the man who had almost succeeding in killing Midnight three years ago was now out of prison.

"He escaped. Moncarro called me as soon as he'd set every cop he had available on his trail."

"Jesus…" Rick breathed.

"I know, I know," Midnight said, her mind already working.

"He's coming here," Rick said. It wasn't a question.

Midnight looked at him, then closed her eyes, nodding slowly. "They don't know for sure which direction he ran in, but Moncarro told me he wanted to make sure I knew."

Rick nodded. "He'll be gunning for you again."

"I know," Midnight said. "And he'll be looking to take his son. We can't let him get ahold of Ricardo."

"We can't let him get near either one of you," Rick said as he reached for the phone, his voice stronger now.

"What are you doing?"

"Putting out an APB on the son of a bitch. If he crosses the border anywhere populated I want him caught or shot, preferably the latter."

Midnight nodded, swallowing convulsively. She was more worried about Ricardo than she was for herself. Things could get really bad—but that's what happens when the past catches up to the present.

You can find more information about the author and series here:

www.sherrylhancock.com

www.facebook.com/SherrylDHancock

www.vulpine-press.com/midknight-blue-series

Also by Sherryl D. Hancock:

**The *WeHo* series** follows a group of women from Los Angeles as they navigate the ups and downs of love, life, work, and everything in between.

www.vulpine-press.com/we-ho

**The *Wild Irish Silence* series**. Escape into the world of BJ Sparks and discover how he went from the small-town boy to the world-famous rock star.

www.vulpine-press.com/wild-irish-silence-series